NO SECRETS REMAIN

A FAITH MCCLELLAN NOVEL

LYNDEE WALKER

SEVERN RIVER
PUBLISHING

Severn River Publishing
www.SevernRiverBooks.com

ISBN: 978-1-64875-588-0 (Paperback)

Also By LynDee Walker

The Faith McClellan Series

Fear No Truth

Leave No Stone

No Sin Unpunished

Nowhere to Hide

No Love Lost

Tell No Lies

No Secrets Remain

The Nichelle Clarke Series

Front Page Fatality

Buried Leads

Small Town Spin

Devil in the Deadline

Cover Shot

Lethal Lifestyles

Deadly Politics

Hidden Victims

Dangerous Intent

The Turner and Mosley Files

The General's Gold

The Cardinal's Curse

To find out more about LynDee Walker and her books, visit

severnriverbooks.com

For you, dear reader. This book truly wouldn't be here if you didn't love my characters, and if that knowledge didn't make me push myself to create the stories I think you deserve to have about them. Thank you for reading, and for every lovely review and kind message or note—you are the reason I sit down at my computer every day.

"Above all, don't lie to yourself. The man who lies to himself and listens to his own lie comes to a point that he cannot distinguish the truth within him, or around him, and so loses all respect for himself and for others. And having no respect he ceases to love."

—Fyodor Dostoevsky, *The Brothers Karamazov*

1

"Why are we here? Please, just take me home! Please." The girl sobbed, falling to her knees in the cold sand, hands tied behind her back.

"Someone will come for you." The lean, wiry man who'd carried her from the truck crouched beside her. "I'm sorry."

"Fuck you!" she screamed, spitting at him and tossing her long blonde hair, ratty and worse for wear but still somehow shimmering in the moonlight, out of her face. "Do you know what my father is going to do to you?"

"Not a damn thing." From a distance, another man shook his head, watching the other four walk away from her and climb back in their truck. "I seem to have drastically overestimated his humanity."

He watched her fold herself down onto the sand with the practiced strength and skill of a champion gymnast. He couldn't give her a chance to kick him—her legs were probably stronger than most of the men in that truck put together. But he could wait.

From his perch behind the marina restaurant's dumpster, he watched her look around. They'd left her hands bound behind her.

She was almost the same age as his own daughter, but far more beautiful and accomplished. And yet he would've folded like a polyester suit if someone took his kid.

Chuck McClellan had laughed.

Laughed.

That bastard was not cutting him out of the money that was putting his kids through college and would ensure he'd be able to retire before he died. He couldn't allow that.

Chuck wanted to be president, though. And he considered himself better than everyone else. Believed he was untouchable. Well—now he knew his house wasn't as safe as he thought. It had been shockingly vulnerable, come to find out.

The problem hadn't even been finding people on the McClellans' staff who would help him try to put Chuck in his place. It had been choosing from the variety of options that were readily offered, and concealing the fact that McClellan's daughter was the target—the staff loved the two golden-haired girls, the sports star and the pageant queen, as much as they hated the governor.

He'd had to pick the one person who was hardened enough to know the truth about the mission and stomach it. And even then, multiple assurances that this was a ransom, not a kill, were required.

But McClellan had forced his hand. Pushed to the line, just like always.

Over the line was showing him they could get in and out of the house without a trace and they didn't mind killing people to make their point.

Disturbing the governor's sleep. His security. His sense of peace.

He'd seen and done some horrific things, but this one...it was going to be the hardest.

He waited.

The girl got tired. Lay down, curled herself in a ball, and cried.

When she'd been quiet for a long while, he left the dumpster and crossed the sand. She didn't stir as he stood over her, eyelashes fanned across her cheeks, tear tracks dried on her skin.

A silencer in place, he fired two rounds. Her body jerked with each hit, but she never opened her eyes.

"She didn't feel a thing," he assured himself, cutting the ties on her hands and grabbing her feet with gloved fingers, pulling her flat on her back to the edge of the water. "She just went to sleep, that's all."

Pulling a small shovel from his coat pocket, he stirred up sand to obscure blood and footprints, backing up all the way to the grass and covering each of his own.

They would find her in a few hours.

McClellan would get the warning.

But nobody would ever be able to prove he'd been there.

2

"Just one body?" I asked.

"In that location? One so far." Kyle Miller's voice came through the speaker on my cell phone in patchy fits and starts. "Our team at the scene says there was a body cataloged near the front of Zapata's truck." I sped along a middle-of-nowhere stretch of highway, the signal just strong enough to make out what he was saying. "No mention in the report of tattoos, but they're trying to work fast. The Mexican authorities are making things difficult."

"I wonder how many of the Federales' response team are on Zapata's payroll?" I mused.

"From what I'm hearing, I'd say more than a few."

"Where did they take the other bodies?" I swerved to avoid the tumbleweed skittering in front of my headlights.

"That's the bad news," he said, a stronger signal making his voice louder and clearer. "A few places, and my guy wasn't sure who ended up going where. He said there was a lot of back and forth, and half of it was in Spanish, and he was trying to finish tracking evidence markers before they blew away in this wind or got picked up by someone else."

My brain replayed the scene of the man falling to the ground when ATF

Agent Miller shot him, the large tattoo of a monster with dripping fangs on his forearm standing out like it was branded there in neon.

I had seen the same tattoo in my sister's bedroom the night she disappeared—three days before her body was found on a lakeshore—more than twenty years ago.

"I'll find a way to track him down," I said.

"You really think this guy killed your sister, McClellan?"

"This guy? I don't have any idea. A guy with the exact same tattoo was there in the room. That's all I know, but it's the first real lead in her case in years."

"We have a brewing shitstorm of international proportions here," Miller said. "I'm not sure how much of my time that will take for the next few weeks."

"I'm sorry." Miller and I had led a small team into Mexico—Jesus, was that just a few hours ago? I shook my head and blinked at the long, flat highway my old truck's tires were gobbling up entirely too fast. We had gone with the intention of disrupting a weapons transaction between suppliers in Texas and Mexico's largest and most feared cartel, and we had done it—but the gunfight had left a dozen bodies scattered across a small desert highway and one of my favorite humans in the world hooked to half a dozen machines in a border town hospital. I had been the one who insisted we go right then, with backup too far away to arrive in time, because my husband was embedded undercover in the cartel and I was afraid they were going to figure him out. We'd lost two young Rangers and nearly lost Archie, and now Miller was probably going to get buried in review boards and paperwork. But I didn't have time to worry about what was already done—I had plenty of other worries flying at me as fast as my truck was flying up the highway.

"How's Archie?" I asked.

Miller chuckled. "He was asking the nurse when he'd be allowed to have something to drink when I left. He's lucky. They say he'll pull through."

One worry soothed. Now if I only had a way to know Graham was okay.

"Hardin will, too, Faith." Miller read my mind. "We need a plan for extracting him, and my UC, too—and we'll get there. I told you I would stick around and help, and I will."

"I bet not many women speed away from the scene of a shootout worried about their husband because they just shot him," I said. "You think I'm the only person that's ever happened to?"

"I'd say most of the time when a woman shoots her husband, she leaves the scene worried more about prison time than his health," Miller replied. "You, however, are a special case. He knows you didn't have a choice. You were trying to keep his cover. From everything I've heard, Hardin is a smart guy—and a tough one. I told you, my UC said he's good."

I blinked as little as possible because Graham staggering backward after I fired a round into his shoulder was the only thing I could see when my eyes closed. I knew Miller was right. Graham absolutely understood why I did it. That did not make me any less guilt-ridden or anxious.

"What if it gets infected?" I asked.

"What if pigs fly in and stage a rescue attempt?" Miller countered.

"My thing is possible and yours is not," I said.

"But neither is likely." Miller softened his tone. "I know you've had a long, hard day. But we've got this. Take care of whatever you sprinted out of here to do and then get some sleep. Dean and I are going to find a place to crash for a while. We'll circle up after the sun comes up."

"Thank you, Miller," I said softly. Morgan Dean was the head of the Rangers' border patrol unit, and Miller was a field office director for the Bureau of Alcohol, Tobacco, Firearms, and Explosives, who'd chased this case to Virginia and back. I didn't know them well, but after the past twenty-four hours, I trusted them both.

"We've got your back, McClellan. Don't worry."

I ended the call as the lights of the south Austin suburbs appeared on the horizon, pressing harder on the gas pedal and focusing on the road, wishing peace was as easy to come by as Miller made it sound.

3

"Faith, there are dozens of images here of you and Graham, most of them posted by media outlets with decent firewalls and encryption. Removing any trace of them is going to take...days. Hell, it may take weeks, and even then I make no guarantees about archived pages." Trey Morton ran one hand over his face as he shook his head at the Google results. "Why do I have to tell you this? You know computers damn near as well as I do."

"And as such, I know exactly what I'm asking." I stood, unsure why I'd tried to sit in the first place as I paced the five-step length of his shoebox-sized office in the basement of Rangers HQ. I couldn't sit still. I'd only made it through the drive by the skin of my stubborn streak, pushed by an obsessive need to see Trey and kept in one piece by the fact that driving my F-150 on predawn Texas highways like my last name was Earnhardt required so much concentration that I didn't have the brain space to be too antsy. "I'm also not exaggerating even a little bit when I tell you that Graham's life may depend on your ability to do this, and quickly."

"My ability? He's your husband, what about your ability? I know you don't broadcast it, but I also know your hacking skills are formidable." Trey clicked to a page and pulled up the source code, and I wanted to hug him for getting right to work even while he argued with me. He wasn't wrong—this wouldn't be easy—and I had both dragged him out of bed at an ungodly hour and rather unreasonably demanded he stop work on any other case to help me.

I spun back for a tenth pacing pass. "I don't have time to sit in front of my computer and test firewalls. I have to get him back."

Miller's assurance that no one in Emilio Zapata's inner circle currently suspected Graham of being undercover was holding my sanity together by a thin thread, but the memory of Derek Amin's assertion that the drug lord himself suspected that the man they knew as "Martin" wasn't really a former Mexican army officer turned criminal picked slowly at the weak stitches. On one hand, the collection of heads Amin had cleaved from other humans, hidden in a secret lair he had called a "trophy room," was more than enough proof he was severely disturbed and enjoyed playing with people's lives. On the other, he had worked closely with Zapata for decades and had nothing left to lose—possession of the deceased's taxidermied head is pretty much a slam dunk as far as murder convictions go, and we had him for multiple counts, plus defrauding the State of Texas by using his appointment as commander of the Texas National Guard to sell off weapons to Zapata.

And then there was the plain, age-old truth: the scariest thing is always the easiest to believe.

"You still haven't said back from what." Trey leaned closer to his widescreen monitor, typing and frowning. "I assume that's because it's either above my pay grade, or it could get me killed." He glanced up and I just nodded.

"So it could get you killed, too?"

I couldn't think about that right then, so I went back to the problem at hand. "Would it go faster if I could get the press photos—or most of them, anyway—down and you could concentrate on whatever is left?"

"Sure, but how are you going to do that?"

I pulled in a deep breath, tapped my foot on the scarred linoleum floor, and pointed to the phone on his desk. "May I?"

He pushed it toward me.

I checked my watch and dialed Skye Morrow's cell number. She answered on the second ring, her voice offering no indication of the early hour, which didn't surprise me—Skye was the walking, sniping reason "how do you sleep at night?" was a cliche.

"It's Faith McClellan," I said. "I need a favor. And more coffee. Meet me at Epoch in twenty minutes."

"Why—" She stopped, seeming to think better of whatever she'd been about to say. Maybe I should panic more often. "The one on North Loop?"

"It's the only one open this early. See you there." I hung up and turned back to Trey. "Start with the newspaper—those are the most recent. They ran a society spread on our wedding and they don't like Skye. She can't help there." I didn't want to be mad at my mother, though I'd told her I didn't want the press for the wedding, and she'd invited them anyway, insisting that we'd get entirely different photos that I'd probably like better from a photojournalist and made prints the price of admission. She'd been right: the one he'd snapped of us on the dance floor, foreheads touching, with a candle framed just perfectly between our chins, was my favorite image of the day.

Trey grinned. "Their servers are pretty easy to crack."

"Not that you do that often," I said.

He winked before he cracked his knuckles and started typing. "Good luck with Cruella."

"She doesn't scare me." Not anymore.

Focusing on Skye allowed me to avoid thinking about what did scare me right then, handy because I couldn't go there—pissed off drug lords be damned, Graham was coming home. I wouldn't entertain any other options.

And if I had to beg for Skye's help on both knees to make that happen, well...at least the coffee shop had some cushy rugs scattered around.

Skye walked in like she owned the whole damned city, not so much as flashing half a smile at the college kid who made her sugar-free almond milk latte while she pecked at her phone screen with one finger.

I stood when she approached the table I'd settled at in the back corner of the shop, taking a breath to settle my nerves. I wasn't planning to tell her more than I absolutely had to, but she'd made quite a career of pulling information out of people who didn't want to talk, and I wasn't sure how far I'd have to go to get what I wanted.

One of her perfectly threaded eyebrows went up as she sipped her coffee. "I'm not sure I've ever been this intrigued by what someone is going to say. And I interviewed Castro once when I worked in Miami."

"I think that's my first personal correlation to a fascist dictator." I took a long drink of my coffee, thinking maybe I should have asked the kid behind the counter to spike it. "I need all the images and video of me and Graham together taken down. From Channel Two's site and everyone else's, too, and I need it done this morning." I put the cup on the table and willed myself not to fidget with it, holding her gaze without blinking.

I could see the wheels turning behind her blue eyes—Skye is a lot of things, but stupid isn't one of them.

She put her coffee on the table and leaned forward, resting her elbows on either side of the cup. "What's in it for me?"

Neither is charitable.

But I was ready for that. "The story. The whole story, maybe the biggest one you've ever covered. We won't talk to anyone but you."

"That's not going to help me get colleagues at other stations to do what you're asking. And I have no pull with the newspaper."

I just stared at her, trying to keep my face as blank as I could. Offering Skye an exclusive was the best bait I had. If she was telling me it wouldn't be enough, I wasn't sure what my next play was. All I knew was that half a dozen of Zapata's men got a decent look at my face in the desert five hours ago, and I needed to make sure no one who thought to try to figure out who I was would accidentally find out who Graham was in the process. They wouldn't just kill him, they'd make it hurt. I'd been in Texas law enforcement long enough to hear cartel torture stories that would make normal people puke.

Not happening.

I leaned forward, too, and grabbed her hands so suddenly and tightly she flinched.

"Please, Skye." I swallowed hard. "I have no one else to ask. Our cyber crew is badly understaffed and I can't go anywhere else. The fastest way to do this is for the people who put them up in the first place to take them down. I need your help."

She didn't speak for a full thirty seconds, and when she did, she got right to the point. "He could die, then."

"I'm trying with everything in me to keep that from happening." I let her hands go and she picked up her cup, twisting it instead of drinking it. Skye Morrow didn't fidget.

"Who's after him?" She looked up. "Or are they after you?"

"I can't tell you that today." I widened my eyes for effect when her lips disappeared into a thin line. "I truly can't. But when I can tell someone, you'll be my first call. I give you my word."

"He's been gone on an undercover assignment for weeks, and now here you are, looking like hell and asking me to erase photos of the two of you two hours after I got a tip that Archie Baxter was shot in Mexico last night." She tapped a manicured red nail against the cup, watching my face carefully. I knew that look. I had perfected that look. Just slightly quizzical, but unruffled: she knew about Archie and wanted to see if I'd lie about what had happened.

Which meant I couldn't.

"Archie is stable, recovering in a hospital after surgery," I said, keeping my voice low and leaning in for effect. "The doctors say he'll pull through." I heaped drama on a throwaway confession to gain credibility with her. It was an easy bet that whoever tipped her off was either law enforcement or hospital staff, so she should already know Archie was recovering.

She nodded slowly, etching an S in the side of the coffee cup with her nail. "And how did he get there?"

"I can't tell you that," I said. "Today. I would if I could, but I truly can't. Yet."

"What can you tell me, then?" She sat back in her chair and folded her hands in her lap. "I need more than a promise of a story someday if I'm going to call in this many favors for you."

"I can offer you a different exclusive today," I said, picking at a chip in the table with one fingernail and lowering my voice like this was a major concession. "Another Ranger was murdered yesterday. We found him bound to a chair in a trailer in the middle of the desert, his brains blown all over the wall. There were several other bodies at the same location, all likely drug overdoses."

She pulled a notebook and pen out of her bag. "The name of the officer who was killed?"

"Drew Ratcliff," I said. "He was most recently assigned to a small outpost near the border."

"Tied to a chair and shot doesn't sound like an accident," she said. "Was he kidnapped?"

"He was."

"How long ago?"

"Monday."

"And no police reports were filed?"

"We are the police, Skye."

"You also like to keep attacks on the rank and file close to the vest, which I will never understand if I live to be three hundred and ninety. Why wouldn't you want as many people looking for your missing guy as possible?"

Huh. I'd never really thought of it quite that way before. Ratcliff had called me to consult on a murder investigation just over a week before, disappeared shortly after I arrived at the border, and been executed in a trailer full of Gen Z wannabe arms runners—and addicts, by the looks of the place when I arrived with Miller, Dean, and Archie—probably about twenty-four hours ago. One more reason for Zapata's empire to crumble.

"Brass is always reluctant to cause a public panic," I said.

"Oh, come on, Faith." She looked up from her notes. "They don't want the bad press. Even the appearance of someone having gotten the best of one of their agents is untenable. We don't always have to be mortal enemies, you know. I can help you on occasion—like today, for instance."

I nodded, not sure that would ever be true, but I needed her help.

"Any survivors at the crime scene?" she asked.

"One. He was part of a group of low-to-medium-level black market gun dealers operating out of South Austin. Gavin...I can't remember the last name. Should be in a local lockup in Terrell County. I can't imagine he'll be hard to pinpoint."

"So you were down there investigating a weapons ring?" she asked, tapping one nail on the notebook before she reached for her phone. "I just saw something yesterday..." She nodded, brandishing the phone. "Was this guy part of the same group?"

I waved for her to hold the phone still and she handed it to me. The brief story on the screen was a write-up she'd done about a shooting at an old metal warehouse south of Austin where at least most of the weapons being traded were stored.

"Victims Jesse Daniel Lopez, Lucas David Lobban, Brandon Brown, and Micheal Ann Ross," Skye said. "The report said there was an officer on scene at the time of the shootings, but only one shooting was officer-involved. The officer was not specified." She watched my face with the don't-lie-to-me look again.

"It was me. Mikey—sorry, Michael Ann—took me there at gunpoint..."

One of Skye's eyebrows disappeared into her hairline.

"Don't get too excited," I said. "She was a skinny little junkie who was trying way too hard to get her no-good asshole boyfriend to approve of her. She pulled a gun. I went because I wanted to know where he was. I was looking for him when I met her in the first place."

"So who did you shoot? The asshole?"

"No, actually he shot himself in the crotch first fighting with her over a gun, which was mildly entertaining in the moment, but then we called paramedics so he wouldn't bleed out, and right after they got there, Lobban showed up. Walked in the door shooting heavy ammunition from an assault rifle." In full tactical gear. But I didn't have to tell her everything.

She wrote as fast as I talked, then looked up, counting on her fingers. "That's not enough bodies."

"Pardon?"

"You said 'they' when you said paramedics. "But the report lists a woman, the guy you say was the shooter, and only two other bodies: I assume one is the asshole boyfriend and one is a paramedic."

"You don't miss much," I said.

"You don't win almost sixty Emmys by skipping details."

"Two medics showed up. One got killed, one did not."

"So you took out Lobban?"

"I did. He killed the other three."

"And the other paramedic?"

"I imagine the county has her name."

"Which is the dead paramedic?"

"Brandon," I said, feeling a pang of sadness as I remembered his partner saying he was supposed to be married in a few weeks.

Skye put her pen down. "You called me," she muttered. "Which means you really don't have anyone else to ask."

"I said that already." I tried not to snap at her, but I didn't have any more time to sit there. Archie was in the hospital, Miller and Dean were sleeping before they went to their COs and asked for more time on this case, and I was supposed to be figuring out where Zapata's compound was and how we were going to get Graham back. But I had to keep him alive until I could get there. If Skye wasn't the way to do that, I would figure another one out.

"I have a few favors I can call in to get footage and photos removed from every broadcast station," she said slowly. "But I need enough to know whatever you're into is going to be a story big enough to make that worth it." She waved one hand at the notebook. "This is fine, but it's a one-cycle news story. Two if tomorrow is slow."

"I know you, Skye. I know your bread and butter, and I know what lights you up and makes you keep doing the job when the lines around your eyes get a little deeper every year and every new girl has thicker, shinier hair and better boobs than you. What I'm into is the kind of story people win awards for. It's the kind of story you put up with all the bullshit for."

She held my gaze for five beats before she nodded. "One condition."

"I can't promise an exclusive if this blows up." She had guts, Skye Morrow. "And I'm not giving you our firstborn or anything."

She wrinkled her nose and shuddered. "Christ Almighty, don't even joke about that. Babies are loud, messy and smelly. I can't believe someone like you would ever consider having one."

"It was a figure of speech." Mostly. Graham wanted kids, and though I'd never considered it until I thought he might die, it had danced around the edges of my thoughts all the way back to Austin. "Name your price, Skye. I have other shit to do today."

"I want you to wear a camera."

"Today?"

"When whatever you're so scared of goes down."

I gave it a beat to make sure she thought it was a difficult concession. "Done."

Her whole face lit up in a smile that always reminded me of Sylvester the Cat right after he eats Tweety, and she pulled a yellow rose lapel pin with a built-in micro camera and onboard battery out of her bag and handed it to me. "They'll be down by noon. Put your guy on the newspaper."

We stood at the same time and she followed me to the parking lot, turning toward my truck before she opened the door of her silver Mercedes. "Don't die before I get my story, McClellan."

It was probably the nicest thing she'd ever said to me.

My phone lit up in the cupholder before I made it to the stop light at the corner. Dean.

"I thought you were going to bed?" I said, putting the call on speaker.

"I thought I was, too." I could hear the exhaustion in his voice. "I just got a call from my friend at Border Patrol. Dakota Grady, the guard you met at the detention center?"

I turned toward headquarters, sighing. "Please don't tell me that kid is mixed up in this. I liked him." He had shown me back to see an inmate who'd been mauled and disfigured, and actually treated the guy like a human being—Grady was a big-hearted kid to be working as a guard in that particular ring of hell.

"He's missing. He's been a no-show for his shifts for two days, and they sent someone for a welfare check last night. Signs of a struggle at his place, and his truck is parked out front undisturbed. Neighbor reported a disturbance before dawn on Monday. Said he heard shouting in Spanish."

My insides turned to ice. "Morgan." I cleared my throat. "Amin saw me with Grady. And two of the officers on staff there saw Grady give an order for Timmy Dushane to be left alone."

Zapata's crew couldn't be putting things together this fast. Surely.

"Any of that could be a reason for this, or it could be something totally different. You only talked to him the one time, it's not like you really know him. Did you even know his first name?"

He had a point. But it didn't chase the fear off completely. "I did not. But he's a good kid. My gut is rarely wrong about people," I said. "Any other news?"

"Miller is trying to see if he can safely get an updated welfare check on Hardin from his UC, and we're on this thing with Grady. I told you I'd keep you in the loop and that's what I intend to do."

"Thank you," I said. "I'm going back to headquarters to see what I can dig up on people who might know where to find Zapata. I'll have my phone handy. Let me know what you find."

"Will do."

I hung up, saying a prayer for Grady's safety, and for a little bit of luck for the rest of us.

4

I tossed my empty cup into a bin just inside the double doors, the sunrise behind me lighting the lobby in a soft orange glow because Trey and I hadn't bothered to turn the lights on earlier. I flipped them on now, knowing people would start to trickle in over the next hour.

Settling at Archie's desk, I dug my laptop out of my bag and looked up a phone number for the medical examiner in Laredo. It was still early, but Jim was often in his office before six, so maybe they would be, too. I needed to talk to someone before my day got any busier.

The phone rang eight times before a slightly out of breath voice came on the line. I introduced myself and tried to keep my voice even as I asked about the body.

"Hispanic male, probably six feet tall, medium muscular build, with a large tattoo of a creature with blood dripping from fangs on his left forearm," I said. "Cause of death a gunshot wound, possibly multiple GSWs. He would have come in with half a dozen other bodies from a scene outside Ciudad Acuna about four or five hours ago."

"Looking now," she said, keys clicking in the background. "We only had two fatalities come in overnight, both from a high-speed car crash."

"Are you sure?" My voice went up an octave.

"I haven't inspected the cooler or anything, but this logbook has never been wrong," she said. "Where did you say the scene was, again?"

"Off a highway outside Ciudad Acuna," I repeated, trying not to sound impatient—or desperate. Could one simple thing in my life this week actually be simple?

"I bet they sent them to Bexar County in San Antonio," she said. "It's closer than we are to that location." A clicking that sounded like a fingernail tapping on the back of the receiver started, then paused. "You said 'Hispanic male.' Was the guy a Mexican citizen?"

"I don't know for sure but would lean toward yes if I had to answer that," I said.

"That could mean he was taken to the morgue in Mexico."

"How would I go about finding that out?" I asked.

"It would depend on which authorities were first on the scene, mostly," she said.

"Ours were." I picked up a pen and played with it. "We had federal and state officers there and a backup air response team."

"Then if I were you I'd try San Antonio and hope for the best," she said. "If you don't find him there, you can call me back. My name is Lucy Strider, I'm an assistant ME here. I can try to help you locate a set of remains in Mexico, but it's not easy. They have a patchwork of clinics, hospitals, and government facilities there, and the time a body sits and what's done with it depends a lot more on location, status, and local corruption than anything we're used to here."

I blew my hair out of my face and clicked the pen a final time, writing down her name and the lab's phone number. "I appreciate your help, Lucy."

"Hope you find your guy," she said.

I hung up, whispering, "Me too," not entirely sure which guy I was even talking about.

I went to the break room for more coffee and brewed a fresh pot, returning to Archie's desk with a full mug and dialing the Bexar County ME's office. At least if the body was there, the transfer I wanted would be simple.

I got voicemail. Leaving a message with only my name, title, and badge number, I eyed the clock: 6:18. Not what most would call a respectable business hour, but if I could find the body I was looking for, I needed Jim Prescott on board for what came next.

I called him from my cell phone.

"Do I need coffee for this?" he asked by way of hello.

"The stronger the better," I said.

He sighed, his feet shuffling on the hardwood floor in the background. "Is everyone still alive?"

"As far as I know right now."

"Jesus Christ, Faith." I heard his coffeemaker burble to life and a spoon tinkling against a mug a few seconds later. "Okay, go."

"I want to start by saying I'm being careful to only tell you what you need to know to help," I said. "And I am asking for your help, Jim. Not demanding it, but being honest: no one else can do this job as well as you can."

"That's true of most things." From anyone else that would sound egotistical, but from Jim, it was just honest.

"There's a body that I hope was taken to Bexar County last night," I said. "Cause of death is a GSW, but I know how the guy died and who killed him."

"Okay so...what do you need me for, then?"

"I need to know who he is and anything else the remains might tell you about him."

"You know who shot him dead, but you don't have an ID on your vic? Maybe I need more coffee, but something seems to be missing here."

"How much do you want me to tell you?" I asked.

He was quiet for a long beat. "Just what I need to know for now. Description?"

"Hispanic male, around six feet tall, medium build, large distinctive forearm tattoo. I left a message at the Bexar County lab, but I talked to them just last week and they're moving bodies through quickly because they've got a gang war raging and they're out of cold storage. A John Doe with a hole blown through him and some battle scars won't sit there for long."

"I know a guy who owes me a few favors," Jim said. "Let me get him out of bed and I'll call you back when I'm more awake."

"Thanks, Jim."

"Anything for you, McClellan. I hope you know what you're getting into."

"I have a good idea," I said. "And no choice in the matter at all."

"Go do what you do and let me handle the dead guy."

I hung up and sucked in a steadying breath. Jim had been reluctant to wade into this case in the first place for good reason. I just hoped I was doing the right thing by curating what information he was getting until he asked for more.

I can't reach my guy, but working back channels is tricky. We can't push too hard or we might put them in danger. No reason to believe things have changed in the few hours since I heard something, so just stay the course.

I stared at the text message from Miller, the letters running together on the screen in front of my sleep-deprived eyes.

Stay the course. If I'd ever had the urge to get a tattoo of my own, that would have been it—it had been my motto since I understood what it meant, from Ruth's pageants, to navigating my sister's death largely alone, to clearing the highest percentage of murder cases of any detective in the state, to joining only a handful of women who had served as Texas Rangers field officers.

I knew how to stay a course. And right then, I had no choice but to believe I could keep Graham alive and get him home by the sheer force of my will—and maybe some help from Miller's connections. Somehow, in the middle of that, I needed to find the remains of the man with the tattoo and see if something about him might finally get us a break in my sister's murder case after decades of zero progress. I rubbed at my eyes and set the phone on the desk, reaching for my coffee. I could sleep later—I wasn't good at trusting other people to take care of things that mattered to me.

Oh yeah—and somewhere in there I needed to figure out what the hell happened to Grady. He was a good kid, and I did not need to add responsibility for his head ending up in a glass case in some sicko's panic room to the list of reasons I could run on so little sleep.

I dove into my computer, searching the dark web for any mention of Zapata that might add to a list of allies—or enemies. In an hour, I had nearly a dozen of each and a crick in my neck from hunching over the keyboard. I stretched both arms back over my head and then typed the address to a forum on weapons trade, sort of a dark web craigslist for criminals, that I had used to track illegal guns moving around Texas in past murder cases.

Making sure my IP was cloaked, I searched for Zapata's name and got more than a hundred hits in the past 120 days.

"Christ Almighty, this guy wasn't getting all the weapons he needed from the smugglers?" I muttered, clicking to the first post and reading the Spanish with a fluent eye thanks to the parade of nannies who came to our family from Mexico while I was growing up, my jaw loosening as I clicked through.

Armored Humvees. Drones with weapons capabilities. Tanks, for fuck's sake.

War. Amin's words floated through my head. *He wants out. With who is immaterial, really. Disappear once the battle begins.*

I took screenshots of all the posts and wrote down amounts and dates. Money wasn't a problem for a cartel boss, clearly—he'd paid some corrupt military officials somewhere a fortune for this equipment, and from the posts, I couldn't even tell which side of the border they were on.

What I could tell was that the war I'd been warned about was coming. I counted two armored cars purchased two months apart, three Hummers, five drones, and a real-life honest-to-God tank purchased in the past three weeks, plus the gun shipment from last night...Whatever Zapata was doing, he was moving soon.

I closed the computer and reached for my phone to call Miller, and a hand landed on my shoulder. I looked up to find Graham's boss scowling at me the way he used to when I worked for him.

"Captain Jameson." I cut my eyes to his hand until he removed it. "I didn't hear you come in."

"You were pretty lost in what you were doing there, McClellan," he said. "I can only assume at this point it had something to do with jeopardizing an operation five different agencies have worked on for years in the name of some misguided rescue." His voice had a chill I'd never noticed before, and I didn't care for it one bit. I shot to my feet.

"I'm afraid I must be misunderstanding you, sir. Surely you're not suggesting that I would put Graham in danger?" The edge in my words could have cut glass.

"I'm certainly suggesting that you would put dozens of other officers in danger to get him home," he said. "You did that last night, so it's not like my imagination is running amok."

"How—" I swallowed the "dare you" and pulled in a deep breath. Having Jameson mad at me wouldn't help Graham. He'd always been an asshole and he'd never liked me as much as Graham because he prized following rules over everything else except looking good on TV, and Graham was a rule follower. Well—except the one about being honest with your wife when you're going off on what most people would call a suicide mission. He smashed the hell out of that one.

I glanced up and raised my hand in acknowledgment when Jared Ritter waved as he walked toward the break room, making a "you and me" gesture that meant he wanted to talk when I was through with Jameson. I needed to call a meeting in the bullpen after more people had arrived, because everyone would be worried about Archie and I didn't have time to tell the story ninety-seven times today.

Refocusing on Jameson, I pointed to the conference room. "Let's talk in here."

I walked that way without waiting for him to reply, turning on the lights and waving him toward a chair when he followed me inside. I closed the door and moved to the far wall, leaning against it.

"How dare you lead an unauthorized operation into a foreign country where one of my men is embedded, especially without my knowledge?" Jameson spit the last three words through his teeth.

Ah, so that's what his attitude was about. It wasn't that I went to Mexico or that a couple of our men died, it was that we didn't tell him. I should've guessed when I saw that he was pissed off in the first place. Jameson is self-important above everything else.

"First, I'm not sure where you got your intel, but there was nothing unauthorized about what we did. I was with an ATF field office commander, a Rangers lieutenant, and a decorated veteran field officer, and we were in communication with the DEA."

"So you notified literally everyone in the law enforcement universe but me, when your husband is still my subordinate?"

Breathe.

"Respectfully, sir"—turned out I was a better liar than I thought simply because I got that out without choking on it—"there was no time to set a phone tree in motion, and I knew you would be concerned with Graham's safety above your own ego, as was I."

I held his gaze until he blinked and looked away.

"I heard from him a little after three this morning. He wanted me to tell you he knows you did what you had to, and so did he. He said he's safe."

Of course he did. That didn't make it true, and I could tell by the look on Jameson's face that he knew that as well as I did.

"I just want him home," I said. "That would be easier if you had sent him in with a clear and safe extraction strategy."

"Now wait a minute. I didn't send him anywhere. He was offered an opportunity and he took it. He knew the risk he was taking. Damn federal agencies don't care much about local cops except what we can get for them. Hardin didn't even ask about getting out, he said he was in until Zapata's fentanyl operation was done."

I nodded. It sounded like Graham, and I didn't have time to argue. "I'm not going to put other officers at risk, and I will try to keep you in the loop as urgency allows, but I think we're on the same side here."

"Of course." His face said that was hard for him to say. He closed his eyes and took a deep breath. "I'm...I'm just under a lot of stress. I have a stack of dead bodies, a lab that's backed up, my best investigator embedded in a dangerous deep cover situation, and..." He stopped there, shaking his head. "It's a lot."

"I understand." I tapped one finger on the table, looking to fill the silence. "What do you mean a stack of dead bodies? From what? I'm behind on news."

"They sent the files up late yesterday from the desert because three of the guys lived here," he said. "Overdoses, I think, which has been Graham's wheelhouse lately, but there are several. Plus one guy who was shot."

I raised one hand. "Two men and a woman? Found in a purple single-wide near the state park in Terrell County yesterday?"

"I think that's right," he said. "I can't remember specifics and I don't have the folder, but how many combination ODs and fatal GSWs in the middle of nowhere could there be in one day?"

"I was at that scene. The GSW vic is Ranger Drew Ratcliff. Did you send the bodies to Jim Prescott?"

"Not specifically. They just went to Travis County." He pulled out his phone and held up one finger before he poked at the screen a few times. "This says they did ID the guy who was shot as a cop, they're rushing the ballistics and could have them as soon as tomorrow."

"Can you let me know when that comes in?" I asked. I was pretty sure Zapata sent someone to kill Ratcliff, but considering everything I'd seen in the past week, it wouldn't hurt to be in the loop and confirm that. "And just let me know if you come up with suspects or need help questioning anyone, maybe?"

"Sure thing." He nodded, his entire demeanor different than when we walked into the room—easy and cooperative had overtaken surly and demeaning.

Very unlike him. I didn't trust it.

"I appreciate that." I stood, lightening my tone. "How did you know I was here?"

"I didn't until I saw you out there at the desk." His brow furrowed.

"Why were you here so early if you weren't looking for me?" I studied his face. It's true I'd never liked Jameson, but I'd never suspected him of being anything but a narcissist with a bit of a John Wayne complex. Until right then.

"I'm interviewing for a position here," he said.

I blinked. That, I did not see coming. Yet it made so many things make so much more sense: that was why he'd been here so much lately, and why he was being more of a jackass than usual this morning, too. Being cut out of an operation involving a UC under his command might make him look irrelevant to whoever he was trying to suck up to.

"Appreciate the enthusiasm," Jameson said after I let too many seconds go by without a word.

"I've had a lot going on the past few days," I said. "What position?" My brain hunted for openings in our command staff, but there weren't any that I knew of. No way he was going back to the field.

"Boone is retiring at the end of the year."

If he had told me Jesus himself was waiting at the front door with Elvis and John Lennon I might have been less surprised.

Though I'm not really sure why. Of course he was.

Boone was my boss. He was finally starting to respect me, maybe like me a little, and I respected the hell out of the fact that he cared about the work and not his own image or ego after years of working for Jameson.

I nodded, some kind of bred-in-the-bone Miss Manners thing that would probably make Ruth proud taking over. "Good luck," I lied again. Maybe it was just him I could be convincing with?

"I hope I get the chance to work with you again," he said. "I'm sorry we got off on the wrong foot."

I gulped back a "which time?" with a considerable amount of effort. More than I had to spend on this right now, that was for damn sure.

"I appreciate that, sir. And thank you for keeping me in the loop about the Ratcliff investigation. He was a good man, and I will help any way I can to make sure justice is served there." The words spilled out like someone else was saying them, and he smiled before waving me out of the room ahead of him.

Two weeks ago the idea of working for Jameson again would've at least mildly rocked my world. Today? I had so many more important things that needed my attention that I just bolted from the room. The number of voices out in the bullpen was growing, and I needed to get everyone rounded up for an announcement about Archie.

5

I went to the wall and flashed the lights off and on, putting my fingers in the corners of my mouth and whistling.

Twenty heads turned from computer screens lit up with emails or raised from steaming coffee cups.

"Jesus, McClellan, are you okay?" Ritter asked, half rising out of his chair when he got a good look at me under the fluorescents.

"Keeping up with you, Ritter." I put one hand up. "This is need to know only at this point, and as usual, no comments to the media. I'm sure a few of you have seen the reports this morning of an agent-involved shootout in Mexico last night." Murmurs and a few nods, with some wrinkled brows mixed in. "Baxter was hit and we lost two men from the border unit," I said.

Hands went to hearts, some heads bowed in prayer.

"Baxter came through surgery like a champ, and he'll be back before we know it," I said. "I can't tell the story nine hundred times today because I have a working case where lives are at risk, but I wanted y'all to know. The fallen officers' families would appreciate your prayers, I'm sure. That's all."

I went back to Archie's desk and grabbed my laptop, moving to the conference room so I'd have a door I could close. I needed to let Miller know about the massive loads of concerning artillery Zapata had collected. Miller had been able to round up a decent response on short notice the day before, so I was hoping he could do better with a little more lead time. Whatever they were doing, we needed to be ready to squash it if he wanted Zapata caught and I wanted to get Graham back without getting anyone else hurt.

"Miller." He sounded half-asleep.

"I'm sorry to wake you, but the guns we saw are the least of our worries where Zapata is concerned," I said.

"Huh?" The phone clattered like he dropped it. "Sorry."

"I did a little more digging based on what Amin said last night and the guy has a tank, Miller. A real one. Armed drones, armored Humvees...I think Amin was telling me the truth. He's going to start a war and slip out the back once the carnage starts."

"Damn, what happened to people faking their own deaths? Isn't that easier?"

"Cheaper at least. But would you really let it go if there was no body? Would the DEA?"

He sighed. "No."

"Like Amin said, Zapata knows that."

"Shit. Can you send me screenshots of the messages you saw for our cyber guys?"

I opened my laptop. "On the way now."

"You hanging in there?" His tone changed, softening, as a cabinet door clattered and a spoon scraped against a mug with a muffled ringing sound.

"I'm okay. Jameson heard from Graham around three, so not long after I left to come up here. He says he's safe, but..."

"You think he's lying?"

"I think he doesn't want me to feel bad or worry."

"But that can be true and he can still be safe."

"I know." I sighed. "It's just hard for me to believe."

"What you said last night, about the guy with the tattoo and your sister —" Miller began, before I cut him off.

"I'm looking for his body and have some leads."

"I remember when she died," he said. "I'm really sorry no one ever caught the people who did it."

"Me too."

"That's why you're so relentless." He didn't bother with the question inflection. He didn't need to. It was obvious to people who knew my story. It just sometimes took something glaring for folks to make four from that particular two and two.

"Not much about my life has ever been normal except Graham," I said.

"We'll get him home."

The door to the conference room opened and I stood when I saw Lieutenant Boone and a trio of Rangers brass flanked by a pair of dark suits I didn't recognize.

"Thanks. I'll check in later."

Putting the phone down, I closed my computer. "Sorry, sir," I said to Boone. He couldn't have gotten much sleep if he was here in a meeting when I'd left him outside the hospital near the border where Archie was just a few hours before.

"Sit down, Faith," Boone said. My eyebrows shot to my hairline. He rarely sounded so stern, and he never used my first name. I couldn't have sworn five minutes ago that he even knew it.

I lowered myself slowly back to the chair and put my computer and phone on the table. "Is there a problem?"

One of the dark suits coughed while the brass flanking Boone pinched their lips into identical thin lines.

What the hell did I do?

"Faith, this is Smith and Jones." Boone pointed to the dark suit guys in turn. "And you know our command staff, of course."

I did: Abbott, Brinker, and Cooper. The alphabet jokes made their names easy to remember.

Smith and Jones for the solemn guys in the well-tailored black suits I didn't buy for half a second, but I was far more concerned about Boone's behavior than their identities.

Boone flipped on the projector mounted on the ceiling and plugged a computer into it while Assistant Chief Abbott pulled a projection screen down. Smith killed the lights.

"This hit a federal agent's inbox thirty-four minutes ago," Jones said, his voice deep enough to be generally ominous.

I stared at the screen, not entirely sure what to expect, but praying for

Graham harder than I'd ever prayed for anything—even Charity. Surely to God if they sent us a video of something awful happening to my husband, this isn't how Boone would go about showing it to me. He was task oriented, he wasn't heartless.

Like he heard me thinking, he took the seat next to me and put one hand on my forearm under the table.

Shit.

Someone pushed play, and a grainy image full of filtered light and deep shadows filled the screen. "Is that a...dungeon?" I asked, for lack of a better word for what I was looking at. The slanting Sunny Delight–colored beams danced around a stone wall with shackles hanging from it by iron chains and highlighted some suspicious dark spots on the concrete floor.

"Looks that way," Abbott said. Everyone's eyes were glued to the screen.

A man stumbled in from the right side, hands tied behind him, as someone shouted, "*Muévete, cerdo*," which was Spanish for "move, pig." My stomach plummeted to my knees. The shadows melted into the blood and bruising on the detainee's face such that it took me a minute. Another man jogged in from the left, raising one combat boot and driving it into the battered man's knee, sending him into a heap on the floor. A chorus of laughter and garbled words I didn't make out came across, and then another man, the same one who'd dragged Graham back into the box truck last night, stepped in and hauled the prisoner to his knees by one ear. At that height, more light hit the man's face and I gasped.

"Di tu nombre!" Say your name.

The prisoner's mouth moved but nothing came out. The guard stepped forward and smacked him across the face before he spit on him. I couldn't say which made me feel sicker, and I didn't need him to make the kid talk.

"That's Dakota Grady," I said. "He's a guard at the border detention center."

Boone nodded as Grady said his name, his voice breaking at the end of the first word.

"I don't want to watch any more," I said. I knew what was coming. "You said it came to an inbox at your agency. Where do you work?" I turned to look at Jones.

"You will finish watching, Miss McClellan, and then we'll talk." His voice was low, the kind of gravelly that comes from years of three packs a day or a couple of swift kicks to the larynx.

Boone squeezed my arm under the table and I shook his hand off and turned my chair around. "I met that kid five days ago at the detention center and found him to be the only competent and human guard in the handful I interacted with. If it's all the same to you, I'd rather not see him die this morning."

"It is not all the same to me." Jones paused the video and stepped forward. "Turn back around."

"Who the hell do you think you are?" I started to stand and Boone grabbed my hand.

"Do as he says." He widened his eyes in an imploring look I'd never seen on him. "That's an order."

Who the fuck were these people?

I sank back into my chair, holding Jones's gaze until I spun back to the screen. The video resumed playing.

Grady held up a newspaper. I couldn't see the date but I was sure it was yesterday or today.

"My name is Dakota Grady. I was taken from..." He doubled over, grabbing his side below his ribs and breathing in ragged, shallow gulps. "My apartment two days ago and am only alive today by the grace of Emilio Zapata and his men."

I swallowed hard.

"Do you wish to remain here as a guest?" The guard's voice was way too cheerful.

"No." Grady's voice came through clearer.

"Look at the camera, Mr. Grady, and tell the people back home what you want."

"I'd like..." Grady pulled in a shaky breath. "To go home. Please."

"Tell them how you can accomplish that."

Grady dropped his chin to his chest and swayed, looking for a minute like he might pass out, but he stayed upright.

"Zapata wants a meeting with American intelligence officials." Grady paused, took a deep breath, and continued. "He wants to talk about his son."

Zapata's eldest son had turned on the cartel, working for Miller and the ATF as an informant. Until Amin killed him, anyway. It seemed that Zapata hadn't known for sure Freddie was dead until the past few days. The anger and grief, I understood. But why in the world would he think nabbing a prison guard would make anyone in the federal intelligence community give a flea's ass what he wanted?

"How old are you, Mr. Grady?"

"Twenty..." Grady turned his head and coughed, stifling a scream. Surely among God knew what other injuries, he had broken ribs. "Three."

My God. He was a kid.

I shook my head, and Boone clamped his fingers around mine. I realized he wasn't watching the video. None of them were. They were watching me watch the video. So they had already seen it.

Grady swayed into a beam of sunshine, his face a sickening blue-purple wreck in the light. Was that a...tooth...poking through his top lip to the right of his nose?

My coffee came back up with zero warning. I was pretty sure it splattered Smith's shoes, which made me think karma might work quickly in some cases after all.

Boone gasped and most of the rest of the men in the room groaned. Boone shoved a handful of paper napkins at me from a stack someone had left on the table and I wiped my face with one and dropped the rest on top of the puddle spreading on the thin carpet.

"I don't even think I owe you gentlemen an apology," I said. "I tried to leave."

"I'll get someone to clean it," Brinker said.

"You'll bring no one else into this room." Jones stepped in front of the door. "I'm sure you're capable of taking care of it."

The brass blanched, looking amongst themselves for five beats before they all shot looks my way that would've opened the floor straight into the second ring of hell if any of them had the power.

I stared straight back at Abbott, not blinking.

Smith thumped a fist on the table. "Enough. The floor will wait." He pointed to the screen and started the video again.

“Zapata wants a meeting within seventy-two hours or they’ll kill me,” Grady said, staring straight into the camera. “They’re not bluffing.”

I’ve heard people talk about out of body experiences, but I’m not sure I’ve ever felt anything resembling one until I realized that sitting there in the chair, I couldn’t feel...anything. Except that in a rickety old building in the August heat in central Texas, I was freezing. No heartbeat, no post-vomit empty stomach, no bullet wound in my shoulder. It was almost like I was floating in the chair behind my eyes, listening to Grady’s words through a tunnel.

“Mom, if you could just get him what he wants,” Grady said. “Please.” The screen went black.

The lights came on.

I still couldn’t feel anything but cold.

Boone stood next to me, his voice farther away than Grady’s had been.

“McClellan?”

My knees collided with something hard about half a second before my head did the same. A sticky dampness seeped through my shirt and into my hair.

“Her lips are blue!” Boone cried. “She’s not breathing.”

“She’s just in shock.” Smith sighed like a fly had landed on his steak, putting his feet on either side of my legs and leaning down.

“You’re fine.” He stared into my eyes. His were so dark I couldn’t make out the iris from the pupil, and flat, like there was nothing behind them.

Something stabbed my leg and I sucked in a deep breath, my stomach recoiling, my shoulder on fire, and my thigh throbbing.

“You are also suspended immediately and until further notice.”

6

Smith and Jones filed from the room, taking the laptop containing the video with them.

I had taken three more breaths when my whole body started shaking like I was walking around the arctic in a string bikini. Boone knelt next to me, avoiding the puddle I was lying in.

"It's just epinephrine," he said. "The tremors are a common side effect. They'll pass."

"They can't suspend me, sir." The words fired out between chattering teeth. "I can't walk away from this case."

"They just did."

"Why are you being so calm about this?" I hated that my voice was shaking. I sounded weak and ineffectual when I wanted to roar at pretty much everyone in my general vicinity. I took a deep breath and managed to steady it a bit. "I work for you, not them. Since when do you let strangers walk in here and tell you what to do with officers in your command? Or do you just not care anymore because you're leaving anyway?"

Boone flinched like I'd slapped him.

"Who told you?"

"Jameson did."

"That little weasel," Boone muttered, glaring up at the brass.

"Get her out of here, Boone," Brinker barked. "She's not a member of this department until this is over."

"Do we have to bring her back then?" Assistant Chief Abbott muttered.

"She catches more murderers every year than a lot of cops do in whole careers," said Cooper, who was the new chief as of June 30. "We can't fire her."

"She also causes more trouble in one day than some people do in their whole careers," Abbott shot back.

"And Chuck McClellan is her father," Major Brinker added, though I wasn't sure if that was a pro or a con for these guys.

"I can hear y'all. Just in case you were wondering," I croaked, the tremors subsiding some.

"We weren't." They left the room without a backward glance, leaving Boone to get me off the floor himself. He managed, and pretty well for as little help as he had from me.

"You need to go home and clean up," he said.

"I need to get back to work." I grabbed the edge of the table to stay upright.

"Sleep, too." Boone ignored me and continued his evaluation.

"Graham...sir, I have to go get him out of there. Zapata is unstable—grieving over his son, obsessed with anxiety about traitors in his ranks. It's only a matter of time before they find out who Graham really is. You saw..." I covered my mouth with one hand and pointed to the screen, standing on my own and pulling in a deep breath.

Boone shook his head. "I want him back too, and I will see to that, McClellan, but you can't be part of this."

"Why the hell not?" I paused. "Did he say 'mom' toward the end of that?"

"He did." Boone looked at the floor.

Dakota...Grady.

"Oh, Jesus," I said. "His mother is..."

"Alexis Hutcherson Grady. He is her only son."

Alexis Hutcherson Grady was the Speaker of the US House of Representatives.

And Zapata had her son as a prisoner. But I still wasn't sure why the feds wanted me off the case.

"I can help her get him back." I met Boone's gaze, leaning on the edge of the table. "Nobody wants Zapata taken down or our people out of there as much as I do. Did anyone tell her that?"

Boone sighed. "Of course I told them that. You...have a reputation, Faith."

"Because I get shit done," I said.

"By being impetuous, sometimes."

"You don't solve murders by moving slowly, sir."

"Alexis Grady is not a cop. She is a politician. Her entire life is carefully choreographed, every move considered from ten different angles. She's not like you. She's not like your father. She knows everything that happened in Mexico last night. She knows it was your idea to go down there. She knows we lost men and you didn't get Graham back. And she doesn't want you anywhere near this while Zapata's people have her son."

My shoulders slumped. That woman was not the kind of enemy I needed.

"Sir, please." I widened my eyes and shook my head, knowing as I said the words there wasn't a thing he could do to help me.

"So the Speaker knows who Graham is?"

Boone just nodded.

"And you expect me to just go home and...what? Watch TV? Pick up knitting? While I wait to see what happens to him?"

"We will get him back."

"Who is 'we'? The feds are in charge of your investigation now. The clock is already ticking on the seventy-two hours, and politicians who consider everything from twenty different angles can't pick out shoes in three days' time." I smacked one palm down on the table. "She could trade Zapata Graham for her kid and you know it."

"She won't want the bad press of compromising an undercover officer. I can make sure they know you'd take that straight to Skye Morrow."

"Giving Skye a story wouldn't make my husband any less dead," I said. "Though in a few months, none of this is your problem anymore, right?" That was mean, but I was mad and he was the only nearby target.

"I'm sorry Jameson told you something you didn't need to hear right now, Faith," Boone said gently. "And I'm sorry I have to ask for your badge and your sidearm." He pushed a button on the phone and Ritter appeared, picking up my laptop and phone.

"Those are my personal property," I said.

"You can have them back when Trey Morton has cleared them of sensitive intel," Boone said, looking alternately at the table and his shoes. "Abbott's orders. I'm sorry."

Ritter tried to reach for my arm, presumably to escort me from the building.

"If you'd like to keep that hand attached to your arm, I'd rethink that," I said, striding from the room on legs far too shaky to be fueled by anything other than willpower.

Ritter followed me all the way outside, where I whirled on him.

"What exactly do you think I'm going to do, Jared?" I snapped. "Break a fax machine? Kick in a door? He took my weapon and I'm not stupid enough to take on fifty cops in hand to hand when I'm shaking like a baby leaf in a tornado."

He raised both hands, wrinkling his nose when the wind gusted and he got a whiff of the mess soaking the back of my shirt. "This is the least fun thing I've ever had to do at work. And I've told too many people to count that their kids are never coming home. I just can't get my head around this, like, at all. We see some fucked up shit here, so that's saying something. What the hell happened out there last night? How could you make a mistake like that?"

My brow furrowed. "A mistake?"

"What else would you call it?"

I watched his face. His eyes narrowed more as he talked, his nostrils flaring, lips tight when he wasn't talking.

He was mad at me.

I put one hand on my hip and cocked my head to the side. The cloak-and-dagger routine: of course they didn't tell anyone about the video, or who Grady's mother was. But they had to give the rank and file some reason for suspending me.

"What did they tell you guys?" I asked.

"That you're suspended and restricted to fifty feet distance from all DPS property and employees until further notice."

"I can't even talk to my friends?" I asked.

"You really think you're going to have a lot of friends left here?"

The brass knew I wouldn't slink off quietly. So they were trying to make sure I was completely ostracized by my colleagues. My empty stomach twisted.

"What did they say I did, Jared?"

"Abbott said you shot Baxter."

7

I sat in my truck in a diner parking lot down the street for ten minutes beating up my steering wheel, trying to figure out where to go next. They took my phone, so I couldn't call anyone, and my laptop, so I couldn't review my notes and figure out what the most urgent step was.

I hadn't spoken to her in hours, but I was sure my mother was at Archie's bedside by then, which left me with one person I completely trusted in the whole city.

I put the truck in gear and sped toward the crime lab, stopping at a convenience store to buy a prepaid cell phone and get some water to help flush all the caffeine and meds out of my system.

I knew exactly six phone numbers by heart thanks to the miracle of contact lists and speed dial: the long-disconnected one that used to be my Granny McClellan's, the residence line at the Governor's Mansion, Graham's, Jim's, Archie's, and because I'd looked at it just hours before, Trey Morton's cell phone.

I dialed before I backed the truck out of the parking space.

Voicemail.

He didn't know the number. It probably showed up as spam.

I dialed again.

He picked up and clicked off in the same second.

Dammit, Trey. I pushed the talk button a third time.

The line connected, but before I could say anything, a tone blasted in my ear, and then the call ended.

I tossed the phone into the cupholder and kept driving. I couldn't call the office line. They had tracers and recorders on everything coming into the building and I'd only cause trouble for us both.

I was three blocks from the lab when my dinky burner phone started blaring a tune far too jaunty for my mood.

Robocalls are the scourge of modern technology.

I picked it up and started to kill the noise, then clicked Connect just in case.

"Hello?"

"Yes sir, Chief Abbott, I have your report ready." Trey's voice was strained, but he was trying to sound fake-casual.

"You are my absolute hero." I blinked against a sudden onslaught of tears when something about this day finally didn't suck.

"Never a problem, sir, just let me know how you want it delivered."

"I'm going to the lab now. There's a coffee shop on the corner. I can meet you there in an hour."

"Of course, sir. On its way."

I disconnected the call and parked in the lot at the warehouse behind the lab, just in case, jogging across the small side street and around to the front of the building.

I smiled at the desk clerk, who was deep in conversation with a Travis County officer I didn't recognize, and he waved me past the metal detectors that were installed after Jim was attacked back in the spring.

Feeling less shaky, I pushed open the door to Jim's lab just as he emptied the contents of some poor dead guy's stomach into a metal basin. I pulled my shirt collar over my nose and mouth and took shallow breaths, trying not to give my own stomach any similar ideas.

"Morning," Jim said, glancing from the bin to my face. "Sorry. You know the risks of dropping in here."

"Well aware," I said through my shirt.

"Masks in the box on the counter. Some Vicks, too." His eyes skimmed my bloody, torn clothes and dirty face. "You look like you've been to hell and back. Is that your blood?"

"Yes, but it's not bleeding anymore." I smeared the menthol ointment under my nose and donned a surgical mask that matched Jim's, turning back to the table.

"What happened to him?" I asked. The body on the slab couldn't have been more than thirty-five years old, and the face was battered by recent serious injuries. Shaking Grady out of my head, I looked into the open chest cavity instead of at the face.

Jim bent over the table, prodding at something inside the body cavity and pulling a magnifier he wore on a headband down in front of his eyes.

"Well, he showed up here last week after a car accident—crossed the yellow line and hit a minivan head on, but he's the only one who's dead. Not high priority, I had other cases to get to first." Jim looked pointedly at me. "But APD homicide called this morning and now I'm looking for evidence of foul play. Pretty sure I found it, too—cleverly hidden by trauma from the crash." He pointed to a gash in the dead guy's lower right quadrant with a rounded end, then to a hole in the guy's liver, and finally to a shredded aorta. "I was looking for evidence of poison in his last meal and checking his liver for signs of damage when I noticed this."

"Is that a bullet hole?" I asked, my eyes going back to the gash. I leaned down, careful not to touch it, examining the edges. "And a knife wound?"

"It is a bullet hole, the bullet is right there." Jim pointed to a silver basin on his rolling instrument cart, prodding the edges of the gash and leaning in with a microscope. "Nice catch—I believe you're right. This needs to be swabbed for particulates. Maybe we'll get lucky with the metal in the knife."

"You'd have to find a knife to compare," I said.

"Likely in this poor sucker's kitchen." Jim took the swab while my eyebrows shot to my hairline. "Cops got a tip from a friend of this dude's after he heard the news, said he's known him since college and never seen him have so much as a beer, but his bride of three years has been having an affair and recently took out a very large accidental death policy on Adam, here. The buddy who reported it works at the insurance company. So far I'd say the evidence supports his theory."

"Jesus, ever hear of a divorce lawyer?" I sighed.

"Why pay a divorce lawyer when you think you're smart enough to get paid yourself instead?"

"She wasn't smart enough to get away with it," I said.

"Probably. Depends on what else I can find," Jim said. "I'm sure she thinks she's home free with her boyfriend on easy street."

"I wonder if the boyfriend will visit her in prison?" I tapped one foot. "Probably not. He was shitty enough to sleep with someone else's wife. I say he's gone before the trial is over. Sucky people are gonna suck."

"This gig skews your opinion of the general population for sure," he agreed. "What brings you by? I told you I'd call when I had something."

"It's a long story and the less of it you know the safer you'll probably be, but they kicked me off the case," I said. "Which means I need a mole, because I cannot be kicked off this case, Jim. I will lose my mind."

"Kicked you..." He trailed off. "You know what? You're right, I don't need to know. All I need to know is that I already know you didn't do anything to warrant that."

I smiled. "Thank you for believing in me," I said.

"You make it easy. So how can I help?"

"I need to know if you've heard back from your friend in Bexar County about that corpse. Finding out who this guy is may be vital in more ways than one, including possibly the only way I have right now to find Zapata." My voice broke on the last word, and I looked down at my boots and took a couple of deep breaths.

"Let me improve your day slightly, then. Not only are we pretty sure my buddy Lance has the body you're looking for, it is currently set to be transferred here in"—he turned to look at the clock—"about three hours, which means I need to get these samples bagged up for the lab and finish up with this poor bastard pretty quickly."

I wanted to hug him, but the various bodily fluids on his thick rubber apron were a mighty deterrent. "You're the best," I said simply, scribbling the burner number on a card and leaving it on the counter before I turned for the door.

"That's what they tell me." He picked up his scalpel, pausing before he went back to work. "Faith?"

"Yeah?" I was halfway across the room.

"What you did, for me and Sharon..." He sighed heavily. "Graham is coming home whole and breathing and talking if there is anything I can do to make that happen. And I have a lot of friends."

"Thanks, Jim." I smiled under the mask. "We may need every friend any of us can muster to pull this off."

"But we will pull it off," he said. "Go take a shower, catch a nap. I'll call you when I have your guy ready to open."

I was pretty sure the Vicks was conveniently blocking the stench of the puddle I'd collapsed in back at headquarters, which joined a hole and more than a few bloodstains to make my shirt a special kind of horror show, so a shower and a nap sounded like heaven—but not quite as much as getting my phone and computer back.

Thank God for Trey Morton.

The coffee shop bustled with blue collar guys from the construction site down the way—another parking garage, which was both desperately necessary and somehow borderline evil all at the same time. Austin's explosive growth in the years since my father served as governor was a blessing and a curse on many levels.

I checked my watch. Twenty minutes. Fishing a gym bag from behind the seat in my truck, I ducked into a side door and made straight for the bathroom, figuring even two-week-old clothes left in my gym bag had to smell better than what I was wearing.

Locking the door to the restroom, I stripped the gross clothes off and stuffed them in the garbage before pulling paper towels from the dispenser and using hand soap and water to fashion makeshift wipes I used to clean up everywhere I could reach. Bending over, I turned the faucet on high and rinsed my hair the best I could, blotting it with paper towels before I dug some running shorts and a wrinkled T-shirt out of the bag on the floor.

I shoved my boots into the bag and stuffed my feet into sneakers, slinging the bag over my shoulder and reaching for the doorknob as someone knocked on it. I pulled it open and nearly got knocked over by a young Latina woman who stumbled forward like she'd been leaning on the door.

"Sorry," she muttered, her hair hiding her face, which was pointed at the floor.

"You okay?" I asked.

She nodded and I walked out just in time to see Trey stick his head in the front door. I walked out of the hallway and waved, and he nodded, pointing to the counter.

Tired as I was, I knew more caffeine was a bad idea. I picked up a bottle of water and joined him in line to buy that and his coffee.

Drinks in hand, we looked for a quiet spot that didn't exist inside the crowded shop.

I pointed to a table on the patio.

"No air conditioning," he said.

"That's why it's private," I said. "And it's still early. Come on."

He grumbled but followed me outside anyway. I raised the umbrella over the table and sat in the sun-warmed chair, taking the tote bag he handed me.

"Do I want to know what the fuck is happening here?" he asked.

"I doubt it," I said. "And I can't tell you anyway. I don't need anything else keeping me up at night, trust and believe."

"I do trust you. I wouldn't be here if I didn't."

He tapped his fingers on the table. "Can you tell me why they really suspended you?"

"You don't believe the official line?"

"I run the computers, remember? I've seen your target tests—there's no way you missed by far enough to hit Baxter, on your worst day. I don't care what was going on. That's about as likely as my Granny Rose being crowned Miss Texas, and she wouldn't have been in your league in her prime."

I laughed, pointing to my wet hair and desert-dry, bruised face. "Yeah, my league is pretty rarefied these days."

"You are a bona fide badass, and beautiful to boot." Trey held my gaze as he spoke and I wanted to look away, but it felt rude. "Hardin is damned lucky."

"So am I." I tipped my lips up in a gentle smile. "I'm not sure I can find words to tell you how much it means that you came. Or that you brought my stuff with you."

"And that's not all." His face went solemn. "Good news always comes with bad news, right?"

My smile faded. "What now?"

"I heard Abbott and Brinker talking in the cold case room on my way out. There are federal officials involved in this case who are threatening to end the Rangers division if things don't go their way."

That was disturbing, but not altogether surprising. Speaker Grady was the kind of woman who knew how to squeeze people to get what she wanted.

"I'm doing my damnedest to make sure things do go their way, whether they want my help or not." No matter what his mother thought or did, I couldn't go after Graham and leave Grady to die.

"Brinker said the biggest concern right now is that Emilio Zapata is missing, and whoever they're looking for is with Zapata. He said intelligence usually has a thumb on where Zapata is, but he's completely disappeared in the past nine hours. His truck left the gunfight last night and they lost track of him in the aftermath."

My hand went to my lips.

"Graham was in the back of that truck," I choked out.

Trey looked like I'd slapped him. "Oh, hell, I'm so sorry. I thought you would need to know what they're looking for."

"What I'm looking for," I corrected. "Slippery son of a bitch. Snatch a high-profile kid and make demands while you hide out and watch what happens..."

Maybe Zapata was hedging his bets? Amin had been very clear that he wanted out. An attempt at going off the grid while he had a high-profile hostage would test the government's ability to find him to its limit.

My brain raced through scenarios, with no way to know what was plausible and what wasn't.

"For what it's worth, the bit I overheard sounded like they think Zapata might not be hiding so much as taken." Trey watched my face and when I closed my eyes he stammered around softening the news. "But they don't know anything, really. At least as far as I could tell."

"Thank you for telling me," I said.

"You don't look like you wanted to know." His brow furrowed. "I thought since you couldn't be at headquarters, having information would be helpful."

"It is," I said. "I mean, this particular information is scaring the hell out of me right this minute, but I know how to work a missing persons case, and that's what this just became. Find Zapata, find Graham and Grady. It always helps me to know the mission."

Not that I would've believed a person who'd told me even twenty-four hours ago that I'd be suspended—with everyone thinking I took out Archie via friendly fire as a bonus—and trying to find a way to run a rogue, covert case solving the disappearance of North America's most notorious criminal.

This was crazy even when stacked up against all the other crazy places this job—and the hunt for my sister's killer—had taken me.

But that didn't make it any less necessary.

I patted his hand. "Thank you, Trey. I'm not being dramatic when I say you might have saved a life today. Maybe more than one, even. I appreciate your help, and your trust."

"Anything else I can do? The photos are down from the Statesman site, and as far as I can tell, from everyone else's, too. I don't want to know what you gave Skye to get her to handle that."

"Not my firstborn."

He laughed. "That's a lucky break for a kid."

I stood, picking up the bag. "I have work to do. And listen—when they ask you what you found on these, or ask for them back..."

"You let me worry about that."

"I don't want to get you in trouble."

"You didn't. I did. What're they going to do, fire me?"

Trey was the best cyber forensics guy in the state by a country mile. I laughed.

"Exactly. You just watch yourself."

"I will."

He stood and hugged me. "Good luck."

I hurried for my truck, trying not to think about how much I needed my luck to turn around here pretty quick.

8

An hour of sleep in forty-eight hours of adrenaline-charged ruckus that includes getting shot probably isn't healthy, but it was the best I could do before my phone rang.

Groping between the cushions on my mother's sofa for it, I sat up and patted Archie's dog, Tyler, as I glanced at the screen. Ruth.

"How is he?" I said by way of hello.

"Madder than I've ever seen him." She sounded tired, but relieved, which I took as a good sign.

"He called the office." I didn't bother with asking. I knew.

"Why would anyone say you did this, Faith? Archie says you were nowhere near him."

"He didn't tell them I didn't do it, did he?" I asked.

"He didn't have a chance—I hung up on whoever he was talking to when the blood pressure machine started beeping."

"Thank God," I said.

"He said they suspended you."

"This whole thing has gotten very complicated in the past few hours, and Boone didn't have a choice," I said. "But I don't want anyone knowing they're lying for several reasons. At least not until I have time to think about what good might come of arguing."

"Archie says Graham didn't come back with you last night," she said, her voice pained.

"I'm working on it."

"How are you working on it if you're suspended?"

"They can take my badge, but that doesn't mean I don't still have my skills," I said.

"Give me the phone, Ruth." Archie's gravelly voice in the background sounded stronger than I would've expected.

"I can't even argue. I'm just so damn glad he's alive." She sounded positively teary as she passed the phone off.

"Faith." A warning soaked the word.

"Archie, don't," I said. "I love you and I want you to focus on getting better, and I do not want to hear you tell me not to do what you know I have to go do."

"Who the hell do you think you're talking to?" He sounded so normal he could've been sitting at his desk. "I know better than to try to stop you from doing anything, have since you were little more than knee high. But your mother is worried, and so am I. This isn't some bush league serial killer on a freak show mission. These people are organized, they are vicious, and they are not stupid."

"You remember what I said last night?" I asked. "About the tattoo I saw?"

"There aren't enough painkillers in Zapata's compound to make this old man miss that." He paused. "You think it was really the same guy?"

I sighed. "I couldn't begin to say that was the guy, but the tattoo can't be that common. I mean, we've been over this a thousand times. Ten thousand times. You always say it was so close to the end of his term that people scattered. Memories faded," I said. "I didn't see how that could even be possible until now. Turns out, my memory faded. But I have a lead—the first real lead there's been in...ever, maybe?"

"I had plenty of leads," he said. "And I had help chasing them at first. But they all ended in big fat goose eggs. An alibi here, a dead end there...It's all in the file."

"So what could you have missed?" I asked, knowing I wouldn't offend him. Archie trained me—he was the king of wanting to know what he could do better. "The magic rock on this one is still there after all this time. I hope."

"And you think it's a tattoo?" he asked.

"I think it might get me closer." I paused. "I know you had leads that went nowhere, but I don't remember ever being brave enough to ask you this before: What did your gut say?"

"Ruth, give me the room for a minute, please." His hand over the receiver muffled the words. I heard her heels, sharp on the linoleum, as she left without argument, the door clicking behind her as he uncovered the phone. "Nothing good will come of her knowing this if it doesn't go anywhere."

He fell quiet, and I let it go for as long as I could stand it before I cleared my throat. "Will it do me any good to hear it?" I asked gently.

"I'm sitting here trying to decide that," he said. "You're sure you remember the tattoo? And it's not anything that would be common?"

"I've never seen it again until yesterday," I said.

"My gut says someone let them in," he said finally. "That certainty settled in like a wet blanket about thirty-six hours after we found her and has never wavered. I'm not certain who or why or even how much anyone in the mansion had to do with what happened—there were a lot of people there who would've left a door unlocked for enough cash. Without cameras, that was all it took, really."

Chuck had shut off the security camera system the day we moved in—I didn't remember it, but I'd heard the story a hundred times. He had nothing to fear from the people who elected him, and the governor of the great state of Texas wasn't living under constant surveillance. The latter part was, of course, all he was really concerned with. "I've read the file. I know there was no forced entry," I said. "But I always assumed it was an accident. A door everyone forgot about. A missed check on security rounds."

"But a missed check wouldn't have gotten them straight through the house to her. The maid called the cops the second she heard the screaming. She said she knew that Charity was in danger. Even with me out of the house that night at an engagement with Chuck, they only had minutes to get in and out. They knew exactly where to go to grab her and be gone quickly."

"The tour?"

"Doesn't cover the residence."

"So possibly someone who'd been in our house before?"

"Maybe," he said. "Or someone who was directed by a person familiar with the house and grounds. APD was maybe three minutes behind them running full out and didn't see a trace."

"But people scattered," I said dully. "Memories faded."

"And Chuck was incredibly shitty to everyone who worked for him," Archie said. "There was so much motive, means, and opportunity in that house, it's a wonder that he wasn't the one somebody killed."

"There's a lot I could say to that, but I'll keep it to myself for fear of being struck by lightning in your living room."

"My carpet and my dog appreciate the consideration."

"There's a list of the employees who were there that night in the file?" I asked.

"As well as one of every employee, including the ones who weren't there. But the file is in Cold Case at headquarters and you're on suspension."

"Their file is in Cold Case. I made my own copy and started adding to it years ago," I said.

"This is one of those days when I feel like the student has become the master," he said. "I really have nothing left to teach you, do I?"

"If you say the word *retirement* right now, I will lose my shit."

"Noted."

I heard a sharp rap on the door.

"Doc is here. I'm going to pass you back to your mother. Faith?"

"I know, be careful."

"You don't need me to tell you that." He coughed, and I heard a sharp hiss when something hurt him. "If you find this son of a bitch, land a good one for me, would you?"

"I won't stop at one," I said.

Then he was in the background talking to the doctor, and Ruth was asking me who I was beating up.

"Just a little dark humor, Mom," I assured her.

"I will never understand how y'all think things like this can be funny," she said.

"Hazard of the job, I suppose. Tell Archie I'm taking the SIG out of his safe, and I called the sitter about Tyler. I'll feed him and take him out while I'm here and she'll come by this afternoon. Thanks for letting me crash here this morning."

"You're welcome anytime," she said. "I hope you know I mean that."

"I do." I stared at a photo of her and Archie that sat in the center of the mantel. "I love you both, Mom."

"Please be careful," she said. "I don't like the idea of you chasing killers with no backup."

"I might be suspended, but I have friends. I'm covered. I promise. Tell Archie to rest up and get home, the dog misses him, and even this sofa is more comfortable than a hospital bed."

"Take care of yourself."

"I will."

I shook off sleep, grabbed a Dr Pepper from their fridge, and went down the hall to use the guest bathroom shower, washing my hair three times before it felt clean. I found some clothes I'd left in their guest room a few weeks back and dug my boots out of the gym bag. How many people asked to see my badge in a given day, anyway? I nodded to myself. I could do this, with or without the official support of the State of Texas.

I checked for a message from Jim and found none, so I dug out my notes and my laptop and looked for direction.

Mired in the notes I took interviewing Amin and the screenshots from the dark web, I found it.

I tapped my foot, stroking Tyler's soft ears absently and staring at my phone like it would bite.

Hours removed from a shootout with a cartel in the Mexican desert, I had found something even less appealing to do.

Sighing, I picked up the phone and found the number I needed, biting my lip as I waited for an answer.

"Texas Department of Criminal Justice. Visitation. Can I help you?"

"Good morning, this is Faith McClellan." I reeled off my badge number, hoping the computers at the prison weren't yet updated. "I need a private room for a visit with Charles Anderson McClellan, and I need it in about two hours."

I think I didn't realize it earlier because I just flat didn't want to—the whole idea was downright repulsive. But Amin said himself this whole mess had been building for years, as Zapata built his empire, made more enemies than friends, and grew more paranoid.

And twenty-three years ago, Chuck McClellan, the man behind the idea—a man with dozens of enemies—had been out of town for just enough of the evening for my sister to be taken screaming out of her bedroom thanks to an unlocked door in what he claimed was a well-guarded house.

Archie had always been fond of telling me to start the trail at the beginning, and in this case, the trailhead was at Chuck McClellan's feet.

So I was going to see my father.

The drive to the outskirts of Houston was flat and uneventful, though my eyebrows went up when the GPS told me to turn toward Sugarland. Surely there wasn't a correctional facility near the tiny suburb.

I drove down tree-lined boulevards past wide, sweeping lawns of bright green St. Augustine that hadn't gotten the water restriction summer drought memo, large houses spaced reasonably far apart sporting huge windows looking out over the road—and to the southwest, the prison grounds. I guess urban sprawl really does stop for nothing.

Just past one house that had an amusement-park-style pirate ship waterslide in the backyard emptying into a massive swimming pool that appeared to offshoot into a private lazy river, I turned onto a narrow gravel road that led to the prison gates.

I flashed my ID at the guardhouse and held my breath—this was the first test. Would the guy care enough to ask for my badge? Experience had taught me that there were two kinds of prison gate guards: the ones collecting a paycheck while they played the game of the moment on their phones, because who wants to break into a prison?—and there are two more security checkpoints between a visitor and the visitation room, so someone else will catch a weapon or whatever other nefarious things someone might try to smuggle in; and the ones who think they're Dirty Harry guarding the perimeter at Fort Knox.

This guy barely looked up from his tablet as he waved me through.

Excellent.

I brushed my hair into soft waves around my shoulders in the parking lot and fished mascara and lip gloss out of the console, doing what I could with the cosmetics. No harm in having everything going for me that I possibly could.

I strode to the doors and stopped at the booth outside, presenting my ID and my brightest pageant queen smile. The guard was young, with shaggy hair and acne, reading a comic book. He fumbled with the card, barely glancing at it before he handed it back. A grin spread across his face as he met my eyes, his words tripping over each other.

"What brings you out here, Miss McClellan?" He cleared his throat. "I mean, everyone knows it was you who locked him up in the first place."

While technically Chuck was waiting for a judge to approve his plea deal, his attorneys had finagled a way for him to begin serving his sentence as the agreement wound its way down a river of red tape and review.

"He's made a reputation for himself with the staff already, huh?" I quirked an eyebrow up, not really as surprised as I was acting. The Governor would see the staff here as beneath him. The variable in the equation was whether they would take his nonsense or stand up for themselves.

The kid in front of me? Chuck McClellan would eviscerate him in twelve seconds.

"He's a brilliant man," he said. "I snuck into the back of one of his classes and I think I learned a few things."

"Classes?"

"He teaches the other inmates and some of us guards about politics and investing," the kid said. "He didn't tell you?"

I didn't see it as prudent to say I didn't speak to Chuck unless someone's life depended on it when the kid seemed to like him, so I just nodded. "I didn't realize it was a formal setting, I thought he was just talking to some of the other people here. How often is he doing those?"

"We have one every other week." He leaned close. "I put half my paycheck last month into the stock he recommended and I've made three hundred dollars so far."

I'd bet three hundred dollars was a lot to this guy. Chuck had been known to spend that much on a pair of socks.

"Very impressive." I smiled at the guard, seething inwardly as I figured out Chuck's game. "Just make sure you use his number one secret: don't hold it for more than four weeks. Sell at the four-week mark, take your profit, and move on to another investment."

He nodded solemnly.

"Why don't you write that down so you don't forget," I said, watching him pick up a pen and scribble.

Ever the snake oil salesman, The Governor was inflating what I'd bet were small, localized stocks by playing financial god, buying low and then recommending them to people here, but he would watch the price go up probably through his next two to three classes, and then he'd sell and the bottom would fall out, costing the people who'd trusted him while he raked in profits. Chuck McClellan hadn't done a single good deed in his entire life: there was always a benefit to him, and if he could screw someone else along the way, he enjoyed it more.

I took my license back and reminded the guard to sell. "Don't forget about the four-week rule. He gets so busy talking sometimes he forgets to mention it."

"It'll be four weeks tomorrow," he said.

"If you can sell from your phone, go ahead and do it today," I said, waving as I turned for the entrance.

"Thank you!" he called, tapping at his screen.

Two down, one to go, I thought as I pulled the door to the unit open and introduced myself to the formidable woman at the desk.

She scrutinized my ID and tossed it back across the desk. "Governor McClellan says he's not feeling up to visitors today," she said.

That bastard. I hadn't thought of the possibility that he'd refuse to see me. I was prepared for the guards to be difficult, but I'd expected Chuck to be his normal bored, self-involved self.

I flashed my brightest smile. She didn't so much as blink.

"I'd really appreciate it if someone could let him know that I have some information that could help with the education program he's doing here," I said. "I think he'll see me. Just to help out his students, of course."

She pursed her lips, picked up a desk phone, and relayed the message. Giving me a once-over, she pointed to a chair across from her desk. "We'll see what he says."

I counted to five and her phone rang. She didn't speak, just rolled her eyes before she slammed it down and waved me to my feet. "No weapons," she barked.

"Of course," I said. "I'm familiar with procedure."

She pressed a button to buzz the door open for me without further comment. I walked down a narrow hallway under a low ceiling with yellow bulbs in the overhead lights that made everything in the hall look jaundiced. A guard stood outside a door at the other end, a tall man with stooped shoulders in a charcoal suit and blue tie next to him. Both sipped from Starbucks cups.

I thought the second man was a prison officer until I got closer and he lowered the coffee cup. I swallowed comment until we were alone in the interrogation room, Chuck sprawled chain-free across a chair on one side of a small metal table, the facing wall lined with a sofa that saw better days during the Reagan administration.

"How did you get your own clothes?" I asked as I eyed the sofa and opted to remain standing. Up close, I could see that the suit was his favorite Armani single button, which he thought made his shoulders look broader than a double-breasted cut.

He propped his shiny wingtips on the table and crossed his feet at the ankle.

"I'm not a commoner, Faith. I don't belong in prison garb any more than you belong in those damn jeans, wrestling psychopaths in the middle of nowhere Mexico."

I shook my head. "I'm not having this discussion with you."

"I can call him back and send you on your way," he said.

"Try it, and I'll have the SEC on the phone before I'm out of the parking lot. Your assets are supposed to be frozen, yet you've got yourself a nice little game going here."

"Seems I'm not the only one of us keeping tabs on the other." His face spread into a grin that looked almost...proud.

I had neither the time nor the desire to try to unpack that, but it made my skin crawl right up my arms.

"If you know where I was last night, then you have a pretty good idea why I'm here. I know that Derek Amin carried on your arms dealing scheme after you left office," I said. "I figure you were getting a cut of that all these years."

He laced his fingers together behind his head and leaned back in the chair. "You don't really think I'm going to confirm that?" he asked when I let the silence stretch.

"I don't need you to. But if you want me to refrain from sending some highly politically motivated forensic accountants looking for it, and as such extending your stay here, I'm going to need to know what you know about Emilio Zapata. Everything you know. Homes, strengths, weaknesses, mental illnesses, mistresses...particularly places that might be significant to him where he might hide. Spill it, and let me be the judge of what matters and what doesn't."

"You think you're scarier than Emilio?" He laughed. "Maybe you're more like me than I thought."

"You have a pretty good scam going here, Chuck, all things considered," I said. "I can make two phone calls and have you transferred to a place where scratchy orange scrubs, mess hall coffee, and daily ass kickings are a fact of life even you can't weasel your way out of. Twelve years is a long time."

His eyes were half-hooded as he watched me start pacing. We'd run this race too many times to count: he knew I was thinking as I talked, and I knew he was sizing up my threat.

He didn't bite immediately though, and I didn't have the time or the patience to wait him out.

"Or I can call the prosecutors and tell them you're cooperating on my current case and see how amenable they'd be to a good behavior hearing after sixty percent of your time is served."

"You're desperate," he said.

"I have limited time and questionable resources," I said, spinning to pace back the other way.

"Knock that shit off," he grumbled. "You're making me dizzy, and you're perfectly capable of thinking without bouncing around the room like a broken pinball. You're a McClellan, for Christ's sake."

"Does that mean I'm staying a while?"

"You can't record me," he said.

I perched gingerly on the edge of the sofa, pulling a notebook from my back pocket and realizing I didn't have a pen. Chuck rolled his eyes and reached inside his suit coat, producing an emerald-colored Mont Blanc. "I want it back."

"Of course." I took it and unscrewed the cap.

"You've got some kind of brass balls, taking on the Zapata cartel." There was that look again. I'd only ever seen him look proud of Charity and had never wanted him to really notice me much, so it made me want to squirm in the chair like I was nine years old.

"I don't have much of a choice. But at the end of the day, Zapata is a man who will bleed like any other if it comes to that." I didn't add that he'd seemed distraught about his son's murder, which was more than I could say for Chuck. "I'm still a better shot than most."

"Provided you can get to him," he said.

"That's where you're about to be useful for something." I swallowed the *for once*, but his face said he heard it anyway.

He smirked. "He likes his beach house east of Puerta Vallarta. It's where he goes to recharge. He spent the better part of the past year there after his son disappeared."

I watched his face but said nothing about Freddie Z, since I had no idea who Chuck was talking to or if he'd repeat anything I told him.

Never trust a criminal.

"Where specifically east of Vallarta?"

"I don't have my address book on me."

"I don't have time for sarcasm, either."

"It's right on the water, one of the first stretches of the beach proper that's not a hotel. It looks like a medieval fort—there's a watchtower with a turret at each corner of the property with a brick wall in between. He designed the whole place so those towers would just make it look like it belonged to some sort of eccentric, when really there are armed guards in them around the clock if he's on the property."

I didn't miss a word as I scribbled. "What about when he's not?"

"I'm sorry?"

"Are the guards there if he's not on the property?"

"No. I asked him once and he said they travel with him. He's got three of the top four Mexican army snipers of the past decade, plus another sharpshooter he brought in from Russia a couple of years back. They only need to know you're there for a second before you're dead."

I noted that.

"Where else does he own property?"

"All over," he said. "He's got a fishing place in Panama, and a house in the mountains in Apulo in Colombia, and a ski chalet in Valle Nevado."

I tapped the pen on the table. "He has a plane, right?"

"I think he has two," Chuck said.

I made a note to find the registrations, my shoulders slumping slightly. If he had taken Graham and run off to South America...that was an entirely different level of problem than trying to find someone in Mexico.

"Anywhere else you can think of that he'd go? Women he would look for if he was upset?"

Chuck laced his fingers behind his head. "Well, it's been a while but he used to keep his favorite mistress at the beach house. Her name was Elena. And his wife liked the open-air country house, though she's been dead for a few years now."

"Where is that one? In Mexico?"

Chuck nodded. "About an hour outside Ciudad Carta Rosa. It's remote—no Wi-Fi and no TV, and they hunt and drink and shoot a lot of pool, play a lot of cards. Marta liked that feeling of being cut off from everything."

Promising, given Zapata's current situation. And if there were happy family memories attached to the place, too, maybe he hadn't yet skipped the continent.

"Give me landmarks, roads, something I can look for," I said.

"We went southeast out of the city. I don't know if there is more than one road, because I only saw the one. Rode probably forty-five minutes, then turned through a stone and cast-iron archway that said *Castillo de Ensueño*."

I underlined the last part. "That's helpful." Especially for him. "Thanks. You said the guards travel with him—what do they do to secure this house?"

"They walk the perimeter in a loop, several at a time, when Emilio is there. I've seen them doing it."

"How many? How close? How often?"

"You can't try to sneak between patrols based on secondhand intel from someone who hasn't been down there in years," he said. "I have no idea what they're doing today."

"Has anyone ever breached his security?" I asked.

"Not that I've heard."

"Then chances are good he's still doing the same thing. People are creatures of habit, and no one enjoys fixing things that aren't broken."

He sighed. A litany of emotion flickered across his face in half a minute —maybe more than I'd seen from him in my lifetime.

He closed his eyes and talked to the water-marked ceiling tiles. "If you can get access to my computer, there's a video in a hidden folder called *Conquistador*. It will only show in a search of the D drive that contains the word conquistador and an exclamation point, and it's password protected."

Conquistador? I kept my face blank, but it took effort.

"In there, you'll find three video files. You only have my consent to watch the one called Emilio's 60th, part one."

"You know there's a warrant for everything electronic you own that says we can search every drive and every file."

He took his feet off the table and sat up, leaning forward so fast I flinched backward into very questionable upholstery. "And you know I don't beg. Those files were well hidden by a computer genius just in case something like this"—he gestured to the room around us—"ever happened. I promise you no one knows that folder is there. I'm telling you because I'd rather not have you murdered, too, and you'll never admit it, but you're more like me than you think. But as a witness and as your father, I am begging you, do not open the other videos. Please. In the birthday party video background, you'll see the laser sights on the guards' guns as they patrol. That'll give you an idea of what you're up against far better than me trying to explain it will."

"You have my word." Whatever he didn't want me to see, I was probably better off. The prosecutors would have to be notified that it was there, but what they did with it was their business, not mine.

"The password is CharityFaith, all together, both capitalized."

I nearly fell off my chair.

"Don't look so shocked."

"Why the hell not?" It popped out before I could even think.

"I was a terrible father, Faith. I know that. I'd apologize to you for it, but it made you who you are, and I think you like who you are. Lack of parenting skill aside, I was always proud of you girls."

I laughed. "We're not having this conversation." Just the fact that he had twisted our history enough to sit there and say with a straight face that his years of belittling and abuse were a gift that shaped me into a good person was...We weren't talking about it, because if I hit him I'd probably get shot by a guard who didn't know Chuck was giving him stock tips to try to swindle him.

"I have to see a shrink here as part of my rehabilitation," he said. "My lawyer's insistence."

I blinked. "Are they trying to get you a mental illness diagnosis? Because the plea deal is already done."

"I'm told I have narcissistic personality disorder."

"People have written entire books on that illness that read like your biography." I nodded.

"I'm sure I deserve that."

"Don't go growing a conscience on me now, Governor." I looked down at the notebook, where I'd written the password without even realizing it. Not like I would ever forget hearing him say that.

"If Zapata were looking to start a war, where would he take the fight?" I changed the subject back to the safety of an international cartel leader and murderer because Chuck McClellan trying to be fatherly on top of the rest of this day would likely cost me my sanity.

"You think that's what he's doing?" He leaned back and steepled his fingers under his chin.

"Just trying to plan for every eventuality." I didn't want to give anything away.

He watched my face as I spoke, looking for a tell. I tried not to offer one.

"You have always been thorough," he said finally. "He hated the guy who was the HDIC of the Mexican Army with a purple passion. Never did really say why, but he got drunk one night and listed some truly inventive and horrifying ways to torture a person, all of it aimed at that general."

"Is the guy still the head of the army?" My heart stuttered at the thought that Graham's cover was as a former officer in the Mexican army.

"I believe he's a Secretariat of State these days. His office would be in the government plaza in Nuevo Leon, I think."

"They can't take on the federal government there or anywhere else," I muttered, taking notes. "No matter how many guns they have, they'll be severely unprepared."

He stayed quiet.

"What are his weaknesses? Everyone has them. And I know you prey on them. It's part of who you are."

"His family. Losing his wife and then his son really threw him. Any threat to his remaining relatives would hit him where he lives. He's also afraid of whoever he's dealing with in China. I was there for the front end of that deal and it's the only time I ever heard Emilio speak that he not only didn't sound arrogant, he sounded positively meek."

I scribbled until my thumb cramped, trying to get every word.

"Is there anything else you can think of that I need to know?" I looked up when he didn't reply, and had to hold on to the chair for a second time when I saw actual worry on his face. The look showed every crease and line and called my attention to the gray in his jawline stubble and the loose fit of his suit. Prison was aging Chuck McClellan. He put his hands on the table.

"Emilio is smart, Faith. He's shrewd and heartless and vile in a lot of ways. I know you probably think that I'm all those things, and you probably have a right to, but do not underestimate this man—I'm a purring pussycat compared to him. Whatever you're doing, please keep that in mind."

Something possessed me to pat his hand. "Thank you."

"I heard Archie Baxter gave you away," he said, his gaze locked on my hand covering his.

"He did."

"He earned it." He didn't sound sad, just matter of fact. That was probably better with what I was about to ask. I pulled my hand back.

"I don't have a recorder running, so this conversation would be a he said, she said—just to be clear." I pulled in a deep breath and spoke slowly. "I saw something last night that jogged a long-suppressed memory, and it's clear you know these people well. I'm going back to Mexico, sometime in the next few days. I may not make it back, and I'd like to know the truth before I die. Now it's my turn to beg: Did you have anything to do with Charity's murder?"

Anyone who walked in right then would have thought I'd punched him.

"Go to hell," he choked out, shaking his head.

I tossed his pen across the table and stood. "I might beat you there. If I do, I'll be sure to save you a seat, Governor."

I paused with one hand on the doorknob. "Stop your 'financial education program'—or at the very least don't sell the stock out from under them. I promised I'd talk to the DA, and I will, but I can mention having you brought up on market-fixing charges when I call."

I slammed the door shut and walked past the guard without a backward glance.

9

I steered my truck into a parking space next to a Bentley in front of a coffeehouse with gilded doors, squashed between a Neiman Marcus and a Talbot's in Sugarland's poshest shopping enclave. Grabbing my laptop, I strolled in looking more for free Wi-Fi than caffeine.

Every head swiveled to follow me, my sweaty jeans and button-down sticking out like a crooked front tooth at a beauty pageant.

Seated at a table in the back with a small coffee and a good view of the shop, I opened my laptop and typed a long list of thoughts about everything Chuck had said.

If I wanted to find Graham, I had to find Zapata.

So where did he go?

I closed my eyes, no effort needed to call up the nightmarish video. The chamber was mostly underground, with bare shafts of sunshine coming in high windows. The walls were beige and hard to pick out detail in, but the floor was sand.

I opened my notebook and looked over what Chuck had said about homes. A mountain retreat and a ski chalet definitely wouldn't have a sandy floor, nor would a fishing outpost—Well...a fishing outpost probably wouldn't? I guessed that would depend on where Zapata wanted to fish. I opened a browser and searched for "best fishing in Panama." Chuck always had to have the best, and it seemed his friend Zapata was no different.

I found a list of four upscale areas on the water, but real estate listings showed docks right outside the living room and water coming right up to the dock.

Since the dungeon in the video wasn't a swimming pool, I crossed that one off the list.

Which left his beach fortress and his Mexican country house, as long as he hadn't bought anything new in the past several years.

I googled real estate records in Mexico, thankful yet again that I spoke Spanish before I spoke English as I read the deeds and contracts. Zapata didn't just own the places Chuck told me about. He had seven more properties in Mexico, and Google Earth showed that six of them might have a sandy dungeon underneath.

Great.

I sipped the cooling coffee and rested my forehead on my palm.

Eight properties. And I had no idea what was happening to Graham or how long I might have to figure this out and stage a rescue.

I needed help.

Clicking a pen in and out, I remembered the helicopters from the night before and wondered if Miller could send some federal pilots to spy on Zapata's compounds. Every house had thick walls or fences ringed with cacti around it, and even a deep search yielded precious few photos. Those I found were taken with long lenses and not zoom-in friendly.

No. Zapata was paranoid. Even unmarked choppers might make him do something irrational. It was too big a risk, at least as a first resort. So I needed another plan.

I clicked back to the fishing village in Panama. A video played in an ad in the bottom corner of my screen, of a boy flying a drone out over the water, which was so clear the drone's camera could pick up the fish playing under the water.

Cute.

I paused.

The guards traveled with Zapata, The Governor had said. Everywhere.

I scribbled a few notes and slammed my computer shut, pitching the rest of the coffee and climbing back into my truck. I pointed it toward Laredo, passing fifty miles with six phone calls before I got Trey access to Chuck's laptop.

Might as well ask him for all the favors at once.

I dialed his cell phone.

He stayed quiet as I blurted the entire story and then coughed. "Yes sir. I will get right on that."

I heard footsteps, and then a door closing before he lowered his voice. "You okay?"

"I'm making it through."

"Private drone footage, huh?"

"I was thinking if anyone had flown one near these places yesterday or today, looking for the guards Chuck mentioned might tell us where Zapata went. Or at the very least which homes we can ignore. I can't go search eight mansions in international jurisdictions."

"Did you just say there's something you can't do?" Trey laughed.

"Someone would shoot me by at least the fourth one," I said. "I'm smart enough to know the odds. Can you help?"

I heard keys clicking.

"It looks like there are two main companies who run all the servers for the decent drone equipment apps," he said. "Depending on how well their servers are protected and how lucky we get, I might be able to find what you need. Send me the property addresses or coordinates—whatever you have."

I put him on speaker and forwarded the address file. "You should have it."

"So about your dad's laptop..."

"Dads go to barbecues and run on the beach and walk dogs," I said. "Don't give him that much credit for being a human."

"He's a piece of work, your old man," Trey agreed. "But that has nothing to do with you. I'll find your video and send it to you if you'll promise me one thing."

"What's that?"

"When this is over and you and Hardin are home, you'll take a vacation. A long one."

"Whatever you say, Trey." I paused. "Chuck said there are two other videos in that folder. He pleaded with me not to watch them, so enter at your own risk, but if you choose to and see something the prosecutor needs to know, handle that, would you? And don't tell me?"

"You're a real pain in my ass today for someone who doesn't work here right now."

"I appreciate your help more than you will ever know."

"I know," he said. "Go get your bad guy, Ranger. I've got things shored up here."

"Thank you." I hung up.

Turning up the radio, I let my thoughts roam through everything Chuck had said. The look on his face when I finally asked him a question that had skittered around the dark edges of my thoughts since I was a teenager was certainly believable—but The Governor was a politician through and through, and I had believed for most of my life that he could pass a lie detector test saying the Texas summer sky was brown.

I knew asking him wouldn't get me an answer I'd believe, I had just wanted to see his face. But now that I had, I was having trouble shaking it out of my thoughts. Did he actually care that her life had come to a terrifying and painful end far too soon?

My phone buzzed in the cupholder before I could get too far down that rabbit hole.

"Hi, Miller, I'm headed your way," I said when I picked up. "There's not much else for me to do in Austin today, but I have some information I think will be helpful."

"Did you really get yourself suspended this morning?"

"I wouldn't say I got myself anything. It seems there were extenuating political circumstances and Boone felt like he had no choice but to put me on leave. But if they think that means I'm off this case, they've lost their minds. I am getting Graham back."

He sighed. "Faith, those guys who were in Austin this morning...I shouldn't even be talking to you now."

I froze. "Miller? I'm hearing that Zapata is out of pocket and Graham is likely with him. You said you were going to help me get him home."

"Your intel is good—my UC has gone off the grid, too, and things here have gotten pretty frantic with this latest monkey wrench. Did you know the guard at the prison was the Speaker's son?"

"Of course not," I said. "Though given that Senator Rooney's son was working for border patrol, I'd say nepotism is alive and well in the federal government." I paused. "I can't find him without you and your resources, Miller."

"I'm sorry. I could lose my job, and this case I've been building for years now. I can't risk it. Dean will take over as head investigator for the Rangers and report to me, but I can't talk to you until you're reinstated."

"You can't be serious," I said. "You could lose your case? I could lose my husband! I saw your face when you talked about your fiancé. You know I can't let this go. I don't give one damn what anybody says. I'm sure those guys and their standoffish, dictatorial demeanor were CIA or NSA or some other scary spy acronym commoners like us don't even know. I don't care. I'm going after Graham."

He was quiet for so long I thought he'd hung up on me. "I know Graham is important to the mission, and I would like to think I can consider you a friend. I will get him home to you in one piece. Please just go home and wait."

"Graham is not important to the mission." I modulated the words like nails punching out of a pneumatic gun. "Graham is the mission. Full stop. You want to go after Emilio and his weapons and your DEA buddies want to run down his Chinese connections—and I even know some things that could help you with that. But I care about nothing here more than I care about my husband coming home. I want Graham and I want Dakota Grady, and I can help you get what you want, too, Miller. You know that."

"Look, even if my hands weren't tied by forces far more powerful than I am, your single-mindedness on this case could put other people in jeopardy. The suits in DC are often wrong about a lot of things, but they're not wrong about that."

"I would never—"

"I'm sorry, McClellan. I'll get him out of there."

He hung up.

I pulled off the interstate at the next exit and sat in the parking lot of a QT station, hands shaking. My day had started with one of my favorite people on the planet having a bullet dug out of him, progressed through being half-ass fired, being told by my own father to go to hell, and now being completely shut out of a case I literally could not walk away from without losing my mind. Oh, and let's not forget begging Skye for help, agreeing to wear a camera for her, and the general feeling of unease that went with trusting a reporter.

Wait.

A reporter.

I picked up my phone, googling Miller's friend from Richmond.

Nichelle Clarke, journalist, popped up from Wikipedia. There couldn't be more than one reporter in Virginia with that name, and the Wikipedia entry told me she was at least on caliber with Skye for bird-dogging a lead. But Miller swore she had some common sense and a conscience.

Could he be right about that? I wasn't sure such a thing existed—I'd said more than once that Santa Claus is more real than a reporter with a heart. Maybe she was just nice to Miller because he used to date her.

But what if she really was what Miller said she was?

I was flat-ass out of options. If Dean was taking my spot as lead for the Rangers on this case, the brass would be watching him like they were auditioning for roles in a George Orwell story, and I couldn't risk getting him thrown off it, because Graham needed people who had a stake in this working it, and Dean would be driven by the friends he'd lost in Mexico last night.

Miller said this Clarke woman had helped him with the weapons smuggling case. She'd offered up a tip on the Dixie Mafia during the phone call I'd heard, and as far as I could tell with a quick search, she hadn't published a word about it anywhere.

Plus—Miller talked to her, and clearly he wasn't talking to me.

I remembered her saying she was headed home to see her mom and clicked back to Wikipedia.

Family: Lila Clarke, a wedding coordinator in Dallas. I couldn't check

DPS records without possibly tipping my hand to people I didn't want to show my cards to, so I tried Whitepages.

It showed two in Dallas, one in her seventies and one in her forties. I chose the younger one, though that would've made her a young mom by Nichelle's birthdate, punching in my credit card number and snapping a screenshot of the address on file before I looped under the freeway at the next bridge and headed north toward Dallas.

10

Lila Clarke's house was small but adorable. Nestled in the middle of a gentrifying block on the edge of west Dallas that bled officially into the suburbs just the other side of the train tracks a few blocks away, its almond vinyl siding and cheerful blue shutters were clean and inviting—but it was the gardens that really gave the place top-tier curb appeal.

Even in a drought, hot pink and coral hibiscus danced in the slight breeze, and tall orange and red cannas stood watch over a flowing rainbow of gerbera daisies, creeping purple heart, and sunny lantana.

"This woman could give Ruth a run for her money," I muttered as I climbed three concrete steps to a small but inviting front porch and rang the bell.

Sharp footsteps echoed on the other side of a pretty carved-oak door with a wrought-iron inset at eye level. "I got it, Mom!"

The door swung back and a tall brunette made even taller by the emerald stilettos on her feet smiled. "Hi, I'm Nichelle. Meredith, right? My mom is in the kitchen. Come on in. She'll be right out."

I shook my head, making her forehead wrinkle. "I'm not Meredith, I'm Faith."

Her striking eyes, so blue they were purple in the sunlight, widened.

"Faith..." She pressed two fingers to her lips. "Kyle's friend Faith? The

Texas Ranger?" All the color that hadn't come from a makeup brush drained from her face and she grabbed the edge of the door with both hands. "Oh God, is he..."

"No, no." I raised one hand. "I'm so sorry, he's fine. I should've led with that."

"You know you're letting the heat in, right?" A deep voice came from the room just beyond the door.

She stepped backward and waved me inside. "Sorry."

I laced my fingers together behind my back and rocked up on tiptoes, smiling at a tall guy with dark, thick hair and a completely disarming smile who stood when I walked in.

"Joey, this is Kyle's friend Faith. Faith, Joey," Nichelle said.

A petite woman with gray strands sprinkled through her mahogany hair and the same eyes as Nichelle hurried in from a door in the far wall. "So sorry, Mere—you're not Meredith." She grinned. "Sorry again. I'm Lila." She glanced at her daughter. "Who's your friend?"

"I'm sorry to come by unannounced," I said, years of Ruth's etiquette coaching making the words spill out automatically. "My name is Faith McClellan, and I'm a friend of Kyle Miller's...sort of...I was hoping I could talk to you for a few minutes." I directed the last words at Nichelle.

"Of course," she said.

"Joey, that's your cue to come give me a hand in the kitchen," Lila said.

"Yes ma'am." He stood.

"If you talk him into making his grandmother's Bolognese, you'll never eat in an Italian restaurant again," Nichelle said.

"I don't think I have everything you'd need, but promise me we'll do that before y'all have to leave." Lila's voice faded as she led Joey back through the swinging door to the kitchen.

Nichelle watched the door sway for a second before she turned to me. "I'm so glad they're getting along."

"They both seem pretty great," I offered. "I'm sorry to interrupt your visit. It's—"

"No worries," Nichelle cut in, waving for me to take a chic cream armchair with gray accents while she settled on the lemonade-colored chambray sofa cushion Joey had abandoned. "You look worried."

"I look how I feel, then."

"From what Kyle told me, it takes a lot to worry you, and you really hate the press." She paused, studying my face.

I nodded. "All true, I'm afraid. You are good at reading people."

"Thanks. Comes in handy in my line of work. What can I do for you, Faith? You need something pretty desperately, or you wouldn't have come here."

I barked a short laugh, touching my chin to my chest. "Can you like, see an aura or smell it or something?" I asked. "You're the second person who's said that to me this afternoon."

"I talked to Kyle at lunchtime. I know he's in Laredo. You are clearly not, yet he didn't warn me you were coming, which means he doesn't know you're here. I know y'all could've been killed last night and there's a big arrest announcement coming. I know there was some drama this morning, but he wouldn't tell me what kind. Local TV said at noon that two Rangers were killed and one was injured in a gunfight in Mexico late yesterday."

She glanced at Archie's spare gun and a loose holster I hadn't taken the time to tighten. "Seems like maybe that's not your weapon. If I were booted from a case I'd worked this hard on, I'd be desperate too. Maybe even desperate enough to cold call a 'no-good' reporter."

She leaned back and opened her arms, running them along the arm and back of the sofa.

"Maybe I should get a forehead tattoo when I have a minute to myself," I said. "That was like—fortune-teller level analysis. You ever think about taking your show on the road?"

She smiled. "I'm generally happy with my current gig. I just pay attention to details."

"You pay attention to all the details at once," I said. "I know, because I'm unusually observant myself. It's not easy to piece a whole story together so accurately."

"Yet you're not here to talk about telling fortunes."

"How sacred are the words 'off the record' to you?" I watched her face intently, not quite even believing myself what I was contemplating.

"I get the stories I get by digging deeper than most other people, and also by cultivating good sources," she said. "If you cover cops who don't trust you, it's pretty hard to get them to talk about anything past the surface facts."

I watched her, letting the silence stretch. She held my gaze for what felt like an hour before she smiled. "Waiting for me to fill the silence?"

"You're doing the same thing?" I smiled before I could help it.

"We're probably not going to get very far here if we don't operate on a basic assumption of goodwill and trust."

"I catch murderers for a living, assuming goodwill is a dangerous concept."

"I've been shot more than a few times chasing a story," she countered. "And you came to me."

I tipped my head toward the kitchen. "Joey is your boyfriend?"

"He's my fiancé, actually." Her cheeks lit with a soft smile and delightful glow that I knew all too well. "We haven't told anyone because he wanted to get to know my mom and talk to her before we did that."

"You love him." I could see it on her face, plain as her gorgeous violet eyes.

"With the fire of ten thousand suns."

I sucked in a deep breath and looked down at my jeans, focusing on a tiny red stain above the right knee I hadn't noticed before. "My husband is embedded undercover in a particularly cruel and vile cartel without a safe extraction strategy in place, and now the leader of the cartel is missing—and so is Graham. Graham is wounded, but even if he could try to run on his own, he wouldn't get far before Zapata had him tracked down and killed because the cartel leader is paranoid about traitors in his ranks."

"Seems like he's right to be," Nichelle said.

My lips tipped up at the corners. "Touché. We have reason to believe Zapata is looking for a fight and doesn't much care with who. Graham's cover might be compromised already, and oh, yeah, Miller and the Rangers brass have shut me out of the case at the request of a politician, who may well be inclined to trade my husband's life for her son's. At the very least, international politics adds a slowdown, and the longer Graham is there, the more likely something terrible could happen to him." The words fell out of my face so fast I wasn't sure they were even in the right order until she leaned forward and touched the back of my hand.

I met her gaze and found nothing but compassion and concern.

"I've been there. I'll help you however I can."

"Go back to what you said before, about Zapata being afraid of his Chinese contact." Joey sipped his iced tea and then put the glass on a stone coaster painted with bluebonnets. "Is there a way to get to him that way? Would his Chinese contact have a burner cell number or know where he is in case of some kind of emergency? Do you have any contacts who could find out?"

I studied him across the table. He was almost sinfully good-looking, with biceps straining his blue polo sleeves, broad shoulders, and kind brown eyes.

Nichelle had jumped to her feet and retrieved him from the kitchen with a vague comment about him being an insightful sounding board when she was brainstorming. Seemed like she might be right.

I shook my head. "No, but Miller's DEA friends might. Of course, I can't ask because he's freezing me out."

"Kyle isn't avoiding you to be a jerk," Nichelle said. "I know it seems like it, and I get why you're mad, but he must really think he's doing what's best for the case."

"I'm sure he does, but he's wrong."

Nichelle nodded as she exchanged a look with Joey. "I say that a lot."

I focused on Joey, noting the way his eyes went soft and dopey when he looked at Nichelle, though I could tell he was a smart guy—I'd mentioned Chuck's comment about Zapata fearing the Chinese drug lord only in passing, and he had picked up on something I'd overlooked—something that could be really helpful. It wasn't unlike Nichelle's shrewd analysis of my situation before I'd said a dozen words to her—they were a good match.

"What made you ask that?" I asked. "About the Chinese? Can you elaborate on what you were thinking?"

He dropped his gaze to his hands for a second and cleared his throat. "Well, there's a hierarchy to almost every criminal enterprise on the planet. And it's deeper and more meaningful than most people realize."

"How do you mean?"

He glanced at Nichelle and she nodded so slightly a blink would've obscured it. I wrinkled my forehead and turned back to Joey when he started talking.

"The entire basis of any organized crime unit is fear, ma'am." Hand to God, if he had a hat, he would've tipped it.

I leaned forward as he talked, the same instinct that often told me which doors to open and which to avoid at a crime scene telling me not to miss a word of what he was saying.

"It can't be trust, because how does a killer trust other killers? TV and movies would have you believe there's some sort of honor among thieves, but that's a load of...Well, it's just not true." He flashed a small smile. "The only way any of it works is that the lower-level guys are afraid of the bosses."

"So you think the Chinese guy outranks Zapata in this hierarchy?" I tapped one finger on my chin, intrigued.

"He has to," Joey said. "It's the only way Zapata would fear him."

"So you're thinking to get Graham and the other agents out of there we might...what, exactly? Make a deal with a Chinese fentanyl dealer?"

Nichelle laughed, clapping one hand over her mouth. "Sorry. No, I can assure you no one wants that."

Joey held up one finger. "It's not about making a deal. It's simply about convincing the guy that Zapata is going to screw him over and getting him to go on the offensive. As long as we know when that's coming."

"Which wouldn't be hard if what you said about them not trusting each other is really true," I mused.

"Exactly," he said. "I can promise you that this guy is already at least half-convinced Zapata is screwing him—from half a world away? No chance that thought hasn't occurred to him."

"But how does pissing off Zapata's Chinese contact help Graham?" I asked.

"Remember what you said the national guard guy told you? About Zapata starting a war so he could vanish into the chaos and fake his own death?" Joey asked.

I nodded.

Joey picked up his tea glass and moved the coaster over, putting the glass on the table next to it.

"Essentially, we'd be doing the same thing with a couple of key differences. If Zapata really is screwing over the Chinese guy, he might get killed. You'd have to be okay with that."

"There is a wide berth here of what I'm okay with if it means I get my husband home safe and whole."

He caught my gaze and held it for a beat before he nodded. "So essentially, if we could pull this off and put Zapata's crew on defense rather than offense, their ability to keep their shit together is going to crumble quickly." He stacked two coasters and put his glass back on top, then moved Nichelle's glass to just opposite them. "If my glass is Zapata, he's the highest rank on this side of the ocean, right?"

I nodded.

"So your sources say there's already tension in the organization." He tapped Nichelle's glass, scooting it closer to the coaster tower—and the edge of the table. "Zapata is suspicious—more suspicious than I would say is normal—of the troops. If they're attacked, whoever he's got in the ranks that's a threat will show themselves and likely try to stage a coup."

He put more coasters under Nichelle's glass. I had a feeling he was fiddling with his toy soldier glasses as a way to have something to do with his hands and a place to focus his eyes since I understood what he was saying fine without a schematic model, and I was nearly certain he knew that.

Why?

Any other day of my life I would've asked.

Right then, I could've been talking to the devil himself and if he was offering me a way to get Graham out of Mexico, I wouldn't have left the table without hearing him out.

"That moment is our opportunity: Zapata is shaky, he has no idea who or how many people are out to get him." He moved his glass to the edge of the coaster and kept his hand on it so it wouldn't fall. "If everyone times it right, your husband and the other agent can slip to the other side of the fence in the confusion that ensues, just as Kyle and his guys ride in to dismantle the cartel and arrest the principal players for trial here, not in a

Mexican court where Zapata has owned judges for decades." He pulled one coaster out of each stack and put them on the other side of the table near mine. "Imagine I let my glass and Nichelle's smash and you have the rest of the idea."

He busied himself putting everything back.

I glanced at Nichelle and saw worry lines in the corners of her eyes as she watched him.

"And then getting Graham and the others home isn't dependent on political whims, and Graham's safety is less likely to be the subject of a trade."

"Exactly," Joey said. "If we can put them on defense, we can have some level of control over how this goes down, and what everyone else decides to do matters far less."

"So the thing we don't know," I said, using my sleeve to wipe a half-crescent water ring off the table from the glass, "is how we get ahold of a Chinese drug lord."

"I might be able to help with that." Joey kept his eyes on the table as Nichelle sucked in a sharp breath and shot to her feet.

He kept his seat, looking up at her without a word for long enough to make me avert my eyes. It felt like I was intruding on something intensely private, more so since I couldn't quite figure out what was going on.

"Joey..." she said finally.

"I know. But I need to."

She sighed, sinking back into her seat. "I know, too."

Before I could figure out what to say, Nichelle's mom appeared in the doorway, asking if anyone wanted a refill. She smiled as she leaned over the table, but her hands trembled as she picked up glasses to pour the tea. Had she been eavesdropping?

She nodded when we thanked her and hustled back to the kitchen without a word.

Nichelle looked like she wanted to go after her mother, then looked at me and changed her mind. "Kyle will have to know what we're doing so he can plan an offensive for the right time," she said.

"But not until we're sure everything is set and he has no choice but to join us," I said. "And I want to be part of the offensive. Once we're on site and ready, Miller won't turn me away."

Her lips curved into a rueful smile. "You know him well after only... what, a week? No, he won't blow an operation to keep you out of it, and he will take whatever opportunity we give him to bring this to the close that costs our side the least."

"So our mission is to figure out where Zapata is, if he's still in charge, and what kind of fight he's planning to take where, while we wait to hear from China." I glanced at Joey, who nodded.

"And if your husband, the Speaker's son, and Kyle's officer are with him, or somewhere else," Nichelle added.

"They're with him." I looked at Joey. "Surely they are, right? Graham was in that truck, and he wouldn't trust anyone else with Grady, would he?"

"I'd say that's likely," he said. "But there's no way to know for sure unless we hear from someone, or, like, come across some drone footage or something."

I tipped my head to one side, raising one finger. "I'm not sure how possible it is for us to time the Chinese attack, but if we could have it happen when Zapata's people are in the field fighting and before he tries to vanish..." I shrugged. "It could be a terrible idea. But I was just thinking they would be more scattered and therefore maybe more vulnerable."

"It's a really good idea," Joey said. "I don't know enough to promise anything now, but I'll see what I can do."

"And y'all can talk Miller into this?"

Nichelle rolled her eyes. "Kyle can be dismissive of my ideas, especially when they might put someone in danger. But he usually listens to Joey."

I raised one eyebrow. "I didn't peg him as a misogynist."

"He's not. He just think's Joey's...really smart." She plucked at a loose thread on her shorts.

There's only so much curiosity a person can take. "What did you say you do?" I asked, turning back to him.

"I work for a trucking company in route management and procurement," he said. "And Miller usually dismisses her ideas when they're going to put her in danger, in fairness, which I appreciate."

"I imagine you'd have to be really organized," I said. "For the route management."

He nodded. "At work, anyway."

I sat back after a minute of silence told me no one was going to say more.

"I really appreciate you two offering to help me more than I can say."

"We're happy to." Nichelle smiled and Joey nodded. "I'll call Kyle. He can't know you were here, of course."

"As long as he's talking to you, I will let him pretend I don't exist," I said.

"I think we have a plan, y'all." Nichelle stuck her hand out and Joey and I piled ours on. "Is this too cheesy?"

"We may well be setting out to try to get ourselves killed," Joey said. "The least we can do is start it off as a team. His name is Graham, right?"

I nodded.

Nichelle took a slow deep breath. "Get Graham on three, y'all. One, two, three..."

"Get Graham," we said in unison, a tingle shooting up my arm as we raised our hands high like we were walking out of a huddle on Friday night.

A reporter, her stupidly good-looking fiancé who probably had more of a story than I wanted to know, and a suspended Texas Ranger with a borrowed gun. This was Graham's best hope.

I stood and crossed my fingers, hoping God and my sister would offer a little help.

11

My dinky burner phone buzzed in the cupholder before I turned off Lila's street.

Picking it up, I recognized Jim's number and nearly dropped it trying to flip it open to answer.

"Did you get the remains?" I asked, noticing that the sun was hanging lower than I thought it should be and checking the clock. Almost seven already. And the truck needed gas. I spotted a station two blocks down and turned toward it.

"Two seconds, sorry," Jim said before he muted the call on his end.

I sat through a light and was parked at a gas pump before he came back on the line.

"Sorry about that, it has been nonstop here today," he said.

"Please tell me you got the body from San Antonio," I said. "And that it's the right one."

"This tattoo, it's a vaguely human creature with fangs dripping blood?" he asked.

"On his forearm," I said. "It's big, and the blood drops went all the way to the back of his hand."

"Did you see any others?"

"No, but I was running last night, and obviously my memory from the night Charity disappeared is...fuzzy," I said, starting the gas pump.

"This guy came in wearing a white tank top. Or I think it used to be white. There's a lot of blood."

"That sounds right," I said. "I wasn't exactly studying wardrobe choices with bullets flying, but I could believe that."

"He got here about two hours ago, and I just finished a preliminary. He definitely died of these wounds," Jim said.

"Wounds, plural?" A prelim was a visual exam, so he hadn't gotten far, but he wouldn't call for no reason. I was pretty sure Miller shot him once and I saw him fall.

Jim was still talking like he hadn't heard me. "There are several tattoos, two I think might be worth looking into because they appear to be signed by the artist."

"Can you make out the signature?"

"Not entirely but I just sent you some high-res photos of them," he said.

"Perfect," I said. "Were you able to get prints?"

"I did. I sent them to a guy who owes me a favor."

What? I inhaled for a five count before I spoke, the gasoline fumes burning my nostrils a little in the summer heat. "I appreciate that, but I'm not sure bringing more people into this is smart."

"No reason for concern—I promise. Nick is as level-headed and discreet as they come, and if there's something to be found with this guy's prints, he'll hunt it down. I worked with him on a cold case last year and we actually got the guy—killed a college girl back in the nineties and was living a nice quiet suburban insurance salesman life when Nick found him. All from a DNA sample that was locked up in a storage shed the Austin PD wanted to tear down last winter."

"I trust you." I yanked the pump a little too hard from the tank and spilled a small splash on the ground. "Dammit."

Jim cleared his throat, completely failing at covering a laugh. "I know how hard that is for you. I told you earlier—I have a lot of friends. People owe me a metric shit ton of favors. And I will cash them in however necessary to help you. If anyone—from a fifth grade kidnapping prevention program to a one horse county sheriff in Bumfuck, Mississippi—has ever taken prints from this guy, Nick Ryan will find them. Might take him a minute, but you can trust him."

"If he's that good at this, why doesn't he work for the Rangers?" I climbed back into the truck and started the engine, looking for a coffee shop with Wi-Fi and finding one just across the road.

"I asked him once why he didn't go into police work. He said he likes investigating all kinds of stuff. He's like a secret weapon for finding information."

"He's not a cop?"

"Nope, he works for the state in intelligence gathering, in a little office down in New Braunfels. He pulls together sort of J. Edgar Hoover style files on VIPs and runs background checks on high-profile officials at universities and cities...If there's dirt to be found, he will find it. He likes to say he's better at it than Skye Morrow."

"You're telling me the state employs a professional muckraker?"

"Private information analyst, I think they call it."

"I don't even know why I'm surprised."

"I hear you," Jim said. "I'm going to keep examining this guy—going for X-rays next, though I imagine there's plenty of shattered bone from these bullets, so I'm not sure what I'll get."

"Do a scan, too," I said. "We've found fake bits on corpses before that are great identifiers."

"On my list, along with a full dental." Patience I probably didn't deserve dripped from the speaker.

"Sorry, I'm not trying to tell you how to do your job," I said. "I'll check out the tattoos."

"You are a little bit, but I understand why. I cut up dead people for a living and the number of times I started to try to lecture Sharon's doctors—it's a wonder they didn't have security toss me out."

I laughed. "Thanks."

"Let me know if you need any more photos," he said. "And try to stay calm—if this guy has an identity to find, we'll find it."

I thanked him again and hung up, ducking into the coffee shop. It was cute—local, not corporate, and filled with overstuffed, cozy furniture, tables holding board games, and the delicious smell of freshly roasted beans. I ordered a latte and found a blue table in the corner, scooting the Yahtzee box to one side so I could open my laptop. I clicked through the Wi-Fi connection instructions and into my email, zooming in on the photos of John Doe's ink. The first was definitely the tattoo I remembered, from last night and twenty years ago, too—complete with blood running down onto the back of the guy's hand, which I couldn't help but think was a metaphor for a killer. But it wasn't signed.

I went to the second image and zoomed in on the scrawl beneath a collection of Chinese characters wound around a dragon. It looked like the first name was Alex, which could be a man or a woman, and I couldn't make out the last name except that it started with an E.

I googled "Alex E tattoo artist" and got 268 hits. Tattoo needle in a large haystack. I scrolled, eliminating the ones in New York and Los Angeles at least for now based on proximity. In the twenty-two years since my sister was killed, the guy was still in driving distance of Austin. So setting the search to Texas and the surrounding states seemed prudent.

New Orleans had the most with four, followed by two in El Paso, one in Laredo, three in the Hill Country—and three in the Dallas/Fort Worth metro area. I hit the address for the first one. Fifteen minutes away, open until one.

Every search has to start somewhere.

Nothing notable at the first tattoo parlor except that it was overrun by a passel of drunk frat boys getting Snoopy tattoos on their asses. The harried artist going from one pale backside to the next told me Alex didn't work there anymore because he moved to California with his girlfriend. Strike one.

The second one was in a part of town Ruth would've been horrified to find me in. I strode confidently to the door with my head up and my shoulders back, and found an orange eviction sticker crumpled on the edge of the locked door.

Strike two. Maybe I'd head back toward Austin tonight after all. I checked the address for the third place—twenty minutes west in Arlington, right off the interstate.

"Might as well check it out while I'm here," I muttered, cranking the radio and turning toward I-30.

The sun sank below the horizon as I parked in front of a well-kept but aging strip center smack in the middle of an explosion of new development around the football and baseball stadiums.

I pulled the door open and smiled slightly at a handwritten sign taped to the glass: *Fuck service charges, ca$h only.*

The lobby was small and empty, the walls invisible behind a collage of photographs of intricate tattoos interspersed with sketches of designs offered by each artist. I found the plaque advertising Alex's work, but there was no signature on it.

Footsteps clicked on linoleum and I turned to the doorway to find a petite woman with aquamarine curls and leather pants hurrying toward me.

"Sorry, the guy who works out here called out again today. I'm Pixie. What can I do for you?" She stopped short when she got to the counter and peered up at me. "Your first time?"

"I'm not sure yet," I said, flashing my best put-the-judges-at-ease smile. One thing I'll say for spending my childhood being plucked and groomed and corset-cinched into every pageant in five states—Ruth had taught me a smile for every social situation and made me practice them all in front of a mirror such that I could call them up by reflex even now. It was often handy when trying to get information out of people. "I'd like to speak to Alex if he's available."

"He's working on a calf sleeve in the back, but the big guy is out, so he probably won't mind if you come back. What are you thinking you might want?"

"A star, maybe?" I had toyed with the idea, as a tribute to both my career and my sister, but never too seriously. Graham wouldn't object, but Ruth would flat lose her shit. And we were finally getting to a good place—no need to rock that rickety boat.

Pixie gave me a once-over with green eyes framed by thick, fake purple lashes. "Yeah. That's probably a good fit for you."

I wasn't sure if that was an observation or an insult, so I just smiled, pointing to the rose vine trailing across her collarbone, almost like a necklace above the collar of her sequined sweetheart top. "Your roses are pretty," I said.

She shrugged. "Not enough blood on the thorns for my taste, but I couldn't do that one myself."

"You can give yourself a tattoo?"

"Sure, when I can reach the spot well. It doesn't hurt."

She laughed when I raised one eyebrow.

"I don't think it hurts, anyway," she said.

"Can you cover a scar with it?" I asked.

"You have a scar to cover?" Her turn for the skeptical eyebrow.

"Three, actually, but let's start with one." I pointed to my shoulder. "Nearly perfectly round, about an inch across."

"That sounds like a gunshot scar."

"It might be," I said.

"Huh." She lifted her shirt and pointed to a blue daisy just under her rib cage. "They do better with flowers."

She disappeared before I could ask how she got shot, and then popped her head through a doorway, waving me back through a large room with several stations set up with what looked like dentist's chairs.

"He says you can go in, but keep your voice low so you don't disturb his client. And don't mind the doc."

I stepped into the room.

An actual wall of a man was sprawled on his belly on a bed like the cots most emergency rooms have. Not a thread of the sheet under him was visible, except around his head. A curvy woman in a lab coat sat reading a magazine next to an IV pole, and a lanky guy in shorts and a tank top with so much ink Adam Levine might say he was over the top leaned over a calf nearly as thick as my waist with a needle buzzing in his hand.

"Come around so I can see you," he said, not taking his eyes off his work. I peeked as I rounded the end of the cot—he was shading a familiar star in dark blue, the silver outline already complete.

"Big fan?" I gestured to the guy on the bed. "Football, I mean."

"Sweetie, he's the starting defensive tackle." Alex still didn't look up.

"Strong safety, Alex," the white coat lady said, looking up from her magazine. "He told you three times."

"Whatever. He gets paid a lot of money to assault people on Sundays in the winter."

Lab coat lady pointed to a chair in the corner. "Have a seat. He's not a football guy, but he is the best ink artist in town, so the players all come here."

The buzzing of the needle paused and Alex glanced at me while he changed the color. "You have never set foot in a tattoo parlor in your life," he said. "What brings you to see me? Dare? Early midlife crisis?"

"Hoping you did some work on someone I met recently," I said. It was mostly true.

"They didn't tell you if I did the work?" He turned the tattoo gun back on and started filling in a deep-violet dragon. I kept my eyes on it, trying to decide if it really looked similar to the one in the photo Jim sent me or if I just wanted it to.

"He wasn't in a condition for me to ask."

"Drunks are so fucking annoying." Alex kept his hand even and his voice calm. "We get two or three a night in here, half of them cussing us out when we won't do dumb shit like tattoo 'fuck off' across their foreheads. You know someone would sue as soon as they slept off the booze and found a mirror."

"How does that ever seem like a good idea?" I asked.

"Don't ask me, sweetie. I believe in spreading love." He smiled and I noted the blue heart on his cheekbone, easily mistaken for a teardrop on first glance. He finished coloring the dragon's head and sat back to look over his work, then raised his eyes to mine. "You have a photo of this?"

I opened my computer and showed him the picture. He leaned in.

"Is that your signature?" I asked, checking the football player's leg for one and not finding it, at least on the back of his calf.

"I would not put my name on another person's body without their express permission. Maybe not even then. That is a level of vanity even I don't possess, and I know I'm pretty and I know I'm good," he said. "I've only ever met one person with an ego big enough for that. But I can definitely do that design." He gave me a once-over. "If you're sure it's what you want. I can do it better than that, for sure. Make an appointment with Pixie on your way out. I have all I can handle here tonight."

"Do you know where I can find him?" I asked. "The artist you said would have the ego for a signature like this?"

The gun went silent and Alex stood, leaving the room without a word.

"Was it something I said?" I asked lab coat lady.

"He probably has to pee," she said absently, turning the page. "I've only been here a few times, but he's kind of a quirky dude."

"You're a doctor?"

"Sure am." She looked up and smiled. "A real MD, with all the student debt to prove it. These moonlighting gigs pay well and are, as you see, minimally taxing."

I heard a rustling sound behind the wall and then footsteps. It took me three seconds too long to realize there were two sets. I wasn't quite to my feet when Alex returned with a friend.

"Stand on up slowly with your hands in the air." A tall, buxom woman with neon red hair and biceps that might rival the anesthetized football player's pumped a twelve-gauge and kicked the ejected cartridge out of her way. "And then get the fuck out of my shop and don't come back."

12

I rose slowly, my eyes on the gun. If she had one shell to eject, then she should only have two left, because bird-hunting regulations limit most American-made shotguns to a three-cartridge chamber.

Dr. Easy Money flailed for a second before scrambling to her feet and promptly slipping on her dropped magazine, the chair thudding into the wall when she landed hard on it.

"Nobody move," the redhead said.

"So do I go, or do I stay still?" I asked, keeping my voice and my breathing even.

"How about you shut the fuck up and don't give me attitude?" she snapped, wagging the gun like a finger as she spoke.

"Don't get me wrong, I'm not interested in dying at the moment, but you and that shotgun aren't even the scariest thing I've seen today," I said. "And I've ridden this horse enough times to be almost sure that if you were really going to shoot anyone, you'd have done it already."

"You don't know me," she said.

I nodded to the finger resting outside the trigger guard, keeping my hands in the air.

"I know you don't even want to shoot anyone accidentally right now. Because I do the same thing when I'm handling my weapon."

"I told you, she's one of them," Alex said. "If you're too much of a little bitch to shoot her, give me that thing—" He closed one hand around the barrel and the redhead yanked back and then shoved forward, tossing him to the floor.

"You sit the fuck down and don't ever touch my gun again," she growled. "I don't care how many ballplayers like you, I'll can your ass."

The doctor whined from her seat, her wide eyes still on the shotgun. I turned to her with a calm smile, trying to help her understand that we were in far less danger than a passerby might think.

"Why are you asking about that ink?" the redhead barked, the gun still levied at my midsection.

"Everything okay in he—" Pixie stopped in the doorway, put her hands up, and took a step back. "Never mind."

"Come join the party," the redhead said.

"I have a customer," Pixie said. "Maybe I should tell her to come back tomorrow."

"Or maybe you should come in here and lock the door like I fucking said." The redhead swung the shotgun toward Pixie and I swore under my breath because the distance across the room and over the sleeping mountain of athlete was too much for me to try to leap while her attention was diverted.

"Chill the fuck out, Hannah." Pixie stepped inside and locked the door.

"So, I'm not going?" I asked.

"Who are you and why are you here?"

"She wanted a star tattoo," Pixie said, looking from the gun to me. "You're...what the hell are you mad at her for?"

"What did you think when you saw the gun, stupid?" Alex asked, now sitting cross-legged on the floor.

"I thought your guy didn't want to pay. The shotgun is usually for people who don't want to pay."

"He makes millions of dollars a year. He's not walking out on his bill."

The cot groaned as the leg Alex had been working on twitched, and its owner mumbled something I couldn't make out. The doctor scrambled to her feet, tweaking the flow on two different IV bags. Her patient settled again.

"I can only keep him under two more hours on a cosmetic procedure," she said.

"Everybody shut up!" the redhead screeched, turning back to me. "You, Barbie. You talk. Who are you and why are you here?"

I sighed. No way to know if admitting I was a cop would better or worsen my position, but the truth was the best option I could think of at the moment. How much of it I should offer was an entirely different question.

"I'm a Texas Ranger," I said.

Alex furrowed his brow. "Like one of their wives?"

"Like the kind with a gun who chases bad guys."

"A cop?" The redhead's brow furrowed, but she didn't shout and she didn't wave the gun anymore.

"My name is Faith McClellan. I think the man who had the tattoos I was asking about knew who killed my sister a long time ago. I thought maybe the tattoo artist might be able to tell me a little about the person he'd put them on."

"You put tattoos on a murderer?" Pixie turned on Alex with a gaping jaw, and the doctor followed suit.

"Not me, genius," Alex said. "Alejandro."

"Alejandro, Hannah's ex Alejandro?" Pixie blurted, and for half a second I thought Hannah the redheaded gun wielder might actually shoot someone.

"Shut. Up," she growled, swinging the gun to Pixie, who clapped one hand over her mouth and slid down the wall she was leaning on until her ass met the linoleum.

"I really need to talk to him," I said.

Hannah swung the barrel back my way. "I can't help you, but I can tell you that if your sister has been dead a while, this is not worth your time if you're not looking to join her. You're risking your life going after those guys."

"What guys?" I took one small step forward, aware that she was still holding the shotgun but more certain she wasn't going to use it.

Hannah shook her head.

Alex looked at the floor.

Pixie and the doc clearly knew very little.

I kept my hands up and took another step, moving to the corner of the cot.

"Stop." Hannah poked the gun my direction.

"Sure," I said, pausing. "You know I'm not here to hurt you, right?"

"Shut up—everyone, just shut up. I need to think."

"Why?" I asked.

"Because," she barked, moving her finger to the trigger briefly.

I looked at Alex, who was still looking at the floor. There was something important they weren't saying.

"How long have you worked here?" I asked him.

"Shut up," Hannah repeated, her voice going up an octave.

"Do you know where I can find Alejandro?" I asked.

"Seriously. Shut the fuck up."

I paused for two breaths.

"Why does the mere idea of your ex scare you so badly you need a gun?"

"Because these fucking people you're talking about are dangerous and I don't want to get tangled back up with them," she blurted.

"Are you running a risk of that by talking to me?"

"No—maybe— I don't know."

"You don't know what?"

"How they know what they know!"

"Hannah!" Alex barked.

"You think they're keeping tabs on you?" I tipped my head to one side. Why would Zapata put money and effort into that?

Hannah glanced at Alex, still on the floor, then shook her head at me.

"Nope. You gotta go. Get the fuck out before I decide I am capable of shooting you."

"I can help you," I said as I moved toward the door.

"Nobody can help me," she said. "I've been a lost soul for a long time, Ranger, but I'm not quite ready to meet the devil. I look out for me and mine, and you are neither. There's the door."

I kept my hands up until I was well out of the room and slammed the front door open a little too hard.

Another hour gone, and all I had to show for it was a name. Better than nothing, but not by much. I gunned it hard enough to squeal the tires as I left the lot, spotting a hotel on the other side of the freeway.

If I didn't sleep at least a little I was going to pass out and crash the truck.

Hoping Miller's reporter friend had better luck than I did, I hauled my bag and laptop upstairs, flopped onto the king-sized bed, and fell asleep with the light and my boots on.

Sunbeams danced through sheer curtains when my dinky burner phone's shrill ring interrupted a dream that involved Graham and a beach and a pink drink with an umbrella in it. I'm not sure I've ever been so resentful of an electronic device.

"McClellan," I mumbled, shoving my hair out of my face.

"Oh good, you slept." Jim sounded like he hadn't.

I couldn't be frustrated with Jim. Not today.

"Like a rock. With boots on." I sat up and pulled them off, wiggling numb toes. "A little coffee and a shower and I might feel almost human."

"Are you at home?"

"No, I'm in Dallas. Or close anyway."

"I was going to ask you to come by." He paused. "This number is a prepaid phone?"

"It is. What did you find? Just tell me."

"A few things. Some I really think I'd rather say in person, but the scan showed..." He sighed. "In the fight the other night, did you see this guy go down? Who shot him?"

"Miller did. Hit him hard in the chest, near his heart—spun him around and put him right on the ground."

Jim stayed quiet for so long I thought he might have hung up, and the burner phone had no connection counter.

"Jim. Are you still there? Seriously, I can't do more suspense than necessary today. Kind of maxed out."

"I'm just thinking," he said. "There are two wounds here. One that could've come from what you just described. And one to his head."

"I definitely didn't see him get shot in the head."

"I also found powder on his hands."

"Sure. There was powder on everyone's hands. We were in a gunfight. The place looked like a scene from an old western."

"What kind of weapons were you all using? Tac team rifles?"

"Some. I think Archie switched to his sidearm. I know I switched to mine."

"Caliber?"

"Uh, the rifles are .223 and my SIG is nine millimeter. Seriously, what's with the inquisition?"

"I'm trying to figure something out without sharing speculation."

"Jim. It's me. Please speculate. I'm not a rookie who's going to add anything you say to the gospel according to Jim Prescott. I understand how brainstorming works. What's bugging you?"

"Did he see you?"

"I suppose?" I couldn't keep the exasperation out of my voice.

"I think he might have shot himself," he said. "This was a clean shot to the head at close range—there're powder burns and stippling on his temple too. I don't have the other victims in my lab to compare, but I've seen plenty of carnage from gunfights in my time here and a close-range wound isn't common. Matter of fact, I've never seen one this clean."

"I agree it's weird," I said slowly, blinking and wishing I trusted hotel in-room coffeemakers. "But I'm going to need help with why in the hell a guy with the background this one had would blow his own brains out in the middle of a gunfight. I mean, he couldn't have been more than what...fifty-five?"

"Dental wear puts him in his midfifties," Jim agreed. "And I know this sounds pretty out there, but the scans showed he had cancer. A large mass in the cerebellum and smaller clusters pretty much everywhere. Lungs, liver, bones...I'm not really sure how he was standing out there firing a weapon at all from looking at these, to be honest."

My jaw hung open until my mouth felt like it was full of cotton.

"Faith? Did I lose you?"

"No." I grabbed a bottle of water and gulped. "No, I'm here. I'm just...

What the fuck, Jim? Our first lead in Charity's case in years is a suicidal cancer patient who also happens to be a cartel foot soldier?"

"It's the John Doe that came into Bexar from the fight in Mexico the other night with the tattoos I sent you photos of. You want to come ID him?"

"I really think I do." I stood, glancing at the clock: 7:15. "I'll be there by eleven. Keep looking, and call your tracker in New Braunfels." I tapped one finger on the back of the phone. "I'll see if I can get us some help here if I can figure out how to ask."

"Drive safely. I'm going to put this guy on the table and see if cutting him open tells me anything else."

I hung up, clocked a three-and-a-half-minute shower, tamed my wet hair into a ponytail, and yanked clothes back on, stopping at the coffee station in the lobby on the way out and making two cups to go.

Driving to Fort Worth to pick up the southbound freeway, I turned Jim's words over twenty ways from Sunday in my head. Cancer. Suicide. How was that even possible? I mean, if the guy wanted to die quickly in battle because he was afraid of the slow painful death cancer usually brought, or because of some macho pursuit of glory—Miller shot him. If he didn't think the wound was fatal, why not just get back up and step in front of someone else's gun? He could've shot himself in his living room, right?

Headed south on 35 W, I checked the clock and dialed the number Nichelle had given me the night before.

"Sorry to call so early," I said when she picked up.

"I'm up. I was just about to call you," she said.

"You have something from Miller?"

"No." She paused. "I need you to trust me and not ask too many questions."

"You have no idea what you're asking."

"I think I do. I read about your sister. And I've heard about Skye Morrow—she was actually a case study in the line between informing the public and going too far into invasion of privacy in one of my college classes."

I barked out a laugh and sipped my coffee. "Of course she was. Nice to know someone who's not me thinks she goes too far." I was starting to like Nichelle in spite of myself. "I promise to try my hardest. How's that?"

"I appreciate that."

"What've you got?"

"Joey found Zapata's supplier. He has a phone call with the guy at four this afternoon."

13

The cab's headlights blinded him temporarily as he waited outside the bar, slumping to one side like he was drunk—which was also handy for obscuring his face. Just in case his driver remembered.

He slid into the backseat, listing to the side, head down. "Listen, man." He affected a country accent. "I ain't got no more money with me, but that fuckin' bartender, he took my keys. I just need you to take me out to the camp, and I'll get you paid."

"Camp?" Joe's eyes were wide in the rearview. "What camp?"

"Just a few miles from here, I found a place to pitch a tent. Turn at the light up there. Left."

"This is where you're sleeping, too?" Joe asked, muttering under his breath that he shouldn't have taken this fare. The Bayou Barstool was riddled with bad elements. Fares usually puked if they didn't try to rob him, and he couldn't tell which was more likely with this guy.

But he couldn't skip the fare. This week was slow, and the pay was shitty when it was busy.

"Fine."

The man settled into the backseat of the cab and tried not to vomit as Joe navigated the winding roads. Self-defense was one thing, but killing someone in cold blood...his stomach twisted. He pointed to the tent and Joe turned in.

"I'll wait," Joe said. "Twenty-seven fifty without tip."

He stumbled out of the back of the car, turned to the tent, and came back. Joe put the window down and stuck his arm out for the money.

The man drew an old-fashioned pistol and fired one clean shot right into Joe's head. "Tipping is optional," he said, studying the scene. Joe crumpled over the steering wheel. He was an old bachelor, lived alone with his dog, and had been shot after picking up a fare in a seedy part of town at one in the morning. Nobody was going to look too hard here.

Wiping the door handles and the leather seat, he packed up his tent, walked to the other side of the stand of trees where his truck was parked, and drove away.

14

"That's him."

I stood in Jim's lab a few minutes before eleven, studying a face that had been my own personal boogeyman for more than half my life. I had seen it in dreams, alive and scowling, the only one in the room that night not hidden by a mask. I hadn't remembered the tattoo until I saw it again in the desert, but the face had haunted my nightmares for so many years I knew it instantly, even aged, slack, and pallid as it was.

Jim punched one last staple into the incision in the chest, pulled his gloves off, and turned off the spotlight over the table. "I haven't ever seen anything like this—most of the bodies that come through here are otherwise healthy folks who died under mysterious circumstances. I've found small tumors before that people probably didn't even know they had, but this...he was dying. There's no other way to say it."

"But cause of death was the head wound?" I glanced at the neat little hole in his temple, the blood cleaned away so Jim could work, stitches ringing his hairline.

"Definitely."

"He doesn't look so scary anymore," I said.

"I'd say not." Jim rounded the end of the table and put one hand on my shoulder. "You okay?"

"I wish I'd gotten to him before"—I waved a hand at the corpse on the table—"now. I have a million questions."

"And maybe you might've shot him yourself?"

I blew out a long breath. "I've thought about that so much I used to actively try to picture this guy when I was at the range or working on hand to hand. Could I have shot him if he wasn't a threat to me or in danger of escaping? I sure wanted to. But standing here looking at this, I'm not so sure."

"You don't have it in you. There's a difference between self-defense and murder, even when it's in the name of justice."

"Revenge might be a better word." I couldn't look away from the slack, graying face. "It's a lot harder to hate him now. Is that weird?"

"Eh. The boogeyman is easy to fear and hate in equal measure, right? Because he's superhuman. Real flesh-and-blood people are more complicated." Jim put one finger under my chin and turned my head so he could see my eyes. "This is a complicated thing, a corpse with a connection to your sister's murder."

"Archie is pissed that he's stuck in the hospital. This was his case."

"I know. On both counts." Jim chuckled. "And I feel for the medical staff keeping him there."

"I thought he was going to die, Jim." I swallowed hard. "He needs to stay put. But if anyone can make sure he does that, it's Ruth McClellan."

I clapped my hands. "And I can figure out how all this stuff intersects and who's responsible for it."

He furrowed his brow, sticking out his lower lip. "I thought the cartel boss was responsible for it."

"He's responsible for plenty, I'm sure. I just need to know for sure...once and for all...who ordered my sister killed and why. And I need to get my husband and the other good guys they've got down there back. And figure out which Zapata goon murdered Ratcliff."

"That's a full plate, Faith. And the dishes bite."

"I'm being careful." I tried to smile.

"Who is Ratcliff and what happened to him, again?"

"He was the Ranger who called me to the border in the first place. He'd been assigned to the outpost at the border in Terrell County by himself for a while, and he was trying to figure out who killed Zapata's son when he disappeared. We found him dead in a trailer in the desert day before yesterday. Jameson said yesterday morning the bodies from that scene were all sent here because three of the four had Austin addresses. Ratcliff was a good man, and a smart cop—I can't let whoever killed him slither away under cover of bigger things I have happening right now."

"And no one else can find this particular murderer?"

"Exactly." I grinned. "No—that's not true. Travis County is on it. I'm just supposed to be kept in the loop to offer advice."

"Until they hit a wall and you decide to take over," Jim said.

"I'm hoping it's pretty straightforward. It has to be one of Zapata's guys. I just want to make sure justice is served. Just waiting for Jameson to send reports."

Jim waved for me to follow him to his office. On the way out of the lab, we passed Adam, the poor sucker with the cheating wife from yesterday. "APD pick up his old lady yet?" I asked.

"Got her, got the gun, just waiting for the ballistics." Jim nodded and tapped the spacebar to wake his computer. "Name?"

"Drew Ratcliff."

He typed it in. "GSW to the head, arrived night before last, rushes on all the reports. Let me see who did the postmortem."

He clicked the file and shook his head. "Fuller."

"Isn't he like a hundred and ninety years old?" I asked.

"He's not at his best these days, that's for sure," Jim muttered, squinting at the screen.

"What?" I asked.

"There was a significant quantity of opiate in this guy, Faith," he said.

"They must've force fed him the pills, I guess?" I tapped a finger on the edge of his desk. "There was a bowl of something the kids who OD'd thought was Percocet on the table. I think it was fentanyl."

Jim sat down in his desk chair and scrolled, shaking his head. "No, I don't think so."

I leaned one hand on the desk and craned my neck to see his screen. He turned it toward me slightly. "He had significant damage to his intestinal tract and some bone deformation," Jim said. "He was a habitual user. Probably for some time."

"We take drug tests every thirty days," I said.

"At a one-man outpost in the middle of nowhere?" His eyebrows went up.

"I can't believe..." I leaned toward the screen and read. It was all there in black and white, and if Fuller noted it, it had to have been relatively obvious.

"I know. But that's the thing about a postmortem—they tell all your secrets." He scrolled back a page and pointed. "Tox screen was positive, too. If he was taken from the outpost Monday, he could've taken something just before, and it would still show up here."

"Jesus. Why? Why would he do that? Didn't he see enough of the damage this shit does, working down there?"

Jim shrugged. "I've seen OD victims whose families told me they got it from a dentist after a root canal. For a long time, doctors thought it wasn't addictive." He scrolled some more. "Noted remodeling on a severe knee injury." He clicked the scans and zoomed in. "Looks like it was probably five years ago. Tears of the ACL, MCL, meniscus, bone shaving during surgery. That could do it."

"Jesus." I sat back and pressed two fingers over my lips.

"What's wrong?"

I shook my head. "This...it's entirely possible that something I thought I knew for sure isn't true at all."

"Unsettling. But since he's dead, that doesn't really matter does it?"

"Sure it does," I said. "Because now I have to find the person who killed him before they end up in here, too. Someone is going to answer some questions about what the hell is happening here, and I'd like to start with why Ratcliff is really dead."

"Being a cop investigating the murder of a powerful criminal kingpin's son isn't enough?"

"Maybe. Or maybe Ratcliff's addiction got him in with a really bad crowd and they were tying up loose ends..." My hand went to my mouth. "Or punishing him for calling me. The guy who was running the weapons ring, Amin—he was pissed that I was called into the case. It's entirely possible that I got Ratcliff killed by showing up down there."

"No, playing buddy-buddy with a cartel boss—if that's what he was doing—that's probably the reason he's dead. You carry enough guilt around with you without heaping more on with no good reason. And you said this guy"—he tapped his screen—"was the one who called you, which means he was more concerned with solving the case than covering his own ass. Which means maybe he knew he was in danger and thought you could help."

"Either way, I'm not leaving this to whoever Jameson has left to put on it," I said. "Call me a control freak, but I have to find the person who shot him."

"In all the spare time you seem to be swimming in."

15

Jim said he'd keep an eye out for reports on Ratcliff and forward them to me and his information hound in New Braunfels, and that he'd do the same with the labs on the cancer patient with the tattoo and the two gunshot wounds. I had carried both bullets straight to the lab myself when I left Jim's office.

I needed to know if anyone had a team sweep the site for cartridges, and which weapons were found near which bodies.

It would've been a big job, but as Miller had proven, the federal government is a big operation, and they love their large projects. I couldn't ask Miller, though. So I called Nichelle.

"Hi, Faith," she said when she picked up. "I think I might have found something."

"And you're going to tell me before I read about it on Instagram? Are you sure you went to reporter school?"

She chuckled. "The story is better when you have all the facts, not just one. I believe that, and I'm lucky that my editor does, too. I'll run something when I have it all—not before."

"What've you got?"

"I told Kyle about this the first time you and I met on the phone the other day, but Zapata was buying different guns from the Dixie Mafia than he was from the national guard guy you told me about when you were here, and I think I know who he was buying them through. If I'm right, most of them are registered weapons that were stolen."

"If they were registered, we might have ballistics."

"Right. And you can track them through the system to a certain extent. This whole thing started for Kyle because of a gun he couldn't trace that was used to kill a convenience store clerk," she said. "But these, you should be able to trace. Some of them, at least."

"He stumbled into an operation that could take down a cartel boss because of a dead convenience store clerk?" I clicked my tongue. "And I thought the internet-famous hog that led me to a serial killer was wild."

"I see that and raise you an unidentifiable homeless woman and the takedown of a televangelism empire."

"I read about that! That was you?" I asked.

"I have the bullet hole scar to prove it, even."

"Nice." I fell quiet for a second. She just kept surprising me, and I wasn't exactly sure what to do with it.

"So I know why I was going to call you..." she prompted.

"Right." I shook my head. "Sorry, I'm in one of those situations where I could use more coffee but don't want to, like, have my heart explode or something, so I'm reluctant to get any right now. Anyway—it's sort of the same thing, really. I need to find out if anyone swept the scene of the gunfight for weapons and cartridges, and even better if maybe someone made a diagram of what they found where. I can't ask Miller."

"But I can," she finished for me.

"But you can."

"No problem, I'll work the question into telling him what I just told you. But I should probably know what the end game is for the request. If he says they have that, then what do I ask him? I can tell you there's not a chance in hell he'll let me see it while he's still working this case."

I tapped my finger on the console. "I might have a friend or two who could get ahold of a copy of it." I hoped. "But knowing where it is so they know who to call or where to look would be helpful. See if you can get him to tell you which agency did the work?"

"Easy enough," she said.

"Do you have a line on the stolen weapons you think Zapata was buying? Serial numbers I could start a search with, maybe?"

"I just have a name right now," she said. "I assume I can trust you of all people that any information I share with you won't go to another reporter before my story breaks, right?"

I pushed aside immediate thoughts of the desperate promise I made to Skye. It was a razor-wire tightrope, but I would figure out how to walk it successfully. Somehow. "Absolutely."

"James Warren Hebert. My source says he goes by Jimbo. I'm working on finding location information, but I do have a handful of serial numbers on weapons that he's moved lately. Allegedly."

"Can you email me those? And anything you find about where I could locate this guy?"

"Sure thing."

I gave her my email address and she promised to send a file and call me after Joey talked to the Chinese drug lord.

There's a thought I never imagined I'd have.

"I have another murder I need to spend some time looking into this afternoon," I said. "But I'll be around." I paused. "Thank you, Nichelle."

"I'm glad we can help you," she said. "And appreciate your discretion."

"Likewise," I said. "I know you have a long history with Miller, and I also know he'd be pissed if he knew you were talking to me."

"Kyle gets pissed at me a lot." She laughed. "I'll handle him. I don't lie to him—that's part of why he trusts me. But I won't let on that I've heard from you unless he asks me straight out."

"Fair enough." I would rather she lie, but respected that she didn't want to.

"Talk soon," she said before she hung up.

I didn't get the phone in the cupholder before it started buzzing again.

I clicked it open without looking at the screen, keeping my eyes on the road. "Mc—Hello?" I stumbled over not saying my name, but maybe I should find out who was calling before I did that given my current situation.

"Mrs. Hardin?" a familiar voice asked.

"Bolton? How are you feeling this morning? And...how did you get this number?"

"Jim Prescott over at the lab gave it to me, ma'am. I know the commander says you trust him, and Captain Jameson told me Prescott requested to be kept in the loop on the investigation of the site where they found Drew Ratcliff's body."

"Did you find something?" I asked.

"Yes ma'am. The casings in the room where he was found appear to match the caliber of the bullets they pulled out of him at the lab and the one the techs dug out of the wall down there."

"Anything from NIBIN?"

"Nothing yet, but I just uploaded the images from our evidence about twenty minutes ago."

"Do me a favor and get Jim Prescott to give you the contact information to loop in his tracker in New Braunfels. He says the guy is the best he knows at digging."

"Yes ma'am." I heard computer keys clicking.

"Bolton, you have a wound in your leg still healing from trying to save my life the other night, I think you've earned the right to call me Faith."

"Whatever you say. Ma'am." He laughed.

"Fine." I laughed, and it felt really good for the five seconds it lasted. "Can you email me the file on the crime scene in that trailer? Where did they take the lone survivor?"

"I don't know, but I'll get the file and I'll find out. I'll send everything to you as soon as I have it." I heard keys clicking, followed by a low beep.

My gut said this wasn't as straightforward as I'd thought at first.

I'm always careful to avoid jumping to conclusions because I have lived the consequences. Facts can be lined up to support a lot of theories on any case and seem perfectly logical—looking for proof before assuming helps both with being right and not getting yourself killed.

Shit. This was getting far more complicated than simply assuring the arrest of a colleague's murderer. Absent clear information on whatever Ratcliff might have been into, I couldn't be sure why he was dead. It sure seemed like whoever had given JJ's buddies those laced pills had shot the captive cop in the head, but what if the two weren't related at all? If he was killed by someone who wasn't a Zapata soldier, I needed to know it now, because the motive mattered. Whoever did it could be coming for any of the rest of us, for all I knew.

Leave it to me to find a murder to solve in the middle of the biggest crisis of my life.

"Hey, Bolton, can you drive with your leg injury?" I asked.

"Please. I can power through anything I need to. It's a scratch."

"Scratches don't require surgery."

He sighed. "What do you need, ma'am?"

"Keep your phone handy. If you get a call from this number that's a hangup, pull the LoJack data on my truck and come back me up."

"Where are you going?"

"It's not the best part of town."

"And you're going alone?"

"I seem to be all out of partners at the moment."

"I know full well you understand the risk you're taking. Is there another way for you to find out whatever it is you want to know?"

"Not a faster one, and I don't have time to waste today."

"Captain Jameson said the commander is okay."

"Captain Jameson has no idea if Graham is okay." Because Zapata was MIA, which meant Graham was, too, assuming Zapata took everyone in the truck with him when he ran. I paused. Before he stopped talking to me, Miller said he couldn't get in touch with his UC, either. I didn't think much of it at the time, but with Zapata off the grid, it was alarming. What if he'd taken them as part of a plan C if Grady's mother couldn't get him what he wanted? Not that I could say any of that to Bolton.

Bolton cleared his throat. "Look, I don't know what happened to Archie Baxter yesterday, ma'am, but I know you. No matter what rumors people are spreading, you have more honor in your pinky toe than most people have in their whole selves. So, you know...that's why I called you. Me, Mr. Prescott, I assume Mr. Baxter to the extent that he's able...You might be overwhelmed and under the gun, but you're not really alone. We're on your side."

I swallowed hard. Damn rookie was going to make me cry. "Thank you."

"Call me if you need help."

"I will. You find the files we need on that gun."

"Yes ma'am."

I closed the burner phone and put it in the cupholder as I pulled back onto the road and turned south. JJ's friends were the other dead people in this equation, and I'd seen his whole shithole apartment full of guns not a week ago, all of which could be tested for ballistics signatures and recorded. Maybe there were answers hiding somewhere in there.

16

The splintered door was the first clue I might not find much in JJ and Mikey's run-down apartment.

I nudged what was left of it open with the toe of my boot and held Archie's gun steady in case there was a surprise on the other side of the wall.

The stifling heat inside the rickety old building had sweat dripping from my forehead as I rounded the doorway, finding an empty room save for stuffing and foam that had been cut out of the shabby furniture.

Someone had thoroughly tossed the place. Looking for what?

I moved through the small apartment from the kitchen with it's cabinet doors hanging askew and open through the hallway to the crusty disgusting bathroom, where the lid to the toilet tank was smashed into four pieces on the floor. The closet we'd found full of weapons days before was open and empty, and the bedroom was in the same condition as the living room, all the guns gone out of it, too.

I looked around, trying to think of what else besides the weapons someone would have been looking for—and where it might be that they hadn't known to check.

It was impossible to know for sure even that this was connected to JJ and Mikey's murders—in a neighborhood like this, someone could've broken in to steal thousands of dollars in weapons and ammo whether JJ and Mikey were dead, alive, home, or away. But it seemed like a safe bet that whoever killed them knew what they were into—and might've had associates who cleaned out the apartment after I took down the shooter.

Every common hiding space had been checked and left open, or gutted, in the case of the upended and stained mattress with springs poking out of the slashes in several places.

I closed my eyes and called up the last time I was in this room. Mikey said something about Archie looking under the floorboards.

I went to the small closet in the corner, ducking under the jagged maw of the broken lightbulb dangling from the ceiling and noting the bullet holes in the wall behind the few pieces of clothing JJ and Mikey had bothered to hang up.

She said the closet.

I didn't see an opened compartment in the floor.

Kneeling while trying to avoid broken glass, I used the flashlight on my phone to examine the edges of the worn boards. There. The fourth one from the right had small pry marks on the end. Looking around with the light, I spotted a screwdriver on the shelf, tucked into a corner someone might not have noticed, especially with the light broken.

I grabbed it and pried up the end of the board, finding a hole beneath that held at least two pistols—I grabbed a tank top from a hanger and pulled them both out, then pried up other boards rather than poking my hand down into the unknown.

Aiming the light into the recess under the boards, I spotted a thin black rectangle a little bigger than my hand. Picking it up with the tank top, I turned it over and spotted a USB port. A hard drive.

JJ was probably the kind of street smart that would keep blackmail intel on whatever shady characters he was dealing with, though I hadn't really expected him to be smart enough to have a decent hiding place for it.

"Let's see what kind of secrets you have for me," I murmured, hearing the squeak of the bedroom door hinge just a split second too late.

I didn't quite have time to get Archie's gun aimed at the door once I dropped the drive back into the hole with the tank over it and swept the boards back into place.

"What's a pretty thing like you doing skulking around closets in a place like this?" The question floated on a smooth voice with a Cajun accent, the light in the room so dim with the covered windows and broken overhead that it was hard to make out much except a white fedora and a shiny silver pistol. "Go on and put that weapon on the floor nice and slow, darlin'. We wouldn't want anybody to get hurt."

I nodded, bending slowly to lay the gun in front of my boot.

Standing, I took note of the guy's size—he was probably five-nine without the hat, and lanky—and put my hands up.

He swept a gleaming black-and-white saddle shoe out and knocked my weapon into a corner, then pointed at the two I'd just dug out of the floor. "More than one probably ain't a bad idea around here. Don't get any ideas, though. I see them."

"I just want to go home with the same number of holes I got up with this morning."

"Now that there..." He scratched at his temple with the barrel of the gun and laughed. "That remains to be seen. Who are you and what're you doing here? Right answers will be rewarded, but wrong ones..." He gestured helplessly with the gun. "They'll just have to be punished. And none of us wants that."

"Is there someone else here?" I glanced behind his shoulder but only saw gloom, listening for footsteps or shuffling or that damn door hinge.

"Would that worry you more than me standing here pointing this gun at you?"

"Hard to say."

"Let's start with something easier, then," he said. "Like, who are you?"

"I helped Mikey out with something a while back," I said. "I came back to see if she was okay, and found the place trashed."

He moved his finger to the trigger of the pistol. "I warned you about punishment," he said.

"Every word of that is true," I replied, letting my voice shoot up like I was panicked. Which I wasn't—yet. It seemed he was alone, and I liked my odds in just about any fight. Without the gun, anyway.

"I know I sound like the bayou, but you expect me to be stupid enough to believe you played some kinda white knight savior to JJ's little whore and then came to check on her packing a gun and wound up digging through her closet?"

I fixed my face into Ruth McClellan's iciest ice queen stare. "This is Texas. Soccer moms carry guns to the grocery store. You think I would come to a neighborhood like this with no way to defend myself? Who's calling who stupid here?"

He bobbed his head from side to side. "Fair enough. Fat lot of good it did you, though." White teeth flashed in the gloom half a foot below the brim of the hat.

"You're quiet."

"It comes in handy in my line of work."

"Which is?"

He wagged the index finger of the hand not holding the gun at me. "I'm asking the questions, remember?"

"What good does that do if you don't believe my answers?"

He leaned forward and studied my face. I stared straight into his pale green eyes and set my lips in a defiant smirk.

"How'd you meet Mikey?" he asked.

"My boyfriend needed a gun and couldn't pass a background check," I said. "This girl I know from the gym, she knew Mikey from when they were kids and she put us in touch."

"I thought you said you helped her?" He shook the finger again. "Isn't that her helping you?"

I rolled my eyes and dredged up my best haughty beauty queen voice. "I did help her. She was worried that her boyfriend was cheating and I helped her with makeup and clothes. She knocked fifty bucks off the price of the gun. I saw a couple of bruises that made me think he was hitting her and I've been worried. I came back out here to make sure she was okay. When I saw the place had been wrecked, I looked around. All I found was these clothes and those guns."

He bobbed the gun, thinking that over.

"Say you're telling the truth. What do you think you've seen here today?"

"A robbery in a shitty neighborhood because someone found out this guy had like a couple hundred grand worth of weapons in here?" I pursed my lips and blinked.

"That's exactly right," he said. "And did you see anyone else?"

"Not if that's what it takes for me to get the hell out of here."

He nodded, moving to the side to let me walk out of the closet. "You shouldn't have come here. Bad things happen to ladies like you in neighborhoods like this one."

I backed up, moving toward the corner of the closet—and Archie's gun.

"Don't you trust me?" he asked.

"Why should I, exactly?"

"Fair point." He aimed the pistol. "And good instinct. Should've let it keep you far away from Mikey and her problems."

I waited, my eyes locked on his trigger finger. It moved a millimeter, and I dropped to the floor as the bullet whizzed through the hanging clothes and into the plaster of the wall, the roar deafening in the tiny space. Rolling to the side, I snatched Archie's weapon off the floor and rolled back, aiming and firing in half a blink.

The zoot suit crumpled to the floor, a surprised look on the intruder's face and a neat little burgundy hole in his forehead.

His gun fired as it hit the floor, but no other noise came from the apartment.

I took a deep breath and stood, moving the floorboards and collecting the hard drive and both guns as evidence. I stepped over the body in the doorway, squatting to take a pulse from the other side. Not a flicker. I checked his pockets and found his wallet inside his coat, pulling out his ID and leaving the wallet on his chest. Felix Dedeaux, born 1986, address in a gentrified part of downtown Austin. "Who sent you here, Felix?" I muttered as I slid the license into my pocket.

Closing the door to the bedroom as I walked out, I tucked JJ's hidden hard drive into my back pocket and one gun into my holster, holding the spare from the floor cavity and Archie's both aloft as I stepped back into the hallway and all the way out to my truck.

Felix was right about one thing: this was a dangerous neighborhood.

It was also the kind of place where people like to pretend they don't know each other's business because that's pretty safe, but everyone actually knows everything in detail.

And if Nichelle's sources thought the Dixie Mafia was selling stolen guns, I needed to know where the hell all those weapons went.

17

Watching lanky people with hunched shoulders and stringy, unkempt hair shuffle down sidewalks on both sides of the street, I pulled away from the curb in front of JJ's apartment building with its painted-over windows and graffitied exterior like there wasn't a dead guy leaking blood through someone's ceiling in the heat in there. I could get Bolton to send a cleanup team, as soon as I wasn't nearby for anyone who might call him a friend—or employee—to find.

Three blocks down, I stopped the truck in front of a convenience store with a brown and orange sign out front that read "QuickWay" and a huge Texas Lottery neon sign in the only window that still had glass in it. Wrought-iron bars on the outside of the missing windows hung sometimes by single screws, yanked free of their anchors or peeled back from the broken windows. A small sticker on the front door warned that the clerk was armed. Couldn't say that I blamed him. Whoever owned this joint had to be paying hazard wages to get someone to work the counter. But in a neighborhood like JJ's, whatever served as the closest grocery store was also often the hangout spot—so the logical place to look for information, which, now that I knew more about what was going on here, could be a fair amount. Someone had to know JJ's regular customers—customers who weren't Zapata, anyway. I stashed the spare guns and the hard drive in my duffel bag behind the seat in my truck and smoothed my hair before I locked the truck and crossed the street.

The little store was busy inside despite the lack of cars outside—shops like this one were always busy because in parts of a city where grocery stores don't exist, people who don't have cars have no choice but to shop there. The owners funded the hazard wages for staff by overcharging for basic necessities and robbing people blind on booze and cigarettes, because they had the supply monopoly for the area. It's one of the systems that keeps poor people poor that I never knew existed until I became a police officer.

The clerk looked up from his phone, shaking back the two thick strings of orange hair hanging over his jowls and giving me a once-over. "Your car broke down? Because triple A won't send anybody out here and getting an Uber ain't much easier."

I glanced around. The three guys in the corner were doing a drug deal, and a pale, slender girl who looked the kind of sixteen-passing-for-early-twenties living on the streets will do to a person was scratching lottery tickets at the far end of the counter. Two older women with stooped shoulders were examining items in the narrow aisles between shelves, and a tall skinny kid who couldn't have been old enough to be out of school looked to be playing some version of eeny, meeny, miney, mo with the contents of the beer cooler. The clerk was my best bet. I focused on him, keeping my voice loud enough to be easily overheard and hard to ignore, but not too threatening. It's a practiced skill that serves cops well.

"I'm looking for a fella who goes by JJ, runs with a group of guys who like to hunt, and a skinny chick named Mikey."

"What business somebody like you got with JJ?" the clerk asked.

"I want to talk to him about a gun." Or two...hundred.

He pursed his lips and looked me up and down again. "You a cop? If you are, you have to tell me. It's the law."

I had no such obligation under the law. But I also wasn't a cop at the moment. Not technically.

"No, I just need to talk to JJ." Conversation in the back corner had fallen you-could-hear-a-flea-sneeze quiet when he said the word *cop*, and after a minute, a scrawny guy in knee-length denim shorts with bleach spots and a

T-shirt that was probably once more white than dingy beige piped up. "JJ and his bitch got they asses blowed right up."

A shorter, more muscular guy with a dangling chain-link earring in his right ear who I had immediately pegged as the dealer in their trio shoved Scrawny Guy's shoulder. "Shut the fuck up, dipshit."

"Don't you push me, fuckface." Scrawny Guy squared off and raised both fists. "Your shit ain't even that good."

The clerk pumped a shotgun once and every eye went to him. "Knock that shit off. Icepick, where'd you hear that about JJ? I ain't heard nothing."

"You ain't seen that skinny little broad either, though, have you?" Icepick asked, his voice shooting up an octave.

Dude had some nerve calling anyone "skinny." He could've starred in an ad campaign highlighting the dangers of meth addiction. I didn't even like Mikey, and I was offended on her behalf.

But it sounded like he might know something, and if he did, I wanted to know it too.

"Man, you don't know shit," Dangly Earring said, waving one hand. "She probably went out of town or something."

"Sure, because people here do that all the time." The words were soft, from the girl with the lottery tickets. She handed them to the clerk and pocketed the quarter she'd been using to scratch them. "Twenty bucks, Sammy."

"You spent eighteen on them, Tish." Sammy the clerk's voice softened when he looked her way.

"Then I have two more than I did when I came in here," she said, putting a hand out for her cash.

"Regular people don't win the lottery," he said, handing over the bill.

"They sure do. I see it on the TV every week."

Sammy closed the register and shook his head, turning back to Icepick and his companions. The women in the aisles had moved on to the cooler that held eggs and butter, and the kid had a twelve pack of Keystone Light and was looking from me to the counter like he wasn't sure he wanted to ask Sammy to ring it up. I wasn't there to check IDs, but I wasn't helping a teenager leave with a case of beer either, so I avoided his gaze and turned back to Icepick—zero chance I was asking where the nickname came from —who was talking to Sammy.

"I heard they got into some bad shit, man. Dude JJ was working both sides of the fence, and it caught right up to him. They ain't even seen it coming, they was just gone."

Since I was in the room when JJ and Mikey died, I knew Icepick had the last part of that right—which made me think his information was more reliable than Sammy wanted to give him credit for.

"Shut up, you meth-head freak." Earring shoved again, and Icepick turned and swung before he got his feet planted. He landed a decent punch to the other guy's jaw, but the shock up his arm spun him back such that he staggered, barely staying on his feet. Which was unfortunate for him when Dangly Earring's return blow plowed a meaty fist into a straight, smallish nose that exploded in blood. Icepick went to his knees howling.

Sammy aimed and pumped the shotgun so fast I wasn't even sure how it got back into his hands. "Back the fuck up," he said.

I watched the older ladies, who were putting eggs and coffee creamer in their baskets and muttering about the prices like nothing unusual was happening. I wasn't sure what to make of that.

"People come here because we keep the peace. You fuckers want to go at it, go on, but take it outside," Sammy said, slow and quiet like he wasn't really bothered either.

Earring reached behind his back like he was going for his waistband and I put my own hand on Archie's gun, tucked into my jeans up under my shirt because wearing a holster into a place like this screams "cop" and I wasn't looking to advertise that.

"Don't." Sammy swung the barrel of the shotgun slightly my way, then settled it back on Earring. "Either one of you. Old Rita here will blow you right about in half at this range."

Icepick had gone from yowling to whimpering, watching Sammy over his fingertips with wide eyes.

"You're bleeding all over my floor, man," Sammy said.

Icepick stood without uncovering his face and one of the old women shuffled over and handed him a wad of crumpled Kleenex from her purse. She peered up at him through thick glasses. "You're fine. It ain't broke."

He nodded and took the tissues, shaking one free and using it to stop up one nostril, then repeating the process for the other side.

Earring shoved the bills he'd taken from Icepick as I walked in—hard to believe that was minutes and not hours ago—into a pocket on his faded cargo shorts and made for the door. "Fuck all y'all."

The bell jingled as he slammed his way out. Kleenex Lady shook her head and grabbed Icepick by the ear, dragging his head down and poking her nose an inch from the dangling bloody tissues.

"You stop running 'round with that riffraff," she said. "Your momma wanted better for you."

She let go of his ear and shoved her hand into the pocket of his shorts while he massaged his earlobe, yanking out the little paper packet he'd bought from Earring. "And stop this, too. Don't lead nowhere good."

Icepick yelped when she poured the contents of the packet into the soda fountain's waste tray and held the button for the water, holding his gaze the whole time with her chin jutting out, eyes flashing behind the glasses.

Sammy snorted to cover a laugh.

The two women exchanged a nod and carried their baskets to the counter. Sammy was ringing up the last item when Kleenex Lady turned to me. "Whatever brings you here looking for trouble, let it go."

If only it were that simple.

"You have a nice day, ma'am." I reached up to tip a hat I wasn't wearing out of habit. She nodded and counted change out of a plastic squeeze pouch to pay for her groceries.

"This was a decent neighborhood once." She murmured as she passed me on her way out the door.

I nodded.

The door closed behind them and I turned to Icepick. "Twenty bucks for everything you know about why JJ is dead."

I had assumed Zapata sent the guy who shot up that warehouse as a way of tying up loose ends, but maybe I was wrong. That seemed to be happening with this case more than it usually did.

He narrowed his eyes and sized me up. "Fifty."

"Thirty, if you know something helpful."

Tish the Lottery Girl shook her head and slunk out the door, letting the heat in when she opened it.

"Deal," Icepick said. "I know plenty."

I glanced at Sammy. He put his shotgun down and picked up his phone. "There's some bad elements around here, lady. You don't look like you got no business at all here, but I believe in freedom of choice, so you do you. I run the register and keep the peace."

Icepick leaned in, his voice nasal from the blood and Kleenex. "He means he don't listen and he don't talk. Sammy's tight as a vault. You know the commercials about things happening in Vegas? That's Sammy. He sees a whole lot, but he knows keeping his mouth shut keeps him from getting his ass shot off."

I nodded. Seemed sensible.

"Have you seen any of JJ's friends in the past forty-eight hours?" I opened a refrigerator case and pulled out a Dr Pepper bottle, gesturing to ask if he wanted one. He nodded, and I bought them both and opened mine, taking a drink and waiting for him to talk. My phone buzzed in my pocket, but I ignored it for the moment.

Icepick tipped his head to one side like he was thinking and tried sipping his drink, making a face when it washed blood down his throat from the still-dripping nose. "See, it's like this—JJ is an arms man. Any kind of gun you could ever want, he could hook you up." He paused, blinking at me. "That's why you're looking for him, ain't it?"

"I said that already, didn't I? But it sounds like I'm out of luck," I said, turning my lips down and ducking my head just enough to look disappointed.

"Not if you don't want to be." Icepick winced when he tried to smile.

"Do you have guns to sell, too?" I tried to sound earnest. Not sure it worked.

"I know where to take you."

"I'd appreciate your help."

"We have to go see Rocky."

"Where would we go to do that?" I wasn't afraid of a scrawny little junkie—if Icepick had been armed, he'd have produced the weapon when the dealer punched him, and I could take Icepick and half a dozen more like him in hand to hand without breaking much of a sweat.

He shrugged. "There's a couple places to look." He widened his eyes and stared pointedly. "I believe we had an agreement?"

"Right." I pulled out the cash. "That's all you know about JJ?"

"I said I'm taking you to see Rocky, didn't I?"

Sammy snorted from behind the counter, but offered no comment, so I couldn't tell if it was directed at us.

"Rocky has guns, right?" I said slowly.

"Rocky has JJ's guns." Icepick sighed. "He was the wheel man, see? And they all took off when JJ and Mikey got blasted, except Rocky."

This was suddenly far more interesting. And well worth thirty bucks.

I stepped out of the way and waved at the door. "Let's go find Rocky."

Icepick pointed to the restroom. "Give me one minute."

I pulled out my phone as soon as his back was turned, finding three texts: Archie wanted to go home, according to my mother; someone was trying to reach a burner phone about my car's extended warranty; and Jim thought after our conversation about Ratcliff that I might want to know the Austin PD had found the weapon that killed Adam the sucker because a kid fished it out of a pond in Bee Cave. Subsequently, they'd found the owner of that weapon—and it wasn't Adam's wife. *APD says this weapon was stolen from a collector, that's why the bullet looked so wonky. She was trying to buy something that couldn't be traced. Figured that might be useful to you in some way.*

I nodded, an idea blooming. It very well might.

Thank you, I typed back as Icepick reappeared, shaking his hands and then drying them on his shorts. *Will keep you posted.*

"You sure you want to come with me?" Icepick asked as he moved toward the door.

"Some reason why I shouldn't?" I asked.

"Lots of them," Sammy said from behind the counter without looking up from his phone.

"Following you," I said to Icepick, pointing at the door.

18

We checked a vape store, an auto shop with a sagging bay door stuck in a half-open position, and two apartments before Icepick threw his hands up and directed me to a motel I flat would've taken for closed up if he hadn't told me to turn into the lot.

The building was blue and green. A line of a dozen or so rooms faced straight out over an asphalt parking lot and a small crater that was once a swimming pool but now sat empty with weeds poking up through cracks in the concrete, surrounded by a chain link fence full of holes.

I stepped out of the truck. "This place looks like it came straight out of a bad horror movie."

"It probably could, but I ain't got no place left to look," Icepick said. "I know Rocky used to know a girl, she stayed here sometimes. Maybe he's here."

Or maybe whoever got JJ already got to Rocky, too, and I was wasting my time.

Icepick strode to a heat-warped green door and knocked. "It's Icepick, man. Open the door if you're in there. I got something for you."

A chain skittered across the back of the door and it cracked, greasy dark hair with a brown eye peeking through it appearing in the space.

"Who the hell is she?" a rough voice demanded.

"She was looking to buy from JJ, man. I figure you need the cash. Less my finder's fee, of course."

Icepick was a piece of work. In Chuck McClellan's world, this guy would've made an outstanding lawyer.

I focused on the eyeball peering at me through the crack. "Why are you scared, Rocky?"

"I ain't scared of nothing."

"The door shaking from you holding it says otherwise." I kept my voice calm.

"You think insulting me is gonna get you what you want?"

"I'm not insulting you," I said. "But I do need to know exactly what JJ was into, and I'm running out of time for bullshit."

Icepick jumped backward. "You said you needed a gun."

"Can't I need a gun and some information on the guy I'm trying to buy it from, too?" I snapped. "You say this JJ guy got himself killed. I'd rather not follow suit."

Rocky peered through the gap. "Who are you?"

"Someone on the same side as you, I think," I said. "I can help you if you help me."

"How am I going to do anything to help anyone?" He shook his head. "Couldn't help nobody. I'm the driver, my whole fucking job is to keep them out of trouble, and trouble found them anyway."

"Yeah." I poked the door and he flinched. "And you're afraid it's looking for you."

"I'm probably right about that, too."

"Maybe. The bitch of getting yourself in jams like this is there's no way to tell."

He rattled the door. "I ain't opening it. But if you got questions you can ask."

"Who had JJ killed?"

"Jimbo did." Rocky's voice was dull. Certain.

"Oh, man, he crossed it up with Jimbo?" Icepick's voice was at least an octave higher.

Nichelle's voice rang in my ear so loud she could've been standing there. *"My source says he goes by Jimbo."* And her source was probably Dixie Mafia, because that's who she said sold the stolen guns to Zapata.

So I wasn't wasting my time here at least. Especially since the rest of JJ's crew—except this guy, apparently—was either in jail, scared shitless, or dead in the same trailer with Ratcliff in the south Texas desert. Maybe this Jimbo person was behind all of that? And if he was, maybe there was a relatively short road to why Ratcliff died and if he was into anything shady. And how that might impact my personal safety.

"Why?" I asked.

Rocky shook his head. "JJ was fucking stupid."

"He seemed to think he was pretty smart."

"Don't mean he was right. He's dead, ain't he?"

"Can't argue with that."

Rocky looked up. "I don't want to die, man."

"Then why are you still in Austin?" I asked. Not that I wasn't glad.

"This is home." He blinked like he didn't understand the question.

"And this is where they know to look for you. You said you're the driver. So...drive." It seemed obvious to me, but Rocky looked like it had genuinely not occurred to him. Not the sharpest knife in the block, this guy.

"To where?"

I closed my eyes. "Another motel in another place. They have them everywhere, you know. People will only put so much energy into hunting you if you didn't directly wrong them."

"I ain't done nothing to nobody," he said. "I fucking told JJ he was being stupid. Greedy fucker. Look where it got him."

"Greed will fuck you over every time." Icepick nodded like that was sage wisdom and I thought about what Kleenex Lady said about his mother. Working the kind of cases I tend to catch, it can be hard to keep mindful of the fact that guys like Icepick had mothers who loved them and wanted the best for them.

"Was he asking too much money for what he was selling?"

Rocky waved one hand. "Boy was a lazy-ass liar. Selling Jimbo stolen guns that could be traced if the cops got ahold of them, saying he got them from his contacts in Mexico, when they ain't come from no Mexico, they came from a cleaner his girl knew."

"A cleaner?"

"Yeah, like a maid? Housekeeper, I guess people call them. Girl can pick any lock, anywhere. Lifted the guns right out of these rich people's safes and fenced them to JJ for half what they were worth."

"Why not sell them herself?" I asked.

"People with even a little sense don't want to mess with the kind of folks who buy stolen guns, ma'am."

I nodded, thinking about the crates of weapons in JJ's warehouse. No maid stole those guns. But the stuff in the apartment that was missing—I could buy that came from a thief.

So JJ was dealing with this Jimbo guy and with Amin in some capacity. Possibly directly with Zapata, too, though I wasn't sure of that. And each hand probably wasn't supposed to know about the others. Crooks and killers are weird about loyalty for people who do the terrible things they do.

"I might be looking for the wrong guy anyway," I said. "I need something big."

Rocky raised one hand. "You're not in the wrong place. This here is where JJ got in the killing kind of trouble. Jimbo found out JJ was moving guns to the Mexicans—not from them—using a dude and some whore he met down near the border. Jimbo had been trying to get in with some big shot Mexican dude, runs one of the big drug cartels, to upsell him the guns he was buying through JJ. Other folks too, but JJ a lot of the time. And just when he gets in good with this character, he finds out fucking JJ has bigfooted him and has shit like drones and rocket launchers coming through his place."

My guessing game was on today, anyway. "Whose place?"

"Jimbo's. He had a warehouse outside town that he wasn't using. JJ told him we wanted it to chop up cars and sell the parts on the side, and Jimbo let him use it as a nice gesture."

"Jimbo is big on gestures," Icepick agreed.

"Who is Jimbo connected with?" I asked.

"He runs this part of the city," Icepick said.

"For what?"

"For himself, I guess." Rocky looked thoughtful, then made a face like something pained him. "You ever see that movie, the one with Fredo and the big dude who says he's making you an offer you can't refuse?"

I nodded.

"That's Jimbo. He thinks he's the big guy. I mean, he is a big guy. But you know what I mean."

A person could get a headache trying to follow that. "Sure."

"That's all I know. JJ fucked Jimbo over, Jimbo found out from someone, and now they're all dead." Rocky looked at me. "You think I ought to leave?"

"I would if I were you."

He disappeared for a minute and returned to open the door, a backpack strap on his shoulder, his clothes faded but clean.

"My car is around back where you can't see it from the road."

"Good luck, Rocky. Stay away from trouble from now on."

"Thanks," he said.

I nodded and he jogged toward the corner of the building.

Icepick folded his arms across his chest and flashed a row of remarkably straight and white teeth. "That's gotta be worth more than thirty bucks, but you can keep the rest of your money because I like you."

I held up another twenty. "Where can I find Jimbo?"

"He owns most anything that makes money around here, but he usually stays at the Bayou Barstool a few blocks up." Icepick glanced around. "I better take you over there. There's some badass characters in there."

"I don't want to put you in danger." I meant every word.

Three hours ago, this guy went to a corner store looking to score meth, which was probably a pretty regular occurrence for him. I didn't need his death on my conscience or Kleenex Lady's stare haunting my dreams. I figured he had to know I wasn't really looking to buy a gun by now, but I would've also figured Rocky knew to get the hell out of Austin and it genuinely seemed he hadn't.

"I been taking care of myself since I was eleven, ma'am, and Jimbo ain't nobody you want to say the wrong thing to. It's this way. We're better off walking. The only parking lot there has a knife fight or two a day." He strode across the parking lot to the road and waved for me to follow. "What you looking for a serious gun for, anyhow? Your man screwing around on you or something?"

Maybe he didn't know I was lying. Which was pretty bad, because I was well established as a terrible liar.

"Something."

Icepick shook his head. "Some people just flat got no sense."

"Maybe I want to take up target shooting," I said, walking beside him at a practiced speed—fast enough to have business and not want to be messed with, but not so fast that we looked scared. I had learned it, and Icepick seemed to default to it by instinct. Eyes up, but not too far up—confident, but not challenging.

Living in a place where every move has to be carefully calculated must be a whole other level of exhausting.

"Lady, nobody who looks like you comes here looking for the likes of JJ unless they're up to no good. If you wanted to shoot bottles or targets, you'd go to a store. You need to do damage and not have anyone find out."

I slid my eyes to him. "You're smart, Icepick."

"My name is Thomas." His voice was quiet. "Miss Ruby was right. My momma would be ashamed of me, and she hated folks calling me Icepick. She used to be proud of Thomas."

"I bet she still would be," I said softly.

We turned a corner and he pointed to a squat brick building with a gravel parking lot that held four cars and two motorcycles. A yellow-and-green neon sign over the door blared "Bayou Barstool," the letters in a circle around an alligator with big yellow eyes.

By the time we were a block from the bar, I had sorted through enough of what had happened in the past week to have a story. But I couldn't lead Icepick in there completely blind.

"I need the information, not the gun," I said. I didn't even know why, really, but something about him made me think I could tell at least part of the truth.

He stopped dead and turned a skeptical look my way. "If you're a cop, they'll kill me," he said matter-of-factly.

"I'm not." And in that moment it was as true as it had been before I stepped foot in the academy. I had been suspended, run afoul of the federal government even if it was accidental, and was waiting for information on how I might be able to work with a Chinese drug lord while possibly murdering several foreign nationals in the process of getting my husband back. What kind of cop does that?

Not the kind I'd ever thought I wanted to be, anyway. Funny how circumstances can allow a person to justify one little step over a line here and another questionable decision there until you look down and can't figure out exactly how you ended up where you are.

Like, say...about to go alone undercover to possibly buy a gun from the Dixie Mafia, looking for information on the murder of a colleague who may or may not have been a dirty cop.

I didn't have time to think too hard about any of it, and if I had, I probably would've chosen to avoid those thoughts anyway. One aspect of the streets growing up in Chuck's house had prepared me well for: once you're into something shady—and plenty about politics á la Chuck McClellan was shady—you better be all in. Second-guessing or losing a confident façade could get you killed.

Despite the look I'd seen on The Governor's face yesterday, I wasn't convinced his politics hadn't gotten my sister killed. Maybe he didn't order it, which I'd lost many a decent night of sleep to wondering about, but that didn't mean it couldn't be his fault. Finally, Jim had a body in a cooler that might get me some answers there. When I had time to go looking.

"We're here to buy a gun, because you brought me to see the man in charge," I said as I pulled on the door handle. "I have the cash. You play it straight like that, and nothing will go wrong."

I ducked inside, hoping to God I was right about that.

19

Smoke hung thick enough in the air to choke a horse, making my eyes burn from the minute I stepped into the room. I blinked, shaking my head. George Strait crooned from a neon-fronted jukebox in the far corner, and my boots slid in the mixture of sawdust and regular dust coating what looked like a relatively new raw pine floor. Looking at the planks, I bet I'd have been able to smell the wood if the air had been even a little clean.

The whole place had an old saloon feel, but everything except the floor was three decades in need of an update. The swinging half doors in the back were slightly askew, and the neon "Restroom" sign had three letters out, so it lit up as "Re...t...om."

There were more people than I'd expect in the middle of the day, with three at the bar, four playing a game of darts in the back that got louder with every throw, and probably a dozen men gathered at tables in groups of three or four.

Not another woman in sight, though, and while the bartender raised an eyebrow my way, a couple of the men at the table closest to the door looked annoyed by my presence. But that could be because I was a stranger, not because I was a woman. Impossible to tell.

"Where'd you kidnap a woman looks like that one, Icepick?" called a burly guy with a bushy black-and-gray beard wearing a leather vest over a pearl-buttoned shirt from behind the long cherrywood bar, where he was wiping a glass with a rag.

"How is my bony ass going to kidnap so much as a dog?" Icepick asked, slightly indignant. "Lady needs a gun. Told her I know the best place in the entire state of Texas. We need to talk with Jimbo."

"Nobody talks with Jimbo. Not unless I say so."

"So then say so, fucker. She got a man screwing around on her—Can y'all believe that shit?" Heads shook and murmuring ensued, and it was all I could do to not roll my eyes. "She needs a weapon that can't be traced. I ain't seen JJ in days, so I figured Jimbo is the place to bring her."

"Ma'am, is this meth-head telling me anything that even sounds familiar to you?" the barkeep asked.

"He's right about all of it. I went to a store a few blocks from here looking for a guy someone I know told me to see, and"—I glanced at my wingman—"Icepick, right?"

He nodded, folding his arms across his chest.

"Icepick here said he knew a better place. And he brought me here."

The bartender rounded the end of the counter and walked about halfway to us, his eyes squinting as he gave me a once-over.

"The kind of friends people who look like you got only hear about us one way," he said. "And I ain't fixing to get on Jimbo's shit list by not walking you back there. Come on."

Icepick ambled next to me, keeping his stride unhurried, and I worked to keep mine similar, when I wanted to run past the burly guy into the area behind a slightly less askew set of swinging doors in the far back corner of the large room.

The bartender pushed through them and the conversation on the other side cut off so abruptly it deserved a record scratch.

"I got a lady here, Jimbo. Icepick brought her in. She needs a gun. Got herself a cheating man."

"Don't they all?" A deep voice floated out, but I couldn't see inside. A round of loud laughter at a joke that wasn't that funny told me the voice belonged to Jimbo.

"Icepick?" the same voice said after the laughter stopped. "That's the skinny little meth freak used to run with Donnie until his momma..."

The bartender nodded. I turned to Icepick, who was suddenly very interested in the sawdust flecks covering the floor.

"Sure, let's see her."

The bartender stood aside and waved me in.

I picked Jimbo out of the four men at the table with cards in front of them in half a blink. Big, barrel-chested, with a gut hanging over his belt and protruding from under the bamboo cotton blend white T-shirt he wore under an open cream-colored linen button-down. The Stetson on his head made the outfit equal parts Fort Worth and Biloxi. He grinned and tipped the hat when I stopped a few feet short of his table.

"Well hello there, darlin'. I hear you're in need of a weapon."

Showtime. I had rehearsed what I was going to say in my head half a dozen times between the street outside and this room. Now I just had to pull it off convincingly—and lead this guy to ask me the right questions.

"Well, sir, that's kind of true and kind of not." I cast my eyes down, looking at him through my lashes. "I did hear that I could find a gun here that couldn't be traced."

"And where did you hear that?"

"This girl at my gym. I live outside Dallas." Somewhere between Nichelle mentioning Jimbo earlier and the bartender saying people who look like me only hear about this from one place, I remembered the story Sheriff Nava told me about the Dallas gym owners who were at the border getting drugs to sell when their toddler woke up and wandered out of their camper and drowned. Since everything else seemed to be far more connected than I would've thought even a day ago, I figured they might be the safe bet for a link.

The way Jimbo's posture relaxed as he nodded and waved a dismissal at his card buddies said I'd guessed right. That was three in a row.

The Governor would've told me to go to Vegas. I've never been the gambling type, though. These three bullseyes certainly didn't begin to make up for the string of misconceptions and errors that had riddled the past couple of months and landed me in this godforsaken beer joint in the first place.

He waited until Icepick and the bartender had left, too, and gestured to the seat opposite his. "Can I offer you a drink?"

"Some iced tea would be wonderful if you have any."

"Sweet?" he asked, snapping his fingers over his head and producing a man in board shorts and a Señor Frogs T-shirt from...I wasn't sure where. He wasn't there, and then he was, and I couldn't tell where he'd come from.

"Is there any other way to drink it?" I asked, smiling.

Jimbo's face wrinkled as he bellowed a laugh at the ceiling, throwing his head back and slapping the table.

"Javi, bring the lady an iced tea."

Javi disappeared and Jimbo focused on me again. "I like you. Miss...?"

"Robicheaux. Charity Robicheaux."

"I don't like many people, Charity. But I like you."

Good. I needed him to talk. People talk when they like you.

"We have two things in common, then," I said in my haughtiest tone.

Javi scurried back in with a glass and set it in front of me. "Thank you," I said before I took a sip. He nodded and returned to a chair at a table in the corner, nearly out of sight. When he'd put the glass down, I'd gotten an eyeful of a serious .357 in a shoulder holster.

Manservant and bodyguard. Check.

"So why did you really come here?"

"My friend told me I could buy a gun," I said. "She also said I might be able to buy a service." I stared straight at Jimbo for half a second, noting that his expression didn't change when I spoke, before I dropped my gaze to the table, studying the etching in the wood. Not afraid, but not challenging, either. It was a hard line to find.

"I'm guessing you don't mean an oil change or a pedicure?"

"I have people at home for those things."

"I do have a great car guy. Keeps my Caddy running like it just came off the line." He leaned back in his chair and rested his arms on the wooden rails.

I hadn't figured he'd just come right out with it.

"I'll keep that in mind if I run into car trouble while I'm in town."

"You have plans to travel anytime soon?" He traced a water ring on the table with one finger.

"I thought I might head to a beach somewhere for a while." I held his gaze.

"What'd he do, anyway?"

Actually, he lied to my face and put himself in the kind of mortal danger that forced me to follow him into battle and nearly got one of my favorite people in the world killed. But I needed to get him home before I could be mad at him, and I definitely didn't want him dead. His current situation had shown me that much.

One of Ruth's friends had come to the mansion crying when I was twelve—just barely old enough to decode the situation. It would have been enough for a certain kind of person to find themselves in this room with Jimbo, especially if the adulterer in question had a good life insurance policy.

"She's pregnant," I said.

Jimbo's eyebrows went up. "Which one of 'em you mad at, darlin'?"

I pretended to consider that. "I suppose I hate them both. But I hate him more. She didn't promise me anything."

"Not someone you know, then?"

"His boss's secretary."

"She can't be prettier than you are."

I flashed just the right ghost of a humble smile. "She's easy. Manipulative. Makes him feel important, I think."

"You don't?"

"I thought I did. I suppose maybe my mother was right, and the blush wears off every rose. She used to tell me men were all the same, never would stop chasing skirts. I thought he was different, that I knew better than she did." Lies rolled off my tongue so easily it was slightly unnerving, but I needed it right then, so I considered it a gift from my sister—Charity was always a better liar than I could ever dream of being; she used to laugh and say The Governor gave her one gift—and brushed a stray lock of hair out of my face, keeping occasional eye contact with the crime boss across from me.

"Nah." Jimbo waved a hand. "I got broads in this joint every night throwing themselves at me." He laughed and patted his gut. "Throwing themselves at my wallet, anyway. But my old lady, she's been with me through a lot of rough shit. They got nothing on her, even if her tits sag a little more than they used to, you know? We stood in front of my mother,

God rest her soul, and Jesus and everybody and made promises. When a man has honor, that counts for something."

I didn't so much as flinch at the irony of a man I was pretty sure had ordered at least three people killed in the past few days—maybe more—talking about honor and fidelity.

Then again, I was pretty sure he knew I knew he was a badass, and if I'd been telling the truth, his speech would've made me like him on a pretty deep level. Guys like Jimbo knew how to read people, and a woman this wronged by her husband would be far more likely to protect a criminal who professed to be everything she wished her husband was—so maybe he wasn't being any more honest than I was.

But if he was, good on him.

I went in there chasing a hunch I thought might get me some valuable information. About which case I was currently chasing, I wasn't sure. But I still had cards to play to get Jimbo to tell me what I wanted to know.

"So you'd like him to be punished for his indiscretion?" Jimbo's voice dropped and he picked up the hand of cards he'd been playing when I walked in.

"More than I've ever wanted anything." I put some fire in the words, feeling heat rise in my cheeks.

He caught every nuance, nodding slowly. "You told your friend at the gym you needed a gun."

"I think she's pretty good at being discreet," I said. "And I know a couple of things about her she wouldn't want made public. Or reported to the proper authorities." I arched one eyebrow and he stared for a split second before he busted up laughing.

"I really do like you, Charity." He wiped at the corners of his eyes and nodded. "Rare to find a broad with a face like yours and some real brains behind it. Rarer still for the same woman to have the balls it took you to come here. Your husband is a goddamn fool."

"Thank you?" That came with a full-on, the-judges-are-watching smile.

"You are most welcome, little lady." He laced his fingers behind his head, still-beefy muscles flexing in arms that I would bet had been more than formidable a couple of decades back. His face was lined and guarded, but not unkind, and his eyes held the kind of depth that meant he had seen some bad things.

Maybe I liked him more than I should have because he was a fellow traveler—just on the wrong side of the law. I needed to keep that last part in mind, because if things went the way I wanted them to, he would go down for his hand in JJ and Mikey's—and maybe Ratcliff's—murders.

"How much punishment are you looking for? You planning to take out his kneecaps—or maybe another part of him he likes a little too much? Or something more than that?"

I didn't flinch. "I want him dead."

"You're sure about that?" He raised both eyebrows so high they disappeared into the shadow of the Stetson, holding the look for several beats. "It's the kind of thing you don't get to take back."

"I understand." I held his gaze straight on, keeping my face flat. "Truly, better than most people, probably."

"He got money? Insurance?"

"Of course."

"And you're sure it's set up to go to you? Because people change shit like that all the time, you can do it now with a phone call or a few clicks on the computer. I wouldn't want you to get surprised by him leaving everything to the mistress when it's too late to change anything."

"I can verify the current wording, but I'm pretty sure." I bit my bottom lip for effect.

"The less pleasant part of this conversation is that these sorts of... services, as you said...they don't come cheap. Got to pay for quality talent. Got to pay for discretion. Got to pay more for experience. Can't have your contractor getting caught and giving you up to the DA in exchange for a lighter sentence."

"Why would they give a contract killer a lighter sentence?" I asked. I knew why, but him thinking I didn't helped my story.

"The same reason your husband might have changed his will. The same reason I got to bring this up with you: money. Darlin', you would make some kind of court TV. A beautiful family torn apart by infidelity, an illegitimate child, a contract hit. That's the kind of shit that channel my old lady watches makes movies out of, even."

I nodded slowly. "So how much does that cost?"

"How much can you afford?"

"Probably enough to hire the best guy you have." I leaned forward. "Who would you hire to do this for yourself or your daughter?"

I held my breath and waited for him to answer. He tapped the cards on the table three times before he spoke. "The answer I would have given to that a week ago, I can't anymore."

I tipped my head to one side and pinched my lips together, waiting for him to say more.

"Got himself killed," Jimbo offered finally. "But I got another guy, just did some work for me, pretty clean, untraceable. I can call him if you got the cash."

"How much?" I asked.

"Seven fifty."

"Hundred?"

He laughed again. "You got a wicked sense of humor, Charity. I like a wicked sense of humor on my girls."

"Glad I can amuse you, even if I'm not sure why."

"Seven hundred fifty thousand, darlin'."

I sucked in a sharp breath and pretended to think that over.

"It's not cheap, what you're asking someone to do. Takes a special kind of person to be able to take another man's life. More still to do it and get away clean."

I nodded. "I'm sure that's entirely true."

"I can understand if you don't have the resources. We never had this conversation." He tipped his chin down and stared without blinking.

"I can get it, but it might take a day. They won't trace anything back to me?"

Jimbo shook his head. "Not a whisper or a single hair. Zero evidence. You gotta pay up front."

"Three quarters of a million dollars is a lot of money," I said. "Half up front, half when the cheating bastard is dead." I spit the last few words like they tasted bad. Probably because they kind of did.

"Sixty forty," Jimbo countered.

"Done. How fast can your guy pull this off?"

"Within a week, usually. I'll get in touch with him. You should get the money somewhere it can be wired quickly, but a word of advice: it can't come from any account a cop is going to check that belongs to your old man. Is that going to be a problem?"

"Nope." Because it would come from the Travis County Sheriff's Office evidence locker courtesy of Deputy Bolton. I hoped. Not that I was telling Jimbo that. What I really wanted to know was who Jimbo would send to make the kill.

"Good. Set up a dummy account, get it ready to send, and get yourself out of town and far away from your husband. Somewhere you'll be using a credit card plenty so they can see you were there."

"How will I know when it's done?" I asked.

"I'll be in touch." He snapped his fingers at Javi, who I had completely forgotten was in the room. Jimbo read that on my face. "That's why I love this guy. Nobody is better at blending into the scenery than Javi."

Javi produced a notebook and pen without being directly asked, and I jotted down my sister's name and the burner phone number.

"I'd like to talk to him," I said, sliding the paper to Jimbo.

"Your husband? My advice is to act the same way you always do. Does he know you know?"

"She came to my house. Last week. I haven't told him and I bet she hasn't either."

"Just showed up and rang the bell?" Jimbo nodded, sticking out his lower lip. "Man has a thing for women with stones. Problem is, he ought to know you fuck that kind of woman over and you're going to get fucked yourself."

I barked a short laugh. "He thinks he's smart. But no, I'm through talking to him. I want to talk to your...service provider."

Jimbo shook his head. "That's not possible."

"I'm paying someone almost a million bucks to do something and I don't get to interview them for the job?"

"You're interviewing me. Or maybe it's the other way around. Either way, he talks to no one but me. It's safer for him that way, you understand. My momma used to say two can keep a secret if one of them is dead—Well, turns out I'm the exception to that rule. People trust me. I'm asking you to join in. I will take care of your situation and you will never be so much as a gnat on a beat cop's radar."

I held his gaze until I was sure he wouldn't budge on that, and nodded.

"I will be in touch. You should make sure those financial affairs are in order and then leave. Have an umbrella drink for me. I do love those little paper umbrellas on the beach."

"Thank you. It's been an interesting day."

"Glad to know you, Charity, and nice doing business with you. Javi will show you out."

Javi stood and walked me through the doors. I spotted Icepick alone at a table removed from the bar and the other patrons. He was sipping a glass of water and tapping his foot. Probably hitting withdrawal, he'd been looking to score hours ago. I wondered if he'd let me take him to the county hospital.

Five steps outside the door, Javi looked over his shoulder and tugged my sleeve.

"Thank you again for the iced tea," I said.

"You want to talk to the man Jimbo was telling you about?" He kept his voice so low I could barely hear without leaning in, the darkening sky making it harder to see his lips moving.

"I do, but I understand why he doesn't want me to." Was this some sort of test?

Javi put his hand over his heart. "We protect each other, Jimbo and me."

I nodded.

"He trusts me, and I trust him. Real trust is hard to come by." He waved a hand. "Take your husband, for instance."

"Very true." I tried to offer a polite smile since I wasn't sure where he was going with this. Assuming he had a point.

"Jimbo has trouble lately knowing who he can trust."

"I can understand that, given the people he's surrounded by—present company excluded, of course."

Javi nodded like I was finally getting it.

"So what is it you think I need to know before I kill your husband?" He lowered his voice to the barest pitch above a whisper and I leaned toward him to make sure I had heard him right. He raised one arm to scratch his head, and his shirt sleeve ticked up just enough to flash the bottom half of a tattoo.

A tattoo that matched the one on the cancer patient's forearm in Jim's freezer.

Well, shit.

Maybe I didn't know as much as I thought I did.

Hell, maybe I didn't know anything at all.

20

"Make sure it hurts." I held his gaze and hardened my tone, playing the part to the end. No backing out now. "If there's a way to do that, even if it costs more, I want him to suffer."

He nodded slowly without blinking and ran his tongue over his teeth before he shook his head. "I wouldn't want to be the man who fucked with you, *bonita*. That's for sure. You got a stone-cold set of *cojones* under that pretty face."

Icepick stepped outside and then backward when he saw me with Javi.

"I got them from my father." Probably true even if I didn't like to think about it. I stepped back and nodded to Icepick. "I appreciate your help today. I'll take you—"

My truck was back at the motel.

Javi's brow furrowed. "What?"

"My car isn't here. No big deal." I waved one hand.

"You have no business walking here after dark." He pointed to a silver Cadillac in the front parking space. "Jimbo would want me to keep you from doing that." He glanced at Icepick. "Come on, we'll take you home, too."

Icepick looked like he didn't know if it was more dangerous to get in the car or refuse. I caught his eye when Javi turned to slide into the Caddy's leather driver's seat and nodded slightly. He got in the car.

I shut the passenger door and Javi chose a station from the touchscreen set into the rich mahogany-and-leather dash. Beethoven's Fourth drifted out of the Bose speakers.

I studied Javi as his fingers moved on the wheel in time to the music. "Not many people know that one," I said when the music stopped.

"I know them all. Music soothes the savage beast, as they say." He flashed a grin and began shadow-conducting Mozart when the new track came on.

I noted that he didn't ask where to take Icepick, he just pulled up at a building near the store where we'd met and waited for him to get out, which Icepick did so quickly he nearly tripped on his spindly legs.

"Where'd you leave your vehicle?" Javi asked me, eyes on the road as his fingers moved across the wheel in time to Chopin.

"A run-down motel a few blocks that way." I pointed.

"What were you doing there?"

"Icepick was looking for a guy who knew his gun source, JJ," I said. "But the place seemed like it was abandoned."

"Why would you leave your car there?" he asked.

"Icepick said the lot at the bar wouldn't be safe," I said, and his face twisted into something between a grimace and a laugh before he turned onto the street.

"There's not a safer parking lot in town," Javi said. "Jimbo knows bull-shit in the parking lot keeps paying customers away from his establish-ments. And around here, if Jimbo don't approve, shit don't go down."

My stomach twisted as we pulled back into the motel lot.

My truck—which contained my computer and my real phone and my overnight bag that contained my badge—was gone.

"Never trust a criminal, *bonita*," Javi said.

"Aren't you a criminal?" I asked.

"You shouldn't trust me."

"Where did they take my car?" I held his gaze, hoping he liked or respected or whatever me as much as I'd thought.

"Somewhere that's actually not safe," he said.

"I have to get it back." I widened my eyes and tipped my head to one side for effect. "If I have any hope of being able to pay you, I have to get it back."

"And just how do you intend to do that?" He could go longer without blinking than anyone I'd ever met.

"However I have to, I guess." I set my lips into a line. "Can you show me where it is?"

He spun the wheel and shook his head. "I said before I wouldn't fuck with you. This ought to be entertaining."

Javi didn't say another word until we pulled up in front of a rust-splotched metal warehouse on the edge of a more decent part of town.

"There's some rough men in here, *bonita*. You sure you're up for this?"

"I have to get my truck back." I flexed my jaw. I couldn't pull out Archie's SIG, because I'd gone there acting like I knew very little about guns.

Like he read my mind, Javi flipped up the lid of the center console, pulled out a Ruger Max 9, and gripped it by the barrel, handing it over. "You know what to do with that?"

"I do." I took it and put my hand on the door. "Thank you for the ride."

"I hope you make it out. And not just because I want to get paid."

I nodded. "I can take care of myself. My gym teaches classes on self-defense." I tried to sound earnest.

He nodded to the door and tapped the steering wheel. "We shouldn't be seen together any more than we already have been."

He didn't want to go in there. "Rival gang?" I asked.

"You watch too much TV, *bonita*."

I shrugged and smiled like he'd caught me and climbed out of the car. Hopefully, I could get my truck and get out of here before I had to shoot someone. But that depended entirely on what was waiting on the other side of one very flimsy metal door about twenty feet from where Javi parked.

Pointing the Ruger at the gravel under my boots, I crept toward the warehouse, ears on full alert as Javi killed the car's headlights in the deepening gloom.

Outside the door, I flattened my back against the warm metal, still holding the heat of the midday Texas sun, and listened. The snapping sound of sparks flying—maybe a welder—a pneumatic drill, and two male voices, one far deeper than the other.

Two on one with their hands full of tools, I didn't hate my odds of not having to shoot.

I couldn't make out what they were saying over the racket, but it didn't much matter. What did matter was how much of a jump I could manage to get on them if I went in quietly, which was entirely dependent on location and line of sight.

I inched the door away from the frame slowly, steeling myself for a rusty hinge squeal, but there wasn't one. Sliding my foot into the opening, I peered around the wall.

They were taking apart the back end of a Mazda sedan, my truck sitting to one side with the doors shut and the hood open.

Maybe that meant they hadn't seen any of my things yet.

I swept the room in a grid looking for other men and found none, and both of the voices were coming from the two guys who had their backs to me as they worked on the Mazda, sparks flying around their welding masks and aprons.

Whatever they were doing, it didn't look like stripping the thing for parts.

I scurried behind a workbench full of hand tools and crouched, watching. From there, I could see a stack of large wooden crates half again as tall as me on the other side of my truck. I still had the keys in my pocket—all I really needed was to get behind the wheel and drive right through the flimsy metal wall in front of the truck—provided it would start, which I had almost no way of knowing even if I could see why the hood was open.

The taller of the thieves put his blowtorch down and walked to one of the crates. He pulled out a canvas-wrapped bundle, carrying it carefully to the Mazda and settling it into the trunk, though he bent at an awkward angle to do so. The second guy jabbed a finger several times and said, "It'll hold probably seven or eight more."

Whatever that dude had taken out of the crate, it was not one-eighth as big as that car trunk.

Because they were welding a hidden compartment under where the trunk was. And would likely cover it with metal sheeting and thick lining.

They weren't chopping the car up, they were turning it into a smuggler-mobile.

Which improved my chances that my truck would start.

The tall one turned back to the crate and called, "Quit being a little bitch and come help me," over his shoulder. As soon as the shorter guy muttered and put his tools down to move that way, I pulled out my keys and sprinted for the truck.

My boots clacking on the concrete floor were loud, but the fans running over the welding apparatus were louder until I was two steps from the driver's door. I hit the unlock button and reached for the handle and the shorter guy spun, his arms full of three canvas bundles, spotting me through the glass surrounding the cab.

"What the fuck?" he bellowed, the canvas bundles flying up and smashing open all over the floor.

"Amos, you stupid fucking hick, this shit still has to be cut!" The taller guy let his bundles fall back into the crates and yanked his T-shirt collar up to the bridge of his nose as a small white cloud mushroomed out from the canvas.

I yanked the door open, dove into the cab of my truck, and shut off the air conditioning, slamming the vents closed for good measure. I couldn't do anything about the hood right then, so it was just going to have to stay open, because watching Amos drop to the concrete like a stone when the cloud reached him was enough to tell me I wanted out of that building. Immediately.

I didn't even have time to say a prayer before I started it, but the engine turning over was the best rumble I'd ever heard. I slammed the gearshift into drive and stomped on the gas, the tires squealing as the acrid smell of burning rubber filled the space.

If I could smell the tires, was that powder filtering in, too?

Before I could do much besides hold my breath, the metal wall came right the hell off and folded around the front of my truck, open hood and all, as I careened into the parking lot.

"Hey!" I heard the shout, muffled by the closed-up cab, and turned back in time to see the tall guy try to chase after me before he hit his knees, shook his head twice, and pitched onto his face on the concrete.

What the fuck were they running out of this place?

I didn't have time—or nerve, seeing what I'd just seen—to go look at that, but Nichelle could get word to Miller to send his DEA contact. Assuming the drugs were still there with the side of the building ripped off.

I rolled to the far edge of the parking lot, for once thankful for the stiller-than-a-possum-in-headlights air that blankets Texas with oppressive heat all summer. Whatever that white shit was, it wasn't blowing out of there chasing me.

I plugged my dead burner phone into the cord and hopped out, pulling my shirt over my face just to be safe, studying the ripped sheet metal wall that was now bent around the outside of my truck for the least slice-capable place to grab it.

The problem was that there wasn't really a good one. Looking around, I didn't see another person or car anywhere. Good from the standpoint that I was less likely to get jumped. Bad in that I didn't have any possible help.

What else was new?

Pulling my boot off, I hopped on one foot over the gravel and used my favorite ostrich Laredos as an oven mitt to grab the edge of the wall and hop it backward.

I almost burst into tears when it fell to the ground with a whoosh and a small clatter.

Peering under the hood in the dark wasn't productive, but the hood did still close, though slightly misaligned.

Hobbling with my boot half on, I slid back behind the wheel and pulled it up, backing up a few feet so I could drive around the broken wall and out of the lot.

I made it half a block before my phone rang. Nichelle.

"How'd it go?" I said by way of hello.

"The guy is coming here." She didn't sound...anything...about that. Like she didn't know how to feel.

"The Chinese drug lord is coming here?" I closed my eyes but reopened them in time to make the entrance ramp onto 35.

"He's coming here. He doesn't trust Zapata to control his troops, and he said Joey's call confirmed what he's been afraid of for months now." Her voice was dull, and while I didn't get that, I also didn't have time to play therapist for her.

"Which would be?"

"That he needs to take over Zapata's operation and run his distribution with his own people."

I sighed. "So Zapata is looking for a war..."

"And the Chinese are bringing him a surprise attack."

The phone beeped.

"Damn, Nichelle, can I call you back? I'm getting another call."

"No problem. I'll be here."

I clicked over. "Jim?"

"No ma'am, this is Nick Ryan. I work in intelligence for the state," said a pleasant voice that surely should've belonged in radio.

"In New Braunfels, right?" I asked. "What can I do for you?"

"Well, I got a call from Travis County today about a ballistics report—a bullet removed from a Texas Ranger the deputy says was a friend of yours?"

"That was fast."

"I think you might have Jim to thank for that."

"I have to assume you're calling me because the report turned up a lead?"

"Yes ma'am, the NIBIN has a likely match for a weapon used in another murder."

The National Integrated Ballistics Information Network is a kind of fingerprint database for guns that's maintained and staffed by the ATF. The results from a match found this fast wouldn't hold up in court without the weapon, but they might lead us to where we could find it.

"A recent one?" I gripped the steering wheel.

"No ma'am. A taxi driver from 2001."

"Arrest made?" I asked.

"Cold case. Shooting in Austin, not a great neighborhood. Witness was a dispatcher at the cab company who said she sent him the call, and he never came back. Dogs found him three days later still in the cab in a nearby field. From the size of this file, they figured he was in the wrong place at the wrong time, and when there were no immediate clear suspects, they moved on."

"Jim isn't kidding when he says you're good at tracking down information," I said.

He laughed. "Jim brags on me too much."

"Jim doesn't give credit where it's not due," I said.

"I'm still looking. There's no serial number for the weapon because the information in both cases came from fired rounds. The ATF experts are still looking, but I got an email that says it's very likely a match. They moved it to the top of the stack because the victim was an LEO."

"I'm not sure a dead taxi driver twenty years ago is a lot of help for us," I said. "But send me the case file and I'll see if I can find something they missed."

"Yes ma'am. I'll let you know if I find anything else."

"I appreciate your help."

"Anything for Jim."

"I understand the sentiment."

I ended the call and the phone buzzed with a text from Nichelle: *Sunday, 9 p.m.*

Fan-fucking-tastic. The war was coming to Zapata, by way of a guy The Governor said made the drug lord sound "meek." I had no interest in crossing paths with anyone who could cower the man I'd seen fire a gun at Derek Amin. So if I wanted Graham—and Grady—back, I had to find a way to get them before then.

Nothing like a ticking clock your husband's life might depend on to spike stress levels that were already in the red zone to positively crimson. But I would figure it out—if there was one thing I excelled at, it was getting what I wanted. The only real question was: At what cost?

21

The secret to getting away with murder is staying calm. He watched, not so much as a speedy blink giving away that he was about to take a life.

The store was slow. He'd taken a car from the lot before he left work, avoiding the new cameras that had just been installed, and parked at the donut shop across from the gas station, watching people come and go.

He didn't need to worry about cameras out here—in a neighborhood that used to be nice but was sliding toward gangs and drugs faster every year, the brown-and-orange QuickWay sign had two lights out, but it wasn't cracked.

Just after eleven, ten minutes went by with nobody else in the store.

He crossed the street, pausing when two skinny teenage boys strolled up and went in looking hopeful. Some shouting ensued, and the boys came out hanging their heads and bitching about the old broad behind the counter not selling them beer.

They didn't notice the guy slumped against the newspaper rack with his hat pulled low over his face. They just left in the same direction they came from.

People, as a general rule, are way more wrapped up in themselves than anyone realizes.

He walked into the shop, pulled out the gun, and shot the clerk twice in the head just as her eyes widened with recognition.

"Blackmail is a dangerous game, bitch," he muttered, turning quickly back for the door, keeping the hat low over his eyes.

A truck had parked out front, and a pair of cowboys in mud-covered boots, plaid shirts, and black Stetsons chatted about the new Stallone movie as they walked in. The tall one hit his arm with the door as he tried to walk out and pocket the pistol at the same time, and it flew out of his hand, skittering under a shelf.

"Hey, buddy, you dropped some—"

"Rick! This lady's been shot—grab that sonofabitch!" his buddy called.

But he was faster than Rick, and police response times in that part of the city were abysmal. By the time the sirens approached, the stolen car was back where it belonged, his clothes were in his trunk, and he was on his way home.

22

I had clocked my share of twenty-hour days working murder cases, but I couldn't recall ever having been the kind of tired I felt in my bones as I drove toward Archie's house. I didn't have a muscle that didn't hurt, my ponytail was ratty and tangled, and my eyes couldn't decide if they wanted to close or cry.

Standing in Archie's kitchen twenty minutes later, I thanked my lucky stars that my mother had found a new joy in grocery shopping for them when the servants had always done it for us, and that Archie shared my love of peanut butter crackers and Dr Pepper.

Seated at the kitchen table with two packages of crackers and a can of Dr Pepper, I remembered a second thing to be thankful for: it didn't appear any of my bags had been touched when the truck was stolen. I called Bolton and described the not-so-chop shop for him, and the possibility of two corpses on his own case was enough to get him out the door, but I warned him to take gloves and a respirator and proceed with caution.

"You sound like my mom," he grumbled.

"Youth and stupidity go together like peanut butter and crackers, and I'm not looking to have your death on my conscience," I said. "You didn't see those guys drop. Maybe they're just out cold, but either way, anyone approaching the scene needs to use extreme caution."

"Noted. Anything else?"

"One more thing." I pulled the phone away from my head and opened Jim's text from the night before. "Can you check out a domestic situation that turned murderous from APD? The victim's first name is Adam. Case came in last week. MVA fatality upgraded to GSW after the postmortem."

"Someone shot him while he was driving?" Bolton asked. "Hang on, let me get a pen."

"I'm curious about the weapon used. Jim said it was stolen. Can you get me a serial number, since I can't call them right now?"

"Sure. Hey—you said those drug runner guys had your hood open, should I come by and look at your truck?" he asked.

"I have a guy I can call," I said. "But thank you."

"Anytime." And I knew he meant it.

I hung up and opened my laptop, checking the cloak on the IP to make sure the login wasn't being traced. Logging into the spam personal email Jim would've given his tracker friend, I waded through two dozen ads that had landed since I spoke to him before I found the file on the cold murder case.

I wasn't even on the second page before my eyes started to water and I grew quickly annoyed with moving around a zoomed-in screen to read, so I carried my laptop to Archie's shoe-closet-sized study and plugged it into the printer.

The whole file was only sixteen pages.

Safe bet that they hadn't looked very hard for this cab driver's killer, I'd say.

I found an empty file folder and a pen and scrawled the victim's name on the tab, tucking the papers inside. Old habits never really die.

Moving to the couch, I turned on a sitcom that I didn't enjoy admitting was now a staple of Nick at Nite to fill the silence and sipped my Dr Pepper, kicking off my boots and curling my feet under me as I opened the folder.

"Okay, Joe Powers. What happened to you?"

Even a cloaked IP wouldn't save me from detection if I tried to log into the DPS database, and they all knew Archie was in the hospital, so I concentrated on the printed file first.

Lone victim, male, age forty-one, shot dead center in the forehead, slumped over the steering wheel with one arm on the door rest. So maybe he was trying to get out of the car? Why would a cab driver do that?

Because he wasn't meeting a fare. He was doing something else. Except didn't Ryan say the dispatcher told the cops she sent him out there on a call? I flipped pages.

Witness interview one, with the cab company dispatcher, Mandy Eskridge, twenty-seven at the time. The APD officer noted that she had seemed distressed. Statement taken the day after the missing persons report was called in by his neighbor when the dog's barking and whining led him to have the super open Joe's apartment and he found the dog had made a mess of the place and was starving and nearly out of water despite having one of the self-filling jug style bowls in the kitchen. Neighbor said Joe lived alone and kept to himself but doted on the dog.

Mandy Eskridge said she got a request for Joe to do a pickup...huh. I read the address twice before I checked the map on my phone.

The pickup was from the Bayou Barstool.

I pulled out a notebook and jotted that down. It made sense for a bar to call a cab at one thirty in the morning, anyway.

But the field where the car was found three days later was seventeen miles away, near Lytton Springs. Back then, this would've been in the middle of nowhere. Now it was probably a shopping center or McMansion subdivision.

How did they move a cab with a dead body in it that far without being seen?

Limited traffic cameras on the route, probably.

But he was slumped forward. I tapped my pen on the edge of the folder. Any way I could think of to move a vehicle that far would've made a dead body fall backward. Not that any of that was noted in the file as having been investigated.

I flipped to the photos of the recovery site and in a printout could make out only one set of tire tracks, leading through the mud and up to where the cab was parked.

A margin note indicated that Joe's cash bag was empty, particularly unusual for the end of a shift, but maybe enough to make the detectives deem it a random robbery. If they weren't motivated to look for much else.

Back to the photos of the car at the scene. No holes in the glass, driver's window down. Which, paired with the arm on the door, might indicate Joe Powers was talking to someone outside the car. So maybe the bar was the last place the dispatcher sent him, but not the last place he went.

But what happened between the dispatch and time of death? I flipped to the last two pages of the file and checked the name on the autopsy report. Fuller. Great. Though, twenty years ago he wasn't as old as today, anyway.

I scanned. Based on insect activity, lividity, and weather, he put time of death between two and seven a.m. the night Joe went missing.

So maybe as little as a half hour after he was dispatched to the bar.

But why execute a random taxi driver? One thing years in police work had taught me—killers don't just walk around slaughtering people nearly as willy-nilly in real life as they do on TV. Every corpse ups the chances of getting caught, which meant the odds were better than even that whoever shot Joe thought they had a good reason for doing so.

It really was a shame that the detectives assigned to this case hadn't given it more time and attention, but I understood. When you have a stack of files that's too big for the number of people on staff and seventy percent of those files are connected to a loved one who's riding your ass every day and talking to the press every other night...well, squeaky wheels get answers.

Joe's dog couldn't hassle the detectives, so Joe's death got pushed aside.

Flipping back to the witness statements, I read Mandy's again.

She got a request for Joe to pick up at the Bayou Barstool. I flipped open my computer and checked the IP cloak again before I opened the county tax records to see how long that place had been property of the current owner.

October 1989.

So longer than this, then.

My eyes stuck again on Joe's name in the witness narrative. Did she mean she got a request and sent Joe, like everyone had likely assumed? Or did this mean she got a request for Joe specifically? Without a recording, the only way I had to know that was to ask her.

I clicked to Whitepages and typed in her name. Finding people as a civilian is a real pain in the ass.

Four hits. Only one in the right age range—and she lived five miles from where I was sitting. I couldn't put in a credit card number to get the phone number, but I could drive over there.

In the morning. Ringing a stranger's doorbell at eleven thirty isn't likely to win friends or get information.

I jotted a note and went back to the file.

The second witness interviewed was the neighbor who heard the dog whining. He said he didn't remember Joe coming and going much in the week or so before he disappeared, which was odd because they usually crossed paths a couple of times a day. So why wasn't Joe keeping to his normal schedule? Could've been a thousand things, and 990 of them wouldn't have anything to do with why he ended up dead. He was sick, maybe, or his schedule changed at work abruptly, or he was covering for a co-worker who was out. The list was a long one. And I knew better than anyone how fast memories fade and warp in the wake of tragedy. People water down the facts in their minds because it's easier than remembering something horrifying in full-color gory HD.

Not surprisingly, no one at the bar had reported hearing or seeing anything. I read over the list of people the detectives had spoken with in what was likely a short visit, just to check boxes and say they went by there.

No Jimbo. No Javi.

I closed the file and my eyes, just for a second before I remembered the hard drive that had come from under JJ's closet floorboards. Jesus, was that just today? I should really let someone know about Felix, lying dead in that little oven of an apartment. I picked up the burner and called an anonymous tip in to Austin PD's non-emergency number, hanging up before their computers could've triangulated the signal to Archie's neighborhood.

I pulled Felix's driver's license out of my pocket and opened a new browser window, typing his name into Google. I'd probably have to get Bolton to pull his criminal record, but maybe the media had something that would tell me who he worked for.

Seven results, none of them news stories.

But the top result was for felixdedeaux.com. Equally curious and afraid, I clicked the blue link.

Services, Background...Contact us?

I clicked and scrolled through all three pages.

Felix Dedeaux was a bounty hunter. But I had just run JJ's criminal record days before and found no outstanding warrants, which meant Felix wasn't looking for him. I hadn't checked Mikey's, I supposed. And it was also possible that Felix thought one of them knew something that might be helpful to him, or that he was looking to buy himself a new gun.

But it did make me even more curious about what JJ had been into.

Digging in my duffel bag, I found the drive. It took me a few minutes to hunt up a cord, but I found one in Archie's desk and plugged it into my laptop, watching files load. All spreadsheets. I clicked the first one open and scrolled, the screen spinning like the big wheel on *The Price Is Right*—Ruth's daily workout TV program. Charity and I used to hide just outside the solarium in the summers and watch around the edge of the doorway since we weren't allowed TV in the daytime during school breaks.

Eighteen hundred and seventy-three lines.

Serial number, name, date. A gun registry. But for ones he'd had stolen or ones he'd sold? I tapped one finger on the edge of the keyboard for a minute before I remembered Nichelle's email.

I clicked in and opened it, using the burner phone to snap a grainy photo of my screen in case I needed them handy when I was away from my laptop at some point. She had forty-seven serial numbers. I copied one and went back to JJ's drive, searching the file I had opened.

No results found.

I clicked back to the file directory and tried another. Same format, different information. Search.

No results found.

Going back to the directory, I counted twenty-seven files.

That was an awfully big haystack, and I wasn't at all sure what digging in it might accomplish, even. We knew JJ had been selling Jimbo and the Dixie Mafia stolen guns. I might even feel safe assuming at least one of the serial numbers would cross over between the lists.

So what?

The thing about massive investigations is that not knowing what you don't know is particularly anxiety inducing. But what I knew right then was that I could not stay awake five more minutes, much less long enough to cross reference all those numbers Nichelle sent with JJ's longer lists.

I closed the laptop and put the drive in Archie's gun safe. Paranoid? Maybe, but it wasn't like I didn't have good reason.

Seemed that somewhere in my errands tomorrow, I was headed to New Braunfels to ask for Nick Ryan's help wading through JJ's bookkeeping.

23

I'm not even sure a person could call my fitful flopping from stem to stern and back again for the next few hours an attempt at sleep, but it was the best I could do. Every time I drifted off, I saw Zapata waving his gun, but it was Graham lying on the floor broken and bleeding. Twice I sat straight up in a cold sweat, and I finally just gave up and got out of bed a few minutes after five.

Just as well, Jim rang my phone at 5:36, just as the shower was heating up.

"Morning," I said, clicking the speakerphone on.

"The bullet your federal agent friend fired at this guy didn't kill him." Jim didn't bother with pleasantries when he was running on little sleep. "The shot to his head was the kill shot, and I'm 99 percent that it was self-inflicted. You said someone did an inventory of the scene—I'd bet that the weapon picked up near this guy fired the fatal shot."

"Anything else stick out to you?" I asked, trying to puzzle out why he'd have killed himself out there.

"Nothing I didn't expect from the scans. His disease was advanced. He probably only gave up a few months that wouldn't have been good ones anyway. You find out anything about this tattoo?"

"I saw another one like it last night," I said. "So maybe it's more common than I thought. I'm still nearly positive that the guy was there when Charity was killed, though. I remember his face, too, and he hasn't aged enough to change it much in the years since."

"Sorry it wasn't the magic key you were hoping for, McClellan," he said. "There are more than a few of us old guys who'd like to see your sister's case put to rest."

"I appreciate that. I would too—and I'm not giving up, but I have other things that need more of my immediate attention, at least unless or until something else comes up."

"Just let me know if there's anything else I can do," he said. I thanked him again and hung up.

A long shower and some loud music cleared my head and I scrounged some oatmeal and a banana from the kitchen but had no luck with coffee—the bag of fancy beans my mother ground fresh every morning lived in the fridge and had three lonely residents rattling around the bottom. Archie's plastic tub of Folgers in the cabinet was also empty.

I made the oatmeal on the stovetop because our housekeeper had always insisted it was better that way, stirred in a spoonful of brown sugar, sliced the banana over the top, and then poured a glass of water from the pitcher in the fridge before sinking into a chair at the kitchen table to eat.

I tried to separate the threads of the three cases in my head, but they just kept running together. I'd worked homicide long enough to see days when I had more than one active investigation going, but never in my career had I had three felony cases all with sky-high stakes—and all so personal.

I had to get Grady and Graham back, though the kidnapping case wasn't a mystery, exactly. Zapata was gone, sure, but almost certainly hiding out plotting his next move. I might not care that much if he didn't have my husband and an innocent kid with a good heart who couldn't help who his mother was with him. The question was where. Finding Ratcliff's killer mattered because no matter what Ratcliff had been into, he was a fellow Ranger, and my gut said he was a good man who'd had some bad luck. That was the only case with a warm trail left, and I was doing my damnedest to make the most of that while it lasted. But it had intersected with this cold case involving the dead cab driver in an interesting way—so dropping in on the cab company dispatcher before normal work hours was my first priority today. And speaking of cold cases—the threads that linked Zapata's circle to the night my sister died were the first real leads in her case in decades. I hadn't been able to figure out how to ask Javi about his tattoo the night before without blowing my cover, but it had to mean something. No way in purple hell I was letting that slide by without the thorough investigation it deserved. I got up to wash my bowl and spoon and was drying my hands when the doorbell rang.

I crept to the foyer in bare feet and peered through the peephole, nearly falling over when I saw Assistant Chief Abbott staring at the front door like he could see me right through it.

I swallowed hard, reaching for the dead bolt but not turning it. I didn't really know this guy, but he'd made it pretty clear he didn't like me. And how the hell did he know I was here? My truck was in the garage with the door shut.

I had two fingers on the lock when he glanced around and cleared his throat.

"Mrs. McClellan?" he bellowed. "Open up the door here if you're home, ma'am."

I froze. Mrs. McClellan. He was looking for Ruth?

No one in their right mind would think Ruth was here when Archie was in a border town hospital recovering from near death. Would they?

He raised one fist and pounded on the door so hard it shook in the frame. "Mrs. McClellan, are you okay in there, ma'am?"

Oh, for fuck's sake. He was putting on a show for the neighbors. I had used the same one a hundred times—it's a cop trick as old as the badge, to make poking around for evidence look like a welfare check in case anyone is watching or listening—or in this case, the neighbors across the street have a camera on their doorbell.

He pulled out a lock pick kit and called, "I'm going to come in to check on you, ma'am," and I had two seconds to make a decision: open the door and face an unpleasant confrontation, or duck into the closet in the entry hall and see if I could figure out what the hell he thought he was looking for.

I got the closet door closed just as the dead bolt squealed free and Abbott cracked the door open, pausing, likely to see if there was an alarm he'd just set off.

Archie didn't think alarm systems were necessary for cops. "I can protect my house just fine," he had said a hundred times, one hand patting his sidearm.

I curled into a ball in the back corner of the relatively deep closet and pulled a blanket and a coat over my head.

The hinges creaked as Abbot opened the front door wide, and his boots echoed off the ceramic tile when he stepped inside.

I held my breath as he approached the closet door. The steps paused. Door opened, he sighed and it closed, his boots echoing differently off the wood when he stepped into Archie's study. "Here we go," he said, his voice ringing clearly through the wall.

I turned slowly, my tailbone biting painfully into the tile, until I could press one ear to the cool sheetrock of the wall between the closet and the study.

Drawers opened and closed. Papers rustled. Something heavy hit the floor and Abbott swore under his breath. "Where is it?"

My brain raced. All of HQ had been in an uproar over the hostage video and Grady's disappearance, according to Trey. And it wasn't exactly a stretch to think I'd stay here if I was in Austin, or that anyone I worked with could track my truck to the neighborhood via traffic cam in less than an hour's work.

So did Abbott know I had JJ's hard drive? Or—heaven forbid—that Trey had given my laptop back?

But then why hadn't he just called me out from the front porch?

Because he wanted an excuse to come inside.

"No, no...no...no. Dammit, Baxter, who files anything like this?" Abbott roared.

Baxter. Did Abbott think Archie had something here pertinent to the case?

Archie had been in this game forever. Hell, did he have something he didn't even know he had?

Why wouldn't Abbott just ask him?

I had the answer to that before the question fully formed: Because Archie wouldn't tell him the grass was green this morning, that's why. I had half expected Archie to go on and retire after what they'd done the day before, telling people I'd shot him, even if they did say it was an accident—Ritter was proof that no one cared whether I meant to, just that I did. I hadn't talked to Archie in almost twenty-four hours, either. For all I knew he had put in his retirement and that was the reason for Abbott's presence here—maybe he thought Archie had something that belonged to the Rangers, and had come to take it back if Archie wasn't a Ranger anymore.

No. Surely Archie would have called me.

Archie, adding stress in the middle of the shitstorm swirling around me?

Maybe not. Damn.

"He's too fucking squirrelly to keep it in his office," Abbot muttered. "Old bastard thinks he's smart."

Look who's talking, jackass. I didn't say it out loud. Yet.

His boots thudded through every room of the house, the cursing getting louder and more nonsensical as he went.

A couple of crashes made me jump, riling a protective instinct toward my mother's crystal that surprised me.

Steps thudded back through the house.

"Not as smart as you thought." The words filtered through the door as he passed the closet, about seven seconds before the front door opened and closed.

I gave it another minute before I moved the blanket and peeked out of the closet. The house was still and silent.

And a complete wreck. I walked through every room, a progressive trip through Abbott losing his temper that left a trail of increasing destruction in his wake: the kitchen was relatively straight, with a couple of cabinet doors open and the freezer cracked, a pot roast Ruth had carefully wrapped in freezer paper and saran wrap just starting to defrost on the counter. I put it back and shut everything, moving toward the back of the house. The master bedroom had been thoroughly tossed, with particular attention paid to the nightstands and closet. Remembering as I walked across the hall that my duffel bag was on the chair in the guest room with my laptop sticking out of it, I quickened my steps.

The bag was right where I'd left it. The computer was not.

"That son of a bitch," I muttered, digging through my bag. It was gone.

I looked into the closet, which was open when I knew I hadn't left it that way, and straightened a couple of the dresses Ruth kept in it back on their hangers. Alongside her gowns, Archie kept sporting equipment and a hodgepodge of other stuff I'd never really looked at too closely, a privacy boundary I regretted right then. Without knowing what was kept in here, I had no way of knowing what might be missing. It didn't make any sense that Abbott broke into Archie's home muttering about Archie's filing and ego while he was hunting a laptop I'd smuggled back out of the office via Trey. Archie was lying in a hospital. He had less than nothing to do with that.

I closed the closet and went back to the front of the house, grabbing my phone off the counter where it had gone unnoticed between the napkin caddy and the wall. Before I opened it, it started buzzing in my hand.

"McClellan," I said.

"Faith." The word gushed out of Ruth drenched in anguish so thick you couldn't spread it with a butter knife.

I recoiled instinctively, nearly dropping the phone.

"No," I said without really knowing I was saying it.

I couldn't hear what she was going to say next. Not and keep my sanity. Not today.

24

"They said there was a blood clot," she sobbed. "He's in a coma. Nobody here is willing to say he'll wake up."

Coma.

Coma wasn't good, but it wasn't dead.

I could handle a coma.

I pulled in a shaky breath. "What do you mean they won't say?"

"They won't say. They just tell me they're doing everything they can."

"Which is probably not everything that can be done."

"Exactly." She sobbed.

"Mother." I sucked in a deep breath and broke out my best ice queen voice. "Listen to me. I know you're scared. I'm scared too, about a whole lot of things. I can't find Archie a better doctor today, but you can. Pull it together and get to work solving the problem. You went down there to take care of him, right?"

"I don't know how to help him," she said. "Cold compresses and chicken broth aren't going to cut it."

"You are still Ruth McClellan," I said. "I know finding happiness has changed you—Archie has changed you—in so many ways, for the good. But right now he needs the badass bitch who demanded the best and commanded respect from everyone who ever stepped foot in The Governor's mansion, from heads of state to garbage collectors."

She sniffled twice, then pulled in a deep breath. "I'm still Ruth McClellan." She paused, her voice going soft. "I would really, really like to be Ruth Baxter."

"Get a medical team down there. Save the day. Chuck will give you your divorce—that, I can handle." And I would, as soon as I had my world right side up again. But a world without Archie Baxter wasn't a world I wanted to live in. "I love you, Mom. I have things to do here. I'm trusting you to take care of Archie."

"That's not easy for you."

"It's not. But I believe in you." I started to hang up, then slammed the phone back to the side of my head. "Wait—Mom."

"Yes?"

"Do you know what Archie keeps in the guest bedroom closet besides the archery stuff and his old skis?"

"There are some files, I think, in a little cabinet, but I've never opened it."

"Who files things this way?" I muttered.

"What, sweetie?"

"Nothing. Thank you. When he wakes up, you call me immediately."

"Of course."

"He's going to be fine. Because we are McClellan women, and we won't have it any other way." I did a good job of sounding tough until I closed the phone, a tear slipping off my lower lashes. I couldn't entertain the possibility that Archie might not wake up, or I'd just maybe go hide in his coat closet some more. So I didn't. Striding back through the house, I opened the closet in the guest room and moved everything that was in the way of the floor.

No metal box.

Whatever was in there, Abbott had it. And he had my laptop, too.

But I still had my notes, and I had JJ's hard drive and a small band of folks who could help me whether I completely trusted them or not.

And I had a couple of killers to find and some folks to rescue. I checked my watch—five after seven. A perfectly respectable morning hour, especially for people with jobs.

Time to take my own advice and get to work, starting with a visit to the former cab company dispatcher who took the call that Joe Powers never came back from.

Mandy Eskridge lived in a small, sunny yellow house with a low picket fence and a yard full of baby toys.

I rang the doorbell at 7:20 and took a step backward, folding my hands behind my back.

A redhead in a worn blue bathrobe covering a polyester caftan opened the four-panel door behind the green-framed screen door, a towheaded toddler waving a fist full of oatmeal perched on her hip.

"Mandy Eskridge?" I asked, smiling when the baby smashed her hand to the screen, leaving a sticky cereal print.

"I don't have room for no more newborns," she said, a skeptical eye traveling from my face to my feet and back. "I thought you said you had a four-year-old?" She looked over my shoulder at the truck and then back accusingly. "Any more babies and I'll get in trouble with the regulators. I ain't looking to go to war with the state for a few hundred extra bucks a month no matter how high gas prices get."

"I'm not looking for childcare," I said. "I have a couple of questions about your time working for the ABC Cab company several years ago."

Her eyes widened and she took a step back from the screen, the little girl beginning to squirm to get down. "All right, Daisy, hold on," Mandy said, lifting the tail of her robe to wipe the toddler's pudgy hand and pink cheeks.

Once the child was on her unsteady feet and toddling happily toward a brightly colored plastic piano a few feet behind Mandy, the woman returned her attention to me.

"You from the state or the IRS?" she asked.

"The state," I said.

"I tried to tell them they wasn't going to get nowhere getting in bed with drug dealers," she said. "And I ain't saying nothing else until I know you're not fixing to lock me up—I didn't do nothing except what I was told, and eventually I got so fed up I left, when I found out I was going to be a momma. Folks like that ain't no kind of people to bring up a child around."

"I'm not here to arrest you," I said. "Just hoping your memory is good."

She studied me for five blinks before she clicked the lock free on the screen door and opened it. "You can come inside," she said. "I gotta get the rest of these little ones cleaned up from breakfast and get my Charlie out to the bus."

I followed her to a cramped but homey kitchen where four children of various preschool-aged sizes were strapped into chairs, the two smallest in high chairs and two others in booster seats. Four bowls of oatmeal had been overturned, and varying amounts remained on the table—or dripped off onto the floor. A beagle on a plush dog bed in the corner eyed it without moving. I couldn't tell if there was more cereal on the floor or the children, each of whom wore a giant plastic bib.

Mandy expertly released the seat buckles and pulled off the bibs, producing baby wipes from the pocket of her robe and cleaning little hands and faces before pointing the older children to the living room full of toys and carrying the younger two in to plop them in round plastic contraptions with built-in seats and a dozen or so toys attached to hold the babies' attention. A pair of bassinets in the corner began to tremble as the children banged the toys and squealed.

"I gotta get bottles for the babies," she said, waving for me to follow her back to the kitchen.

She plunked two bottles into little things that looked like metal can cozies on the countertop, and leaned against the edge while she waited. Folding her arms across her chest, she faced me. "So what are y'all doing asking questions about this now, anyway? Ain't there a statute of limitations on stuff like this?"

"On some things," I said. "Not others."

I wanted to see how much more she'd say before I started asking the questions I had come to ask, since clearly there had been more afoot at ABC Cab than the death of a driver.

"Welp, I tried to tell Darryl it wasn't a good idea to get involved with them Mexicans, but he wouldn't listen. Greedy bastard didn't see nothing but dollar signs, and even when people started dying, he kept on. So I suppose if he gets what's coming to him after all this time, that there's just Lady Justice taking her time."

"Do you remember the names of any of the people Darryl was dealing with, Mandy?"

She opened her mouth as the bottle warmers both beeped, grabbing both bottles in one hand and shaking them up.

"Only two guys ever came around, though I got the feeling they wasn't really in charge of anything. Javier and Marco. Javi was short and skinny but strong, you know the type?"

I nodded. Pretty sure I'd met him about twelve hours ago. And a link between Jimbo and some kind of drug running activity and the cab company meant Joe's death probably wasn't a random cash grab—but someone could've taken the money to make it look like it was. I stayed quiet and let Mandy talk. She obliged.

"Marco was a big old mountain of a dude, quiet, kind of menacing. I got the feeling from being around him that he could hurt people. I didn't like him."

"You didn't get that same feeling from Javier?" I asked.

"Not as much. He was smart. Talked more than Marco. But he wasn't creepy in that same way."

I knew from experience that gut instinct was valuable around dangerous people, but it wasn't always accurate, either.

"Do you remember if either of them had a tattoo?"

"Several. They both had this weird matching one, though—a monster, kind of, or a vampire maybe. With blood and teeth. I asked them where they got it once and they said it was a gang initiation when they were young in Mexico. They came here to get out of the gang. Maybe they did, but they didn't get away from criminals."

"You sound sure about that."

"If you're from the state and you're after Darryl, you gotta know who Jimbo Hebert is," she said. "Darryl said he was the most powerful man in Texas after Governor McClellan, and I guess if what the news said about the governor is true, maybe they had more in common than a person would've thought."

I managed to keep my face straight through the reference to my father. "Having power doesn't always mean someone is a good person," I said. "Mandy, do you remember much about the last call you dispatched for Joe Powers?"

"Sure do. Darryl told me to send him to pick up from Jimbo's club. Joe got there and said he was taking the guy out off 812. Dude was blitzed and swore he was camping there and needed to sleep it off. And he never came back."

"So Joe called you back after he had the fare in the cab?" I asked. That was not in the report I'd read.

"Sure. I could hear the dude singing in Spanish. Had a nice voice, but he was too drunk to remember the words."

"Was it a song you knew?" I pulled out a notebook and a pen and whipped my hand back and forth jotting notes faster than I could talk.

"It was 'All the Girls I've Loved Before,'" she said. "But the Spanish one. I recognized it right away. My momma loved Julio Iglesias more than she loved whiskey or men."

I swallowed a laugh at the matter-of-fact way she said that.

"Did you tell the detective who came to talk to you after they found Joe's body all this?"

She blinked, her brow furrowing.

"What detective?"

25

I asked Mandy ten different ways about the police report I'd read, and got the same answer every time: no cops had ever come to talk to her after Joe's body was found. She watched the news and the papers daily for weeks, hoping to see that someone had been caught, but she eventually gave up.

"I guess nobody was really around to care about him," she said, propping a bottle on a rolled-up blanket for each infant and turning back to me. "Are you some kind of cold case specialist or something? Like on TV?"

"Or something," I said, switching gears. "Why didn't you ever call the PD to ask if there was an update on the case?"

She picked at a piece of skin on the side of her finger. "I don't know."

"Did you know Joe well?" I asked.

"As well as anyone did. He was quiet. Kind. He had the kind of smile that you could tell he was handsome when he was younger, you know?"

"And you remember the call that night?"

"I told you already, I didn't get a call. Darryl told me to send Joe to that pickup."

Weird that the detail about Joe being requested was in the police report she said was falsified.

And I had no idea which thing to believe.

"Mandy, do you know what kind of drugs Darryl was running? Or how?"

"Sure," she said. "Like I told you, I was clear with him that I wanted no part of that, but I had to keep my eye on what he was up to so I didn't accidentally end up sucked into something that could get me in trouble. I have no interest in spending a minute of my life in jail."

"So what did you see while you were keeping that eye on him?"

"They used the cabs to move the drugs around the city without the cops suspecting," she said. "The mechanics stayed late in the shop for a few weeks when all this got up and running, putting false bottoms in the trunks, with compartments under them they could hide drugs in. Probably thirty or forty pounds at a time. They moved stuff on the second, the ninth, the seventeenth, and the twenty-eighth of every month. I learned to set a calendar by that, because on those days I always got a bunch of calls for certain cars to go to the same locations over and over."

"Pickups and drop-offs." I jotted notes, thinking about the guys that had been operating on my truck the night before. Time had passed, but it seemed like the same tactics were still in play in this particular circle.

"Exactly. And the same drivers always ran the routes. I'm not sure why exactly. I never really got the impression that our drivers knew what Darryl was up to."

"He had them running dope all over town and they didn't know it?" That seemed a little far-fetched to me.

"Not that I could tell. I guess maybe I'm wrong about that. I was a lot dumber back then."

"What else did you know about Joe?" I asked.

"He was nice. Quiet, most of the time, and different from the other drivers. Like, Darryl told me to send him to any call where the people sounded classy or were getting picked up in a rich neighborhood."

I jotted both notes. The apartment where Joe's dog had been found wasn't exactly in a part of town populated by blue blood and old money.

"Did anyone ever complain about Joe?" I asked.

"Nope. His record was spotless, and most people tipped him pretty well. He was always good about tipping me out at the end of his shift. A lot of the other drivers would conveniently forget. At least until I got pregnant. Then they started remembering because I think they felt sorry for me."

"Do you know why he was sent to the bar that night?"

"I've always guessed that he saw something he wasn't supposed to see." She bit her lip and looked down at the babies in the bassinets, still slurping loudly on their bottles. "I guess that's why I dipped out on Darryl when my Charlie was born. Seemed like a good time and a good excuse to get away from all that, you know?"

"You think Joe could have been trying to blackmail Darryl?" I wondered if there were still bank records for Joe somewhere I could lay my hands on. "Or Jimbo?"

"No idea about Darryl. If he was fucking with Jimbo, then he wanted to die." She plucked an empty bottle from one bassinet and picked up the baby, laying him against her shoulder and patting his back until he let out a burp that would do a frat boy proud.

I laughed.

"He's headed for chug contest greatness, this one." Mandy smiled, putting him down and picking up the little girl next to him as a gangly boy with glasses came around the corner from a hallway, stopping short when he saw me.

"Charlie, say good morning," Mandy said. "This lady just had some questions for me about someone I used to know."

The boy's eyes doubled in size behind his glasses. "Are you a detective or something?"

"Or something," I said. "I'm Faith."

"You find lost people?"

"She solves old murder cases," Mandy said.

The kid's brow furrowed and his head swiveled to his mother. "She's asking you about a murder?"

"Never you mind," she said. "Get your cereal and find your shoes."

He walked to the kitchen, shaking his head, and Mandy smiled at me. "Kids don't think their parents are people. I'm not supposed to do anything but take care of little ones if you ask him."

"Funny how that works." I tucked the notebook back into my pocket. "Thanks for your time, Mandy."

"Sure. I hope you figure out...whatever it is you're trying to figure out."

I chuckled. "Me too."

"You aren't going to tell Darryl I talked to you?" A flicker of fear crossed her face.

"I will not tell Darryl a thing."

She nodded. "It would be nice to know what happened to poor Joe."

I let myself out and pointed the car toward New Braunfels, hoping Ryan could make some sense of a few things for me.

New Braunfels had always been one of my favorite small Texas towns. While its unique Eastern European inspired architecture was one of the only remaining signs of the town's origins as a German immigrant settlement in the 1840s, the buildings were pretty and the vibe was friendly. Plus, the county's largest employer from May to October was a massive waterpark that straddled roads and drew visitors in the kind of numbers that can cause a Dallas rush-hour style traffic jam at eight thirty on a Friday morning in August. I loved a good waterslide growing up, though I was only allowed to set foot inside the park once, with my sister. Still one of my favorite days.

I tapped the foot that wasn't controlling the truck as it crawled past a five-story waterslide with several uphill sections, thankful that Ryan had answered his phone and confirmed he was at work when I called. A lot of state employees take Fridays off in the summer.

My phone buzzed in the cupholder, and I checked the text because of the turtle's pace of current traffic. Bolton, sending the serial number for the gun that poor Adam's wife used to kill him, with an added note: *This piece was originally made in 1868, so it didn't have a serial number. But the chamber was replaced in 1979, and the owner opted to have a serial number put on it then in case it was ever stolen. Apparently it once belonged to Jesse James.*

Interesting. Thank you! I typed back.

Finally past the backup, I parked in front of a modest brown brick government building with a state seal on the window glass ten minutes later and grabbed my bag and the hard drive.

"It's an honor to meet you, ma'am." An older man with long jowls and a still-athletic build put a hand out when I stepped inside. "I've read about your cases for years."

The voice coming out of the guy's face was the same one I'd heard on the phone but didn't match the physical appearance at all. I'd been expecting someone roughly my age, and this guy had a few trips around the sun on Archie by the looks of it.

I blinked, trying to hide my shock.

"I know. I sound younger," he said. "Blessing and a curse, I guess. I'm Nick Ryan."

I shook his outstretched hand. "Faith McClellan. I can't tell you how much I appreciate your help."

"Like I said, it's an honor, ma'am." He waved for me to follow him. "Let's talk in my office. I just got a call from the ATF that I think will interest you."

I followed him back, not speaking again until the door was closed. "Did they find something else with that gun?"

"Likely matches for three other murders in a fifty-mile radius of here," he said, nodding.

I dropped into a black vinyl chair. "Three?"

"Yes ma'am. And that's not even the best part."

"I'm sorry?"

"According to the last police report, this gun no longer exists."

26

"How can that be?" I asked.

He turned his computer monitor my way and showed me the records he'd found based on the ballistics results. "I have a couple of theories, though I'm afraid they are simply that."

I leaned in to peer at the screen, the images lining up with as close to identical precision as I'd ever seen. "I don't think anyone can dispute that these were fired from the same weapon," I said.

"It's convincing," he said. "But here's the thing: a duplicate is possible in theory. The advent of artificial intelligence and guns people can make on 3D printers could possibly copy the ballistic signature closely enough to fool the naked eye."

I sat up straight and turned to him. "Has that ever been done?"

"Not that anyone knows of," Ryan said. "But there is growing concern in some sectors of law enforcement that it's only a matter of time before we see a case like this. And if that happens..."

"Ballistics evidence becomes utterly useless." I slumped back into the chair. "I wonder sometimes if computer science has become too focused on what they can do, at the expense of what they should do."

"Someone said that in a movie." Ryan furrowed his brow. "*Jurassic Park.*"

“That chaos guy was the smartest one there.” I pointed to the screen. “When and where were these other shootings?”

“The most recent one was eight years ago.”

“Computers couldn’t have created that ballistics signature back then,” I said.

“No, just the most recent one. And I’m not saying that’s likely. It might not even be possible yet today. But the records clearly show that this weapon, assuming the match holds, was recovered in evidence in a gas station robbery murder and slated for destruction after the conclusion of the trial.”

“Who was supposed to send it through the gator?” Weapons removed from circulation and sent for destruction were fed through a machine called an alligator, named for the power of the metal jaws that chewed guns into scrap metal.

“Says here it was sent through the Travis County Sheriff’s Office.” He pointed to the screen.

“What?” I grabbed the mouse and clicked the report up on the screen, scrolling to the bottom looking for the signature and shaking my head when I found it.

Ryan leaned over my shoulder. “Isn’t that your—”

“Yep.” I couldn’t make myself blink, staring at Graham’s signature on the screen. His case, five months before Jameson assigned us as partners according to the date. “Can you print this for me? And the others, too? Were they also Travis County?”

“No, actually every incident was in a different jurisdiction. It’s not that hard, with all the departments we have around here. I just noticed because I thought it was odd that it’s the same weapon but every shooting went through a different department.”

I shook my head. “I’ve seen this before. It’s not odd, it’s sometimes on purpose. Even with all the technology available now, different organizations don’t share information the way they should. Ten or twenty years ago? Forget it—random cases like this wouldn’t even cross a desk at another department.”

“Exactly.” He tipped his head to one side. “You’re very perceptive, Faith. Not many people from your generation would pick up on that.”

"So how does a person become a professional J. Edgar Hoover, without being a cop?" I asked.

"Luck?" He smiled. "I wanted to work in government where I could help people. Here, I keep people who shouldn't have power from accumulating it. Most of the time."

"Jim says you're better than Skye Morrow at finding dirt."

"I am. And the people I want to help out know where to find me." He winked.

"Touché." I sighed as he pulled papers off his printer and stacked them by case. "So now that we have all this, what do I do with it?"

Ryan chuckled. "That's your wheelhouse. I dig the facts up. People like you arrange them into a case."

"I need a whiteboard." And Archie and Graham, but I didn't say the last part out loud.

"I think I can help with that. Be right back."

Ryan disappeared, and I stared at Graham's signature on the computer screen. He had a memory like a steel trap. I was sure he'd recall this case. Too bad I couldn't ask him. Thankfully, his reports were always the most thorough in the department, so I would know most everything he'd seen from reading the narrative. And at least I knew this one wasn't falsified. I wasn't sure why I hadn't mentioned Mandy's assertion that the other report wasn't accurate to Ryan—force of habit for someone with my trust issues—and it might not matter if I could figure out what I needed to know from the information in front of me, but I could always track those cops down if I needed to.

My phone buzzed and I pulled it out to see a text from Nichelle: *Have some info for you, can we meet today?*

Of course, I typed back. *I can be in Dallas by lunchtime.*

We can meet you in Waco if you're still in Austin, came the immediate reply.

"You're too nice to be real," I muttered. "Reporters aren't helpful people." At least not any of the ones I had ever met.

I sent her the name of my favorite local diner and told her I'd see her in two hours. I paused and added *thank you* to the end of the message, as its own sentence.

Of course, she replied. *It's all going to be okay*.

Tucking the phone back into my pocket as Ryan walked back into the room, I really hoped she was right.

Ryan led me through a short maze of hallways to a large closet with a folding table and chair and an easel holding a large whiteboard, a marker dangling from the top corner by a long string.

"Will this work?" he asked, pulling a short chain on a bare overhead lightbulb. "I know you can't go to your own office, and honestly, I could get into trouble for you being here since you're a suspended state employee, but we have a skeleton crew here until after Labor Day, and there's a back door right out there." He pointed to the hallway.

"Why are you helping me?" I asked. "If you know what they're saying, and this could get you into trouble?"

"What are they going to do? Fire me?" He laughed. "Prescott doesn't talk about anyone the way he talks about you. And for a man who spends most of his days with dead people, I have always found him to be an excellent judge of character."

"Y'all have known each other a long time, he said." I put the copies of the paper files down on the folding table and smiled, handing him the hard drive before I jotted a note with the antique's serial number Bolton had found and sent Ryan the photo of the serial numbers Nichelle had given me.

"I just need to know if any of these are on both lists," I said.

"I'll let you know what I find, and I'll keep looking into the ballistics evidence, too." He stepped back into the hallway and shut the door.

I sat down at the table, found the file with Graham's case, and started to read.

27

"So they had the weapon, but they never made an arrest?" Joey dipped a fry in ketchup and paused with it halfway to his mouth. "Not trying to insult your husband or anything, but didn't you say he's a good cop? Everyone knows leaving your weapon at a murder scene is a pretty decent way to get yourself thrown in prison."

I had read the file on this murder twice before I left New Braunfels and carried it along to get their thoughts because I couldn't make sense of what happened to the weapon. It was processed properly through evidence and slated for destruction when the case was closed. Graham had put all the right documentation in the file just like he was supposed to—he was nothing if not by the book.

So how did this same weapon end up shooting Ratcliff nearly a decade later?

"Everybody knows that, huh?" I raised one eyebrow at Joey but didn't say anything else. I had been a cop too long to miss that he had a past. But I liked him—anyone willing to stick their neck out by popping onto a dangerous drug lord's radar to help a complete stranger was inherently a good person. And I liked Nichelle, too. More than that, I was on the verge of actually trusting her. A fucking reporter. So if she was going to marry this dude, I had to believe whatever he had done that would give him that kind of knowledge was history.

"Not everybody dates someone whose whole life is crime and secrets," Nichelle chided, giving him an elbow to the bicep. But her smile didn't reach her eyes. Should I tell her I had their number—to an extent—and couldn't care less for love or money?

She was helping me, she'd said, because she'd been in my shoes. Which meant she might bolt if she thought she needed to protect Joey. Better to keep quiet, because I needed her.

"From what the witnesses said, the weapon was abandoned when the shooter heard sirens. The men coming in the door hit the shooter's arm when they pushed it open and the weapon slid under a shelving unit. But it didn't matter because the registration was a dead end. The guy it was last registered to had sold it and had a solid alibi for the night of this murder."

"He didn't know who he'd sold it to?"

"Private sales are subject to a dozen loopholes, but"—I flipped pages—"he gave Graham the sales receipt he wrote up himself. Claimed the guy had ID. But it had to be fake—they rounded up every Colter Sellers in the state, put all five in a lineup, and the gun's former owner didn't recognize any of them. The only one who didn't have an alibi for the night of the shooting was a foot too short and twenty years too old to be the buyer."

Joey nodded. "You're dealing with someone who had done this before," he said. "That's the kind of foresight that comes from experience."

"I know," I said.

Nichelle put her burger down and reached for the file. "May I?"

"Be my guest," I said.

She pushed her hair behind her shoulder and moved her plate, flipping slowly through pages of the file. I watched her linger over the victim's information and again over the page with the known facts about the weapon. Pulling a notebook from her roomy leather tote bag, she jotted a few notes.

"What do you see?" I was genuinely curious.

"Not trying to offend you," she said, pushing the folder back toward me.

"You didn't," I said. "I know you're very good at what you do, and I'd bet you're wondering about something specific. Just trying to figure out if you see something I didn't."

"I'm wondering if this woman who was killed had worked there for a while or not. Maybe whether she had a history of an abusive partner or some connection to the other victims. And I'm also curious about this gun and who owned it before the guy who sold it to the presumed shooter in a sale that couldn't be traced—and how much the seller listed here remembers about how and where he got it. How do private sales work here, anyway?"

"Good questions. Graham asked and the gun's registered owner, Rusty, told him he bought it at a swap meet."

"So no record of that sale at all," Nichelle said.

"Do you have time to look into the victims for any possible connections?" I asked, flipping through files. "A cab driver, a convenience store clerk, a carjacking, and a drive-by. They seem random." I paused on the last folder, reading the address and pulling out my phone.

"Something wrong?" Nichelle asked.

"The place this drive-by took place isn't Westlake Hills or anything, but it's not the kind of neighborhood where drive-by shootings are a regular thing. Which makes me think it should've gotten more grease than it did." I flipped pages. Elderly woman and one cat dead, bullet came through the window. New Braunfels PD ruled it an accident. No witnesses identified, no doorbell cameras back then to pick up the car and maybe ID a plate.

Like Joe the cab driver, this lady was left without anyone to advocate for justice. Could that be a link? Who would just go around killing random folks while banking on the fact that the cops would be too busy to pay attention to the case?

"It looks like a couple of these folks didn't have any family," I said. "I suppose if we're dealing with a thrill killer, then that might come into play for targeting victims who don't really have anyone who will miss them."

"It's a weird way to choose targets even for a nutcase," Joey said, pushing his plate away and sipping his soda.

"And won't get me anywhere at all with who might have had this gun a week ago," I said.

"There's a case that we don't have here?" Nichelle asked.

"I don't have the file, though Miller could get it." I finished the last bite of my grilled cheese sandwich. "A Rangers officer was murdered four days ago in a trailer in the middle of the south Texas desert, and the ballistics registry analysts say the weapon used was likely this one."

"But you just said it was destroyed years ago." Joey put his glass down.

"I said it was slated to go to the gator."

Joey and Nichelle exchanged a glance. "I know a little about this kind of thing," she said.

"What kind of thing?"

"I had a story a few years ago. It was more than one gun, but they went missing between the evidence locker and the gator."

"Robbery?"

"Inside job."

I blinked. "You're not suggesting Graham..."

Nichelle put both hands up. "Not even a little. But I would think a check of the chain of evidence control here might be helpful."

"Sorry," I said. "I didn't mean to take your head off. Of course that's what you meant."

"It seems like you have kind of a lot going on here," Nichelle said. "No offense taken."

"I should've thought of that," I said, pulling out my phone. "I do have someone I can ask to look into that."

"I was just about to call you," Bolton said when he picked up.

"What's up?"

"You called me, so ladies first."

"I have a serial number on a weapon that I need you to pull the chain of custody on. The computer will say it was destroyed in 2015, but I need to know who had reason to have contact with it after Graham checked it into evidence up until it was slated for destruction."

"You need information on a gun that was fed to the gator nine years ago?"

"I know it sounds weird, but will you just look it up?" I read him the serial number. "I have a hunch." Well, technically Nichelle had a hunch, but she made a lot of sense, and on a normal day I might've thought of the same thing myself.

"Sure thing, ma'am." He tapped keys one at a time. "Oh. The file is down in the boneyard, ma'am. They didn't computerize the evidence files on guns that had been destroyed."

"Dammit," I muttered.

"I'll go have a look this afternoon if it matters to you," he said.

"You'll have to sign in," I said, more to myself than to him.

"I can write my name real good, ma'am." Bolton laughed.

"That's not what I meant," I said. "If my hunch is right, I don't want your name connected to anything to do with this. I already have Dakota Grady's life hanging over my head. I don't need to have yours up there, too."

Across the table, Nichelle flinched, her eyes going wide.

"Who the hell is Dakota Grady?" Bolton asked.

"Never mind, I shouldn't have said that." I rubbed my temple. "I'm too tired for my own good."

Nichelle scribbled something on her notebook and shoved it toward Joey. She worked at a newspaper two hours south of DC; of course she knew who he was. Damn.

"Please just be careful what you reveal and to whom," I said to Bolton. "I have three different investigations running on single power and very little sleep. Don't put yourself in danger."

"Yes ma'am," he said.

"Why were you going to call me?" I asked.

"The other cases you wanted information on—Jim's guy with the state said he could take over the ballistics hunt, so I let him do that, but it took me longer than I thought to find the guy you were looking for," Bolton said.

I had clean forgotten that I wanted to interview JJ's surviving buddy Gavin. Too much going on. "Wasn't he at the county jail? I'm pretty sure that's where he was taken."

"He was not. I'm fuzzy on the how and why because either the people I spoke with didn't know or didn't want to say, but he's at the border detention center. And from what I understand, he's not in great shape."

28

My granny always said asking people for favors is like using a credit card—there's a limit, and you have to keep an eye on how close you are to it. I put the phone on the table and leaned on my forearms, meeting Nichelle's gaze and hoping I wasn't about to max out with her.

"I have a bit of a new problem."

"What's up?"

Joey leaned forward, like he knew instinctively somehow that I was about to ask his fiancée to do something that was likely dangerous, when I didn't even know exactly how or why.

"There was one witness to Ratcliff's murder who survived, and I need to talk to him. I made some assumptions about how this murder went down the last time I saw this guy, and I didn't ask the right questions because of that. But he's being held in the border detention center and I'm not technically a Ranger at the moment, so I really have no reason to be there."

"But my press credentials would get me in," she said.

"Are you kidding?" Joey turned to her. "You remember the part where this was supposed to be a vacation, right? Visiting your mother, showing me the sights, eating Mexican food, going to the Alamo?"

"You remember the part where I said I was going to help Faith get her husband back?"

He folded his arms across his chest. "She's a cop. You're not."

"Then who better to ride along with here? I will have a cop with me at all times." She leaned her head on his shoulder. "Which is not something I can often say at home."

"Often? Try ever." He rolled his eyes.

"The place I'm going is full of guards," I said. "If that helps you feel more secure."

Joey shook his head. "If anyone could find trouble inside a prison, it's Nichelle."

"Don't I always get myself out of it?" Nichelle sounded indignant, a warning edge creeping into her tone.

"She is pretty good at taking care of herself," Joey conceded.

Nichelle looked at me. "I can call ahead and set up an appointment to interview this person you're looking for, but they will ask for consent from the inmate. They won't make him talk to me."

"Let's hope he's scared enough that he thinks talking to a reporter will help him, then. He won't say a word if he doesn't know there's something in it for him."

"And you still have the problem of how you're going to get her into the prison. She doesn't have a press badge."

"We have a few hours in the car to work on it," I said. "If all else fails, I can send Nichelle in with a list of questions."

"Which means you won't have a cop with you at all." Joey glared as Nichelle grabbed her bag and stood.

"I have an idea," she said, poking Joey. "Don't you think she looks like Mel?"

He looked up and tipped his head to one side. "Not entirely."

"But with her hair up and some drugstore glasses, it could be close enough," she said. "No one is really going to look that closely—who would have reason to believe she's not who we say she is?"

I wiggled my eyebrows. "Especially if we're talking."

"Exactly."

"The desk sergeant didn't care for me last time I was there," I said. "But maybe he'll be off today."

"Or maybe we can make sure he's otherwise occupied," she said as Joey stood up and followed us out of the diner into the oppressive end-of-summer heat.

"My only contact inside the facility is a hostage at the moment," I said.

"One of many questions I have for you, but we can talk in the car." She waved one hand. "I have lots of friends. Surely someone will make a phone call for us."

Joey opened and shut her door when she climbed into my truck, then stopped at the driver's back corner of the bed before I opened my door.

"I'll bring her back safe. You have my word."

He held my gaze for a few seconds, then nodded.

"Ask her to send me the list of victims and the information you have on the gun you think is a match. Having something to do will help me go less crazy, and I know a thing or two about running down information myself."

"Sure thing." I opened the door. "Thank you for your help. Sorry I hijacked your vacation. Look at it this way—I have to get Graham out of Zapata's place before Sunday night, so I can't bug you guys for too much longer."

"Do you understand what kind of people you're dealing with?" he asked.

"Do you understand what kind of people I grew up with?"

He shook his head. "Unless your father is a murderer, this is not the same thing. These people will kill you and your husband and anyone else who annoys them without thinking twice about it."

"I've been a cop a long time. I know that. I also know I have no choice if I want my husband to come home safely," I said. "I appreciate your concern, but I can handle myself."

He nodded. "She'd do the same. Hell, she has done the same. So I will just say it wouldn't hurt for someone to know where you're going and when."

"I'll keep that in mind. And we'll send you the information from these cold cases if you really don't mind."

"I really don't. I'll call you when I have something."

I slid into the truck and cranked the air conditioning, asking Nichelle to look through the files and forward him the information he wanted. She was quiet for a few minutes as she tapped her phone screen, which gave me just enough time to realize that while I knew I needed to go talk to Gavin, I had just promised yet another person I'd be a good steward of their loved one's safety.

Timmy Dushane and his missing tongue filtered through my best attempt at compartmentalizing. Who put this low-level gang member in the detention center, and what the hell had happened to him? I glanced at Nichelle. I had about three hours to figure out how to get us in and out of the lion's den without a scratch, because I had no idea who was corrupt here and who wasn't.

29

"For not having the time to get an actual fake ID, this might just work," I said, looking in the mirror and adjusting the black-rimmed glasses we'd picked up at a drugstore. "We lucked out with the glasses."

"You really do look enough like her that no one will question it." Nichelle looked over my shoulder at my reflection in the gas station bathroom mirror. "Let's leave your hair down, because it's different enough from her photo here." She glanced at the digital image of her friend Melanie's Virginia press ID on my phone screen. "But I think the glasses being so close will get us across the finish line. My friend Aaron in Richmond called an old friend and checked the desk sergeant assigned for today—it's not the guy who hassled you before, so we're at least on better footing there. Odds that the gate officer is a man?"

"It was last time I was there."

She unbuttoned another button on her shirt and handed me mascara and lip gloss from her bag, catching my eye in the mirror. "You were a beauty queen. You can't tell me you've never used your looks to get information you want."

I smiled and shook my head. "I can neither confirm nor deny."

"Yeah, that's what I thought." She brushed on some powder and nodded at her own reflection. "Let's go see a man about some information, Mel."

I met her gaze in the mirror. "Thank you."

"This is going to make one hell of a story." She flashed a grin. "It's what I live for. Ask anybody." She waved me out to the convenience store ahead of her and grabbed two bottles of water from a cooler as I picked up a banana and an apple from a fruit bin that looked surprisingly tempting.

"Have you heard from Miller in the past couple of days?" I tried not to sound mad as I paid for the snack. Not sure I pulled it off.

"No, but he's up to his hairline in planning the final phase of his operation, so that's not unusual." She put one hand on my arm as I reached for the door handle. "For what it's worth, he said part of that is getting your husband out of Mexico."

"Forgive me if I don't think that would be as much of a priority for him as it is for me."

"I get that. And he does have the Speaker's son to be concerned with."

"I can't believe I didn't realize who that kid's mother was the first time I met him." I opened the door and walked back out to the truck. We were twenty-seven miles from the detention center and Nichelle had secured an appointment to interview Gavin in forty-five minutes.

"It's not a terribly uncommon name," Nichelle said, buckling her seat belt. "Nobody goes around making connections like that without a little prompting."

"Yeah, well, watching a video of the kid getting the shit kicked out of him and asking to go home was quite a prompt."

"I can't imagine. And I have a decent imagination. But here's what I do know—Alexis Hutcherson Grady is not a woman you fuck around with. I don't know what Zapata thinks he's playing at, but you don't snatch a high-profile politician's kid and send out videos when your motives aren't political."

"He wants out," I said, as the rest of her comment rolled around the back of my head. "That's what Amin said. He has lived his entire life by bullying and violence and now his son is dead and he wants out. Amin said that's why he was preparing for some sort of battle, so he could slip out, fake his own death. But Amin is a sociopath and a criminal, so I wasn't sure how much to believe."

"He could probably trade an escape and some kind of immunity for Grady's son," Nichelle mused, jotting notes on a long, narrow spiral pad.

"But what made him desperate enough to switch gears that way, I wonder?" I asked, staring at the ribbon of bright yellow marking the shimmering concrete all the way to the horizon.

Nichelle snorted and I slid my eyes her way as she dissolved into a fit of giggles. "You good?"

"You don't understand that it's you?" she asked. "Really?"

"What's me?"

"Zapata needed more insurance when you came into the mix. You spent a week solving a case Kyle has been working on for more than two years, taking down an organized crime syndicate that has been in operation since you were in high school." She shook her head. "It's hard to get the kind of distance needed to see when you're not just good at your job, but you border on superhero status, because we're all only human. But you, Faith McClellan, could convincingly wear a big old red-and-gold S on your chest all day every day."

"I make so many mistakes."

"Everyone makes mistakes," Nichelle said. "Perfection isn't the point here. Results are. And you get results."

"You're not too shabby yourself. Have you really caught several murderers, like all on your own?"

"Takes a superhero to know one." She winked when I glanced at her. "It took Joey a long time to convince me I had a gift. Mine is determination, driven by a desire to help people. I suspect yours is similar, probably with a kick because of what happened to your sister."

I nodded. "I can't shake the feeling that these same people had something to do with her death," I said. "I just can't quite seem to figure out how it all went down. But one of the men who was on Zapata's side of the shootout the other night was there, in our house, that night. He's dead now, though, so I can't question him."

"Holy Manolos."

I laughed. "What did you just say?"

She did, too. "I have a thing about shoes. That started as a joke with my best friend and just kind of became an expression I use without thinking that it sounds funny to other people."

"I noticed the heels. You and Skye Morrow—I don't know how you walk in them. Or why you'd hobble around in pain to be able to wear cute shoes."

Nichelle picked up her phone. "I haven't felt my toes in almost a decade. Though the comparison to Skye might send me running for some Birkenstocks."

"You genuinely don't like her? She gets treated like some sort of demigoddess around here."

"I don't know her, so I'm not sure if I like her or not, but I can say I have no respect for her. Because she has very little respect for the truth, or for public safety, and I care about both—they're what this job is supposed to be about."

I'll be damned.

She shook the phone. "Joey says he might have something for us in a little bit."

"It's nice of him to help."

"He likes to make me happy."

I turned into the drive at the detention center and pulled up to the gate. Showtime.

The guy at the gate wasn't the same one I'd spoken with a week ago, but he checked his list and barely glanced at us or our credentials before waving us through. I put the window up and Nichelle tapped her fingers on the door. "One down."

We parked and walked inside, and I watched her pull a clipboard from her Mary Poppins reporter bag and stride in the door with an approving smile like she'd been there a thousand times. She was good at this. Really good.

She stopped at the desk where an officer, so young and fresh faced I would've mistaken him for a student intern if he hadn't been wearing a badge, was reading a comic book. He glanced up and his eyes popped wide. "Can...um...can I help you?"

Nichelle tossed her mahogany hair slightly and smiled, handing over her press credentials. "Nichelle Clarke, here for an interview with an inmate."

He glanced down long enough to read her name before he tapped a few keys on his computer and nodded, his eyes moving to me. "And you're Miss Parker?"

"That's right," I said. "I left my press card in my other bag, but I have the electronic copy." I handed him the phone and he furrowed his brow.

"Everything okay?" I asked after the silence marked a minute.

"I just don't know if I'm supposed to take this," he said. "I'm still kind of new and nobody has tried to go in with a photo of their ID."

"Do very many people try to break into the prison, Officer Lawry?" I glanced at his name tag and met his eyes with a small smile.

He grinned so wide I thought his face might crack and ducked his head so far I could see the cowlick in the back of his otherwise slicked-down style. "No ma'am, I suppose that's a good point."

He passed the phone back to me and handed Nichelle's card back across the desk. "I'll have someone come to escort you back. You can wait over there." He pointed to a door that led to the interrogation rooms.

Nichelle turned a sly smile my way as we turned away from the desk.

The door buzzed a couple of minutes later and swung open to reveal Officer Bowden, who had not cared for my request that they leave Timmy Dushane alone after he tackled me in the interrogation room. Shit. I knew this was too easy so far. I scooted more behind Nichelle, thankful she was taller than me in her crazy shoes.

Bowden waved for us to follow him without a word, letting the door fall shut after I stepped into the dank, yellowish hallway with the low ceiling.

I stayed behind Nichelle and kept my chin tucked to my chest, glad we'd decided to leave my hair down. Bowden stopped at the door to the same room I'd met with Timmy in and turned to us. "What kind of story you think you gals are going to get from this scumbag?"

"I heard from an inside source that he was a witness to a murder last week," Nichelle said.

"Is that a fact?" Bowden asked. "How is his stupid ass still here, then?"

"Maybe he wasn't much of a threat." Nichelle kept her voice sunny and her smile wide as she spoke. I held my breath, sure this guy was about to look at my face and blow our cover. He didn't strike me as the biggest rule follower here when I met him the first time. If he figured out who I was, we were in trouble.

Bowden looked Nichelle up and down. "Maybe he wasn't." He opened the door.

I put my head at a downward angle and stayed close behind Nichelle as we filed into the room. Bowden turned his back and stood outside the door, pulling his phone from his pocket when I peeked over my shoulder.

Nichelle's gasp drew my attention to the young man hunched over the steel table in the middle of the closet-sized room, and I gasped, too.

Gavin didn't even look like the same skinny drug addict kid I'd met in that trailer. His face was such a mess of cuts and bruises I couldn't make out anything else.

He peered at us in turn out of one half-open eye, the other swollen shut.

"I can't tell you anything unless you can get me the hell out of here." His speech was thick through a split lip, but he was easy enough to understand.

I took the chair across from him and Nichelle positioned herself between the window in the door and the table without even being asked. This woman was going to make me change my mind about journalists.

Gavin leaned forward on an arm encased in a cast, trying to widen his functioning eye. "Do I know you?"

"You might have seen one of her stories online," Nichelle said.

He sat back and nodded, wrinkling his face when the broken arm moved.

"Who did this to you?"

"Why do you want to talk to me?" he asked.

"We're doing a story on violence in America's prisons. This place has had so much bad press, our editor wanted it included for clickbait." I was shocked at how fast and free the lie rolled out of my face.

"They got enough of that here for ten stories," he said.

"How did you wind up here?" I asked.

"Are you going to get me out of here?"

"I don't know that we have that kind of authority," I hedged.

Nichelle cleared her throat. "We can't, but we have friends who can. The federal agent kind."

"That's the kind of friend I could use," he said, his chin dropping to his chest. "All my old friends are dead anyway."

"We can't make you any promises, except that we'll try," I said. "But that's a better chance than you'll get if you just go back to your cell."

He raised his head slightly and appeared to ponder that for a minute. "True." He sighed. "Damned if I know how I got here. I thought this joint was for illegals they were holding for being sent back or whatever. I might not be the most upstanding citizen, but I'm an American."

"What were you arrested for?" I asked.

"I wasn't, not really. These cops, they raided our trailer and my friends were dead—fucking fentanyl-laced pills. I told them not to take that shit. We didn't even know that dude. So they took me to this little dinky sheriff's office with a lady cop who wouldn't give me the time of day, and she locked me up for possession, which I guess was okay but I don't even know really because I wasn't even touching the shit, I was just in the room with it." He looked up at us with his eyebrows raised.

I shrugged, keeping my face flat, though my thoughts were racing. I told Dean not to take Gavin to Nava's jail, because I didn't trust her—and I was right, Zapata's crew ran the county because they had a constant threat hanging over her grandmother, who was in Mexico. So could I trust Dean? Out loud all I said was, "I would think a judge would say that if you'd taken any, you'd be dead too, so you'd probably get off. But they can book you for being in the room, sure."

"Great. Well then, this cowboy dude with a big old gold belt buckle, he shows up and flashes a badge at the lady cop and she tells me he's transferring me because this is his case. And he put me in the back of a car and started driving and didn't say not one word to me. Just brought me here and dropped me off. I don't even know if he got my stuff from the other jail."

I scribbled notes, underlining "belt buckle." While they weren't exactly scarce in these parts, I'd bet my house Abbott was the person who brought him here. But why would he bother?

Gavin had to know something he didn't know he knew.

"You said a minute ago that you didn't know the guy who brought the pills and dropped them off."

"We didn't," he said. "Guy came in and said the pills were a gift. Everyone else started popping them, and then the dude disappeared into the back room where JJ had that cop tied up."

"What did that guy look like?"

"Like half the other old white dudes I've ever met," Gavin said. "Boots, jeans, Stetson shading his face. Gut."

"Did he usually work with Zapata?"

"I assumed he did. Zapata has a lot of people this side of the border running shit these days. But JJ was paranoid about getting screwed over, so he didn't much let the rest of us talk to Zapata's people."

"Did you hear anything from the back room?"

"Besides the part where that cop got his brains blown out?" Gavin sank into the metal folding chair and whimpered.

"How did the cop get there?" Nichelle asked.

"JJ said he took him down," Gavin said. "Favor for a friend, he said. He needed us to watch the guy just for a few days. He didn't say shit about anyone getting shot."

JJ probably didn't think he was going to get shot himself either, to be fair. The only reason Gavin was still alive was because he didn't touch the laced pills, when every indication was that he would've been all over such a thing.

"So you didn't hear anything but the shots?" I asked.

"Yeah, the old guy slammed the door and the other dude, he hadn't said much the whole time we were there, he didn't even look at whoever was taking him water and food, but he spoke when the old guy went in there. Like he knew him."

Which didn't really tell me much, given what Jim had found in Ratcliff's autopsy report, but I jotted it down.

"The old guy was pissed. He said our cop was stupid. Something about calling some broad. I couldn't tell if they were fighting about a woman."

I paused for half a second and looked up. "Do you remember anything else they said about that?"

"Yeah, it was wild, something about the ultimate cover, how this chick was respected. I don't know. Something about no one would question anything with her name on it, and they could control what she saw."

I heard Nichelle pull in a deep breath behind me and tried to slow my own breathing. Gavin was saying Ratcliff played me. And I risked about half a dozen lives trying to save him.

"Anything else?" I asked.

"The cop said if they wanted to get rid of the middleman, this was the only way to do it. The broad, she would handle that." He fidgeted, squirming in the chair. "Was he talking about us, the middleman thing? Because I can't take another ass whooping in this place, so if some chick is going to kill me, I wish she'd come do it already."

"Who beat you up?" I asked.

"The first time it was these two guards," he said. "They didn't talk, just yanked me up off the bed and started swinging." He held up the broken arm. "Hard. But then there was a siren that went off and they dropped me on the floor and took off."

I jotted notes.

"And the other times?"

"Just one other time," Gavin said, and I raised my eyebrows.

"All of this"—I waved one hand in a circle to indicate his face and the broken arm—"was from you getting jumped just two times?"

"That's what I'm saying. These people are serious. The kind of people who would almost kill you and, like, cut out your tongue or some bullshit so you can live in pain but can't snitch. Not that I would snitch."

"So was the other attack also guards?" I asked, trying not to think about Timmy Dushane and his missing tongue.

Gavin shook his head. "That was inmates in the yard. This one guy who runs the big gang here, Valdez, he did a lot of the damage to my face. I got a busted cheekbone under all that swelling. He said to keep my mouth shut about the guns before he spit on me and backed off when one of the guards blew a riot alarm."

"Are the gangs here connected to the cartels?"

"How should I know?" Gavin squinted his better eye and leaned toward me. "But it sure as shit seems like it."

I stood, and Nichelle took a step forward. "At the trailer that day...you're sure you didn't hear a name for the guy who brought the pills and shot the cop?"

"I thought you said your story was about prison violence?" he asked.

"It is, but no reporter can resist a good story," she said. "Curiosity is part of this gig."

"Nobody said names. I would remember." He shook his head, looking back at me. "You must be all over the internet with a face like that."

"I do okay," I said.

"Can you really help me?"

"I will try with everything in me." This kid had made some dumb mistakes, but he hadn't done anything he deserved to die for, and it seemed like he had stumbled onto shit lists for a few people who would have no qualms about getting rid of him. I hadn't been able to save Timmy Dushane, but maybe I could help here.

I stood and followed Nichelle to the door.

"Oh hey," Gavin called. "The old guy, right before the shots fired. He said he was scared of the chick they were talking about."

I turned back with one eyebrow up as Nichelle paused with her hand on the door.

"Afraid?"

"Yeah, so you know, watch your back. He said he went his whole life without getting on her radar. I thought that was a funny way to say that... radar...and he was going to keep it that way."

I nodded. "Take care," I said.

Nichelle opened the door and Bowden tucked his phone in his pocket. "Got what you came for?" he asked.

I nodded reflexively and he peered at my face.

"Don't I know you?"

30

The old lady was the easiest.

Meddling old bigmouth...He was in this too far to have it ruined by her chatter. Thankfully, the cops thought she was crazy, but he couldn't risk her calling back.

Another car that wasn't his, with plates from yet another vehicle. He barely slowed down, spotting her silhouette in the gray light of her old TV through her lace curtains.

Four shots through the window, dump the car, change his clothes. It got simpler every time.

Halfway back to his house, his phone rang.

"You got my money, asshole?" he asked, putting the phone to his ear.

"Did you just gun down an old lady in my jurisdiction, you crazy fuck?"

"She called the cops about the broad at the gas station."

"And they thought she was crazy," the other man bellowed. "Who do you think engineered that?"

"Now she's not a problem."

"You know, I got you your goddamn gun back. I cut you in and made you a very comfortable man. Everything we have done in the past decade will lay right at Amin's feet if anyone is ever even smart enough to know where to look. You could stop shooting random people and causing me headaches."

"You're missing the point."

"Enlighten me."

"They are random. Or at least they look random," he said. "No one will ever put these together."

"Unless someone matches the ballistics on your fucking old-ass gun."

"Who is going to submit records from any of these to NIBIN? No one cares enough to check ballistics in a case like this. And now we don't have to worry about them causing trouble. You should be thanking me, you know."

"Not one more."

"Do I have to remind you that this is your fucking fault? Who had to kill the girl? Sure as shit wasn't me."

"I needed McClellan to know I was serious."

"And where did that get you? I fucking told you he was a coldhearted prick. But you knew better. So stop chewing my ass for cleaning up your fucking mess." He snapped the phone shut and parked his truck in the garage. Just in case.

31

“A lot of her pieces have gone viral on TikTok,” Nichelle said smoothly, stepping in between us and smiling at Bowden as she pointed to the pocket where he’d stashed his phone.

He nodded. “I bet you got a lot of fans, huh? Face like that.”

I shrugged, not daring to speak in case my voice and face together were enough to jog his memory.

“She’s modest,” Nichelle said. “Almost a million followers and counting. I only have three hundred thousand.”

“Maybe I’ll look y’all up. What did Lawry say your names were?”

“I’m Nichelle Clarke,” Nichelle said. “And my modest friend is Melanie Parker.”

He pulled his phone out and we quickened our pace as much as we could without running. Five steps from the door, he looked up from the phone. “Hey, ladies!”

I froze. So close.

Nichelle turned slowly. “Yes, officer?”

“I think you might want to check your Instagram. This says you only have a hundred thousand followers.”

Closing the gap between us and the door, I pulled it open before I answered. “She said TikTok, not Instagram.”

He pecked at the screen with one finger and we hurried outside, jogging the last few steps to the truck and not speaking until we had cleared the gates.

"Holy shit, I thought he was going to figure us out," Nichelle said after chugging the rest of her water.

I plunked mine back into the cupholder. "Me too. He was there last time I was there and I contradicted him about something in front of a superior officer." I turned onto the freeway service road. "Do you think your friend Aaron might know someone who could see about a transfer for Gavin? He's not the smartest person I've ever met, but the last person I came out here and talked to who had been assaulted inside was dead forty-eight hours after I talked to him, and my contact list is pretty short right now."

"I'm not sure what Aaron could do, but Kyle's dad is a retired DPD captain who knows everyone under the sun. I'll call now." She pulled her phone from her bag.

His dad?

"Mr. Miller, it's Nichelle Clarke." She paused, then laughed. "Trust me, once you meet DonnaJo, you won't say that ever again, sir."

That's right, Miller said they used to date when they were kids. It was why he trusted her. It seemed impossible that I'd just heard that a week ago.

My phone buzzed in the cupholder and I picked it up. "McClellan."

"You give great advice," Ruth said. "If no one has told you that."

"People say it occasionally. Is he awake?"

"No, but the team that came from Austin found the problem—there was a second clot and a swollen vessel in his brain. They're closing up from the surgery now. They say it couldn't have gone better, but if I hadn't called this morning, he might be dead now."

My heart skipped a beat and I whispered a prayer of thanks.

"Amen," Ruth said.

"Keep me posted."

"Of course. You keeping yourself safe?"

"Best I can," I said. "I'm okay."

"Make sure someone knows where you are."

"Yes ma'am." It was still just a little weird that she cared. "I'm with a reporter whose fiancé is keeping tabs on us right now. Nichelle Clarke, from Richmond, Virginia."

"You're what?" I knew she had her lips twisted to one side because her Botox appointments made furrowing her brow impossible.

"Yeah, I asked Skye for a favor this week, too. I'm on a roll."

"To the ninth ring of hell." Disdain dripped from the words. I had come by my hatred of journalists honestly, at least.

"Talk to you soon."

"Bye, sweetie."

I put the phone down. "Archie almost had an aneurism," I said. "But she got good doctors there in time to stop it."

Nichelle's hand went to her throat. "Thank God." She pointed to her phone. "Kyle's dad knows a judge in Houston he's going to call. Says the guy is an old friend who owes him big."

"Thank you." I glanced at her. "You really do like helping people. Even when there's nothing in it for you."

"Not everyone operates like everything in life is a transaction."

"I've spent my life around far more people who do than don't."

"Welcome to the wrong side of the tracks." She winked. "Most everyone I knew growing up worked a blue-collar job, and we didn't have big houses or know powerful people, but hardly anybody locked their doors at night, and the whole neighborhood looked out for each other."

"That sounds lovely."

I pulled off the interstate and headed west and Nichelle turned to look at the road sign. "Where are we headed?"

"The lady cop he mentioned is a sheriff down in Terrell County, and I'd like to know who moved him out of her jail after we took him there."

"We can't do that with a phone call?"

"I'm not sure who I trust," I said. "You heard that kid. Ratcliff pulled me into this mess to try to play me, and I fell for it."

She shook her head. "No reasonable person would suspect a colleague asking for a consult of anything so ridiculous. You have nothing to beat yourself up about there."

"I'd rather be able to see her face when I ask," I said. "Graham says I'm a human lie detector. Though clearly it's on the fritz lately." I shook my head, thinking back to the first day I'd met Ratcliff and the remains in the riverbed. "I knew something was weird. I should've trusted my gut. He asked me to come down based on a medallion he found near a set of remains that was typical of the MO of a collar I made years ago. But that guy was executed two years ago, which was an easy fact to find. I just assumed Ratcliff didn't look. But the fact that he was trying to use me to stage a coup in their little criminal organization...well. Nichelle had a point. I never would've imagined that, and I have more trust issues than anyone I've ever met.

"I'm along for the ride as long as you'll have me," she said.

Nava wasn't at her office when we got there, but the lone deputy got her on the radio and she walked in ten minutes later with an order of cheese fries cradled in her arm.

"Faith." She stopped dead inside the door.

"Sheriff," I said. "My friend Nichelle Clarke."

Nava nodded when Nichelle said, "Nice to meet you," before moving to her desk and putting her food down.

"What can I do for you?"

"Morgan Dean brought in a collar from the trailer where all those kids died and Andrew Ratcliff's body was found last week."

"Sure." She flipped through folders on her desk. "Gavin Marks, twenty-four. He was very...chatty."

"He's had the shit kicked out of him at the border detention center twice in the past few days," I said flatly. "I'm very interested in how he got from here to there. And trying to not have him wind up like Timmy Dushane."

She stopped fiddling with the plastic lid on her food and shook her head. "None of that makes any sense."

"He said someone came here and picked him up. Do you know who?" I heard Nichelle's pen scratching on her pad behind me. It was kind of like having my own personal stenographer.

"Yeah. Y'all." Nava flipped pages in her file. "A Rangers Assistant Chief Charles Abbott. Said he was taking him into protective custody."

"Not hardly."

"I didn't ask any serious questions. The kid was dropped here by a Ranger and picked up by Rangers brass, who said he needed to be kept safe. It's not like we really want trouble in here, and no offense, but trouble seems to follow you around."

Nichelle snorted behind me and I slid my eyes her way. "Something funny? At least it follows me and not the other way around."

"Touché." She smiled.

Nava looked back and forth between us. "Is there anything I can do to help?"

I debated for half a second, because Zapata's hold on her grandmother was a problem. But I didn't think Nava was a bad person, and I needed help Trey couldn't offer without putting himself in danger. "You're good with computers," I said.

"I know my way around."

"Mine is missing, but if you could see what you can find out about Abbott, everything in the DPS database, and call me at this number"—I jotted it on a Post-it and handed it to her—"with what you find."

"New phone?"

"Long story."

"I saw on the news you got suspended for misfiring your weapon."

"The news?"

"Skye Morrow Investigates."

"That bitch," I said. "She can forget her exclusive."

"Exclusive?" Nichelle's voice went up, along with her eyebrows.

"She wanted me to wear a camera." I turned to her.

"That would be cool." She poked at her phone screen. "But you shouldn't give Skye the footage."

She flipped the phone around. "Legendary Ranger Archie Baxter fights for life; McClellan fired. Skye has the shocking connection at 10," I read. "She is unbelievable."

"The only thing I hate worse that a defense lawyer is a reporter," Nava said. "I'll call when I have something. You're getting the kid transferred?"

"Working on it. Back channels and all."

"I admire the fact that they tried to kick you out and you're still working the case."

"America loves a rebel." I flashed a tight smile. "Though I have a whole lot of personal stake in all this, to be fair. I couldn't walk away if they threw me in a cell."

She waved as we walked outside.

"So what does your lie detector say?" Nichelle asked.

"That if she's lying, I will hang up my badge. You know...when I get it back." I started the truck and backed into the road.

"But you asked her to look into Abbott for a reason," Nichelle said. "I can buy access to the Texas DPS database and find whatever you need."

"I wanted to see what would happen. If he comes for us, especially way out here, then she tipped him off, which means she's in on whatever the hell he's up to. How did The Governor find so many people in powerful positions who were so corrupt?"

"Well, I think like attracts like," Nichelle said. "And sadly, power does indeed have a tendency to corrupt."

"So it seems, I keep learning."

Her phone rang, blaring a Kenny Chesney song I recognized instantly.

"I thought I was the only person who knew this song," I said.

"It's my favorite." She grinned and put the call on speaker. "Hey, baby. How are things back at the fort?"

"Holding down," he said. "I found a really interesting bit of information. Can Faith hear me?"

"I can," I said. "Please tell me those cold case shooting victims were connected somehow. It will turn this whole day around."

"Oh they had a connection," Joey said. "It took a little luck for me to find it—thank God for society pages and online news archives—but I just spoke to that gas station clerk's son, and he confirmed the whole list for me."

"They knew each other?" Nichelle had her pen in her hand so fast I wasn't sure how she managed it.

I pulled the car to the shoulder and stopped, my gut telling me he was about to say something I shouldn't drive and listen to.

"They all worked at the Governor's Mansion."

32

Nichelle dropped her pen and had to take off her seat belt and fold herself in half to get it back, and I stared at her phone and then at the dusty South Texas two-lane highway, my head shaking seemingly of its own volition.

"When?" It sounded strangled, with good reason, because I felt like I couldn't breathe.

Joe Powers. Mr. Joe, Chuck's favorite driver. The crime scene photos showed him slumped over the steering wheel of the cab, his face obscured, and the last name wasn't something my parents ever used—the staff were always addressed by first names.

I knew what Joey was going to say before he said it.

"Mostly in the nineties. Between 1993 and 1999."

"This is not happening." I clapped one hand over my mouth.

"What?" Joey sounded puzzled.

"That's when her dad was the governor," Nichelle said. "And her sister was murdered in like 1997, kidnapped out of her bedroom in the mansion."

"April of '98," I said.

"Oh damn." Joey fell quiet. "I'm sorry."

"So, someone used a gun to kill a Ranger I was working with last week, that was used to murder four people who worked in our house when I was a kid?" I let my head *thunk* back against the headrest. "How? Why? Who would have motive to do all those things?"

Nichelle tapped her pen on the notebook, her eyes narrowing when I turned my head toward her.

"Hear me out: we were just talking about how the guy, the dead cop, was trying to get you to unwittingly help them take over this sort of crime family of gunrunners that your dad set up when he was in office, right?"

"Yeah." I sat up. "So you're thinking that the person who wanted him dead wanted him dead because they maybe knew about that..."

"And they wanted these other folks dead because they thought they might know something that happened when your dad was in office. Maybe someone tried to stage a coup back then, too."

"It's not unusual in criminal organizations," Joey said. "Or so I've read."

I pulled the car back onto the road and slammed my foot on the gas.

"Thank you for your help, Joey," I said.

"Happy to," he said. "Anything else I can do?"

"Not that I can think of right now."

Nichelle told him she loved him and clicked the End button.

"Where to now?"

"Archie said something to me a couple of days ago..." I banged one hand into the steering wheel. "That *bastard*."

"I thought Archie was your friend?" Nichelle's fingers closed around the handle on the armrest.

"He is—I meant my father. Chuck is the bastard-est bastard who ever drew breath."

"You lost me."

"He said—He looked me straight in the face and said he had nothing to do with my sister's death. But this whole thing stinks of Chuck McClellan. All these years, not knowing how, or why, just knowing she screamed and she was terrified, and I was totally powerless to help her...And that bastard, they were trying to sweep his fucking cash cow out from under him and every single instinct I've ever had as a police officer says it got my sister killed."

"That might be a bit of a reach," Nichelle said gently.

I pressed the gas pedal harder.

"Or not," she said.

"I've taken more than a hundred hours of high-speed driver training. It's dry and clear and there's nobody out here," I said. "I'm not looking to get us killed. I just need to get to the capitol building."

"For what?"

"The archives. My mother made being a good steward of the taxpayers' money an art form, especially when it came to household expenses. Every hour worked by every employee every day we lived there is recorded in a ledger. I can't get into Rangers HQ to get the list of personnel from the cold case file on my sister's murder, and for all I know it might not be safe to go to my own house to see if that's in my file, but I can check Ruth's ledgers."

Nichelle looked at the clock. "I don't think the state archives keep convenience store hours."

"Lucky for us, I'm pretty decent at picking a lock."

"I know someone else who doesn't suck at that." She grinned. "And I'm a good lookout, too. The height from the shoes, you see."

I laughed. "You know, I didn't expect to make a new friend this week."

"Me, either."

I didn't want to take my eyes off the road at the speed I was driving, but I smiled. "Charity would've liked you an awful lot."

"That might be the nicest thing a cop has ever said to me. Including the occasional 'We'll give you the exclusive.'"

"Yeah. She would've liked you."

We pulled into a lower parking deck behind the capitol building at 9:15, the whole garage floor empty and the lights not yet on.

"Where's the thing we're breaking into?" Nichelle whispered.

"Just down the hallway that's on the other side of that door." I pointed, then pulled a lock picking kit out of the glovebox and slid it into my pocket.

"I can't believe this place is so empty."

"Nothing is in session this time of the year, and the day-to-day employees often take off the last couple of weeks of summer. So we shouldn't have too much trouble. There's a guard, but they don't often move from the station in the lobby, and nobody actually watches the monitors."

"Good to know."

"Ready?"

"Let's do it."

We checked the surroundings and pegged the camera pointed at the door we needed to use. "One of the two situations where a BB gun would be handy," Nichelle said.

"Not necessary." I moved the truck out of the line of sight of the camera and walked a wide circle to a taxicab-yellow pipe running up the wall to supply the fire sprinklers.

I shimmied up and grabbed the overhead pipe to test it. It wasn't super thick, but it held.

"How did you do that in jeans and boots?" Nichelle whispered from the ground.

"I won rope climbing six years running when I was in school. The boys said I couldn't beat them because girls don't have the upper-body strength, so I showed them."

"Who'd have thought that rope climbing shit would ever actually be useful in life?" she muttered.

I got up behind the camera and pulled the wire out of the back, moving hand to hand back to the thicker vertical pipe and sliding back down.

"All clear."

We walked to the door side by side, Nichelle's sharp heels echoing off the concrete like muffled shots.

"Those are loud."

"They are."

"Good thing we're alone, but the floor on the other side of the door is tile."

She stopped in front of the door and turned, watching the entire garage floor as I pulled out the tools and got to work. Forty-seven seconds later, the door was open and we stepped inside. Nichelle bent and slipped her shoes off, carrying them by the straps.

I studied the heels swinging by her side as I walked behind her.

"I bet you could hurt someone with that if you had to," I said.

"Oh, I stabbed someone once," she said. "Gorgeous lilac Manolos, ruined by blood."

She grinned when she caught sight of my slack face. "I do love them but have found that the more trouble my stories bring on, the handier they get as a weapon."

"You could just buy a gun," I said.

"Joey and Kyle have taught me how to shoot, but disabling the bad guy is usually more my speed when it's possible."

"Armed with designer heels." I shook my head. "Ruth won't believe it."

We reached the door to the archives from Chuck's administration.

Nichelle peeked around the corner and gave me a thumbs-up. I had the lock open in fifteen seconds, and we shut the door quietly behind us, locking it.

Using the flashlights on our phones, we worked through several cabinets of papers before I spotted what I was hunting. "There." I pulled the thick, wide red leather-bound ledger out and hefted it onto a table.

"There's eight years of expenses in here?" Nichelle asked.

"Her writing is small, but neat." I flipped pages until I found late April of 1998.

"Two hundred dollars spent on chicken, dented cans of tomatoes, Spam, and assorted produce at the Tom Thumb," I said, turning pages. "Here. Staff on duty the evening of the 23rd."

I found all four names. "Joe Powers was driving Chuck though. He was gone from ten til after midnight. They took Charity just before eleven."

Nichelle peered over my shoulder.

"Isn't that the guy the sheriff was talking about?" she asked.

"What guy?"

Nichelle pointed. "Charles Abbott."

I blinked at the words, undeniably there in Ruth's cramped, impeccable script.

"What in the actual blue fuck?" I said.

"Seems like this guy might be our link."

"Sure does, doesn't it?"

I used her phone to take photos of the ledger pages, and put everything back the way we found it before we unlocked the door. And walked straight into a scowling security guard with a key in his hand.

33

"Breaking and entering is a crime," he said, unsnapping the button covering the pepper spray canister attached to his belt.

"We didn't break in," I said, widening my eyes and flashing my most dazzling smile.

"How did you get into a locked room in a locked building without a key if you didn't break in?" He furrowed his brow but stayed where he was.

"The door wasn't locked," I said, turning a confused gaze on Nichelle. "We just came in to look at the historical documents."

"Why would anyone do that?" He kept the same skeptical look.

"A paper," Nichelle blurted. "For our Texas history class."

"Aren't you two kind of old for school?"

"Thanks for the kind words, but no, we're not." She rolled her eyes. "We're seniors at the university."

"What're you studying?"

"Education. Secondary history education. Which is why we have to take Texas history," I piped up.

He moved out of the way of the doorway and tipped his head to one side. "The doors weren't open."

"They really were," I said, putting one hand on his arm. "I promise we would never even bend the law, officer."

"Who's supposed to check them?" Nichelle asked, a slightly accusatory edge to her words.

"I am, but the departments down here always lock up." He ducked his head. "It's creepy as all hell down here at night."

Nichelle and I exchanged a glance, then each shrieked quietly and grabbed one of his arms. "It really is," I said. "Would you mind terribly walking us out to the car so we don't have to be afraid?"

I barely got it out with a straight face, and Nichelle's mile-wide grin wasn't helpful.

"Of course, ladies." The guard straightened his back and puffed out his chest, flexing his arms before leading us back down the hall and out to my truck, which was still the only vehicle on the floor.

"Thank you so much!" we gushed, planting kisses on either side of his face.

He blushed. "Y'all get your homework done and don't go into anymore buildings you're not sure you're allowed to be in. Okay?"

"Yes sir. Sorry about the misunderstanding," I said.

We climbed into the truck, and Nichelle's phone rang.

"I'm still perfectly safe," she said.

Joey.

"Hang on, I'm putting you on speaker." She clicked the screen. "Okay, go ahead."

"I was looking at the records for this gun," Joey said. "I can't find anything anywhere on it since it was supposed to be destroyed, but before that—ten years before that, before the swap meet guy—it was purchased by an eighty-one-year-old man in Bee Cave."

"If he was eighty-one then, I'd be shocked if he's still with us," I said. "Just playing odds."

"His name was Charles Dabney." Joey paused for long enough that I thought we'd lost him.

"Okay?"

"I think Nichelle is starting to rub off on me, the way she finds obscure shit on the internet. Or her computer is enchanted, maybe, but I found a link between the gun and the Governor's Mansion."

"You what?" I gripped the wheel so tightly my knuckles went white.

"Yeah. Mr. Dabney's grandson was an employee. A bodyguard."

"Charles Abbott," I said. "Named after his grandpa."

"How did you know that?" Joey asked.

"It's a gift."

Nichelle shook her head so hard a lock of hair fell out of her bun. "That same guy is connected to this gun now? I know Kyle and Aaron tell me all the time things can sometimes be not what they seem, but this sure seems like..."

"It sure does. Joey, I owe you. Thank you again."

"Just bring my girl home safe."

"On it."

Nichelle hung up and I pulled out of the garage before I grabbed my phone at the next corner and called Ruth.

"He's still in recovery but stable and his brain activity is good," she said by way of hello.

"I'm so glad," I said. "I need to know if you remember a guy who worked at the mansion when we lived there. Charles Abbott?"

"Abbott. Charles...Oh. He was a bodyguard for Chuck for a while. They used to joke about having the same name. I don't remember him well. I don't think he was there long."

"But he worked for the Rangers back then? He was on the protection detail?"

"I think so. Why?"

"That means Archie will remember him."

"Faith? What's going on?"

"I'm just trying to figure something out." I sighed. "I hate to have to ask this, but I need to talk to Archie as soon as he comes to and is able. It's important."

"You sound stressed."

"You could say that." I rubbed my temple.

"Where are you going now?" she asked.

"Rangers HQ," I said.

"Oh, sweetheart, is that wise? With all the talk about your suspension?"

"I'm not going in, Mom." I slid a glance at Nichelle. "My friend is."

"What exactly is it that I'm doing at Rangers headquarters at ten o'clock at night?" Nichelle asked as I merged onto I-35.

"Abbott is one of those guys who works late and sleeps in," I said. "Especially with what I saw this morning, I'm betting he's still there. I'll get my friend to escort you back and ask if you can interview him about the situation with me. Tell him you're from the newspaper. My hunch is that he's Skye's source on her bullshit story and he'll be anxious to trash me to another reporter."

"And then what?"

"Ask him to walk you to the car and I'll confront him about my sister's murder."

"That's it? That's the plan?"

"I don't have a lot of time here."

"Sure."

I called Trey from my burner cell on the way, because I knew he was usually at work if he wasn't asleep when there were multiple big cases going.

"Are you still standing?" he asked. "And is Skye Morrow still breathing?"

I checked the clock. It was 10:09. So they led the ten p.m. broadcast with whatever shit she had been told or made up without asking me for a comment.

"I'll handle Skye later. I'm in a crunch, and I need to know if Abbott is working late tonight."

"I saw him go to his office with a Coke about thirty minutes ago," he said. "But I'm in my office, so I'm not entirely sure."

"That's sure enough," I said. "Listen, I have a friend who would like to ask him some questions for the paper about what happened to Archie. Can you come walk her in to talk to him in about ten minutes?"

"He's just going to tell her the same shit Skye just said. Are you nuts?"

"I'm betting on it. I'll explain later. And I'll call when we get there."

"Whatever you say."

34

I stared at the door to headquarters for the entire sixteen minutes Nichelle was inside. Trey, who had come back out after he showed her inside, gave up trying to talk to me about what was going on after I told him I thought Abbott was a lying and possibly murderous piece of shit without taking my eyes off the door.

"I was sifting through drone footage from the first server company when you called," he said, leaning against the door of the truck. "It took a while to get through their security, but I think this might work. It's just going to take me a few hours."

That got my eyes off the door. "Anything yet?"

"Nothing near the country place your...uh...Governor McClellan mentioned at all. I'm checking the place closer to Mexico City now. I think I have a better chance of finding something there."

"You'll call me if you see anything? Like anything at all?" I went back to staring at the door. I was pretty sure Abbott was crooked as a mountain road and I had sent Nichelle in there alone in the middle of the night, armed with shoes.

"Immediately." Trey followed my gaze. "He warmed right up to her. So whatever you're hoping to get, I hope you do."

"Thanks. For everything this week. Really."

"Always happy to do whatever I can for you." He went back inside.

I counted every smudge on the glass in the yellow parking lot light's glare. Seventy-six, seventy-seven, seventy-eight... On eighty-three, Nichelle walked out a door Abbott held open for her and they strolled to the truck. His face twisted when he saw me through the windshield.

"What the hell is going on here?" he snapped.

"My friend also has some questions for you, sir," Nichelle said.

"I don't know what you think you're playing at here, Miss..."

"Clarke."

"Are you even a journalist?"

"With the awards to back it up, yes sir."

"But right now it's me you owe some answers to, sir." I stepped out of the truck and flanked his other hip. He turned back for the door, shaking his head, and Nichelle stepped into his path. His face went bright red and he put one hand on his weapon. "Move."

I drew Archie's gun. "Calm down, sir."

"Get out of my way." Abbott fixated on Nichelle.

"You will not shoot me," she said. "There's a witness, the computer nerd guy is in there, and this would be far more difficult to explain than your past indiscretions."

Abbott froze, all the bravado going out of him. "What the hell do you want?"

"To know what you had to do with my sister's murder." I didn't put the gun away, but I kept my finger outside the trigger guard and the safety on. "And if you know what's good for you, you will not attempt to bullshit me. Sir."

"What in the hell are you talking about?" he growled. "You have entirely lost your mind, I can see that. Drawing a weapon on a superior officer. You're through, McClellan."

"You're not a superior officer. I'm a civilian at the moment, remember? Thanks to something you made up and have been only too happy to spread far and wide."

"No, thanks to your rash, careless methods that got the goddamn speaker of the US House's son kidnapped." His face went three shades redder in the time it took to say the words. "For a person who claims to hate their old man so much, you are just like him, you know that?"

He could've slapped me and hurt me less. Hell, I've been shot and had it hurt less.

"I am nothing like him." I hated that my voice shook.

"Aren't you? You've built what looks like a very impressive career by being impetuous and headstrong, ignoring the rules you don't like to get what you want. I only worked for Chuck McClellan for four months because it was all I could stomach. And I was the lone vote on the review board that didn't want you here because of what I saw back then and what I read in your case files."

I shook my head, trying to speak without letting my voice quake and failing.

"You're drawing a false analogy here, Mr. Abbott," Nichelle said, watching my face for a minute before she shifted her attention to him.

"What the hell do you know about anything?"

"I know Faith—apparently better than you do even after only a few days with her. Her father is, by every account I've seen, a selfish, greedy, power-hungry malignant narcissist of the worst variety."

"I'd say that's an accurate assessment. And she chases glory above everything else," Abbot said.

"Wrong," Nichelle said calmly. "If she was chasing glory, she'd call the press. She doesn't, though, does she? In fact, she has such a strong dislike for reporters, it took me way longer than normal to win her over."

I snorted and shook my head. "So modest."

"I just understand my value." She poked my shoulder. "And it's about damn time you did, too. Your family doesn't define you, Faith, for better or worse. No matter how badly this jackass wants to redirect your attention."

She turned back to Abbott with a fake-sugar smile. "I noticed you didn't answer the question."

I holstered Archie's SIG and folded my arms across my chest. "She has a point. Sir."

"What is it that you girls think you know?" he asked.

"I didn't remember that you worked for Chuck briefly until I saw your name in my mother's employee ledger. You were on duty the night my sister disappeared."

"Did your mother's log also show that your father was on a trip that day, speaking at a party function in El Paso? Because he was, and I was with him. Baxter was there. He can tell you—if he ever wakes up. We didn't get back to the mansion until the place was crawling with cops."

"Did you know that the ballistics signature on the rounds that killed Drew Ratcliff last week matches the markings from several other murders? All people who worked in the mansion. All people who were there the night Charity was kidnapped. As it happens."

He raised his eyebrows. "Isn't that something? But what does it have to do with me?"

"It seems that the gun in question has changed hands a few times but was originally purchased by a Mr. Charles Dabney a few decades back."

"You're saying my grandfather was a closet serial killer?"

"I'm saying you have this gun. You used it to keep people who might have seen something or done something the night my sister died quiet for good. Maybe you hung onto it as a souvenir or something. It was lost at a crime scene and set for destruction, but...so odd...never made it to the gator."

"You think I stole it from the evidence locker? Who would risk such a thing, even assuming the rest of your crazy story is true?"

"Someone who wanted the trinket that allowed him to get away with four murders designed to cover up a very high-profile kidnapping gone wrong," I said, pointing to Nichelle. "She said something earlier about Zapata kidnapping Grady's son—that no one snatches a high-profile politician's kid without a political motive. But I'm wondering if your motive wasn't a little more selfish. Chuck was getting rich through a backdoor gunrunning scam that has continued for years. Is it really just the national guard who helped that along?"

"You're accusing me of being an arms dealer now?" He threw his hands up. "You have really and truly lost your mind."

"I'm wondering if y'all were trying to force Chuck to let you in on a cut of the profits maybe, or to abdicate leadership of the thing altogether. You couldn't threaten to go public with what he was doing because he would have turned you in, too. So you thought you'd have some scary drug runners from the cartel grab my sister and use whatever you wanted from Chuck as your ransom."

Nichelle leaned in. "That is interesting. Was Charity not supposed to die?"

"I don't have the first fucking clue!" Abbott exploded. "What I do know is that you have theories and circumstance, and not a shred of evidence. Your own mother's log backs up that I wasn't at the house at the time of the kidnapping, and you have not one provable fact that says I ever even saw this gun you're talking about. And every bit of the rest of this is just you two spinning fiction. So I will thank you to get the hell out of here before I decide a defamation suit is necessary, instead of just firing your ass, McClellan."

I glanced at Nichelle. She frowned.

He'd called our bluff. I was more sure that this man had something to do with what happened to my sister than I'd ever been about anything surrounding Charity's death, but without proof, it didn't matter. My gut wouldn't sway a judge or a jury.

"I may not have proof tonight, but as you said, I'm rash and stubborn—and very good at putting murderers in cages." I turned and climbed back into the truck. "Sleep well, sir."

I spun the tires a little pulling out and Nichelle buckled her seat belt and clapped slowly. "This is the first time in my career I wish I'd had a camera running."

"Why? He walked away and he didn't tell us shit."

"You were incredible. And he might not be in cuffs yet, but you'll get him. I am convinced."

"I'm glad one of us is." I dragged a hand down my face, exhaustion settling into every bone. "I am beat. You want to stay at my mom's house tonight and I'll take you back to yours in the morning?"

"Thanks." She smiled. "Let me tell Joey so he doesn't worry."

"That's kind of you."

She dialed. Five rings. Voicemail.

"That's weird. He doesn't usually go to bed this early."

"Shower?" I guessed.

"Maybe." She hit a different contact.

"Hey, sweetie," came Lila's voice, which sounded far too young for her to have a daughter who was nearly my age. I couldn't tell if she was lucky, had found the fountain of youth, or was just super young when Nichelle was born—and there wasn't a good way to ask.

"Hey, Mom, how was your day?"

"I arranged four bands for four brides on the same Saturday without anyone getting upset, found another woman the perfect dress, explained to a stubborn groom that he doesn't have to eat the 'groom's cake' if he dislikes chocolate, he can offer it to his guests as an option and just eat the lemon cake the bride chose for the wedding cake, and played in my garden. So not bad. How about you?"

"It's been interesting. This is going to make one heck of a story." She bit her lip. "I wanted to let Joey know I'm staying here in Austin with Faith tonight and I'll be home tomorrow morning, but I didn't get him. Did he go to bed?"

"He was watching the baseball game when I went to take a shower. Hold on." Muffled knocking came through the speaker. "Joey?" Lila's voice was soft. "Nicey honey, I don't see him, but the car is still out front."

We heard a door open and close.

"Mom?" Nichelle prompted.

"He's sitting on the patio by the fountain," Lila said softly. "Looking at the stars. Hold on...Joey? Nichelle is on the phone. She's looking for you."

"Hey, babe." His voice was low. Subdued. "I left my phone in the house, I think."

"What's wrong?" Nichelle sounded alarmed.

"Chen's people," Joey said. "His sort of consigliere guy, Tian, called me tonight. They're on their way to Mexico a day early, and Faith's husband is still there. I called Miller, but he says his team is locked down by the Speaker's office. She won't green light them to go in. She thinks she can negotiate to get her kid back. Miller thinks her people are working back-channel intelligence to get Zapata and his money out of Mexico, which fits with what Faith said Zapata wanted."

"Does Miller know where Zapata is?" I asked, my voice too high.

"That was the other thing he said. They didn't know where to look. He's gone off the grid or some shit. So his boss wants them to hold and wait for the Speaker to give a go-ahead."

"What is it you're not saying?" Nichelle asked.

I turned to her, eyes wide. What he was saying was scary enough. There was more?

"Tian said they have someone inside, someone Zapata trusts. They know Zapata took Grady's kid. Chen has gone from wanting Zapata out to wanting Dakota Grady. Or rather...his people in Beijing want Dakota Grady. Where he lives, the cartel and the government aren't at war, because the drug exporting business is profitable, so the government takes their cut and stays quiet as long as the product is shipping out and not being sold domestically. The government is sending a regiment of soldiers with Chen to ensure this goes the way they want it to. And if the Chinese government takes the Speaker's son hostage..."

"Political motives," I muttered, every kind of international disaster right up to nuclear war flashing through my thoughts in half a second. "Jesus."

"Yeah," Joey said. "But I'm not sure what to do with this information if Miller can't even get them to act on it."

35

At least there was no finesse needed this time.

Fucking Faith McClellan.

He banged on the door of the trailer, the last of JJ's regular crew opening it.

"Oh, hey." The kid pointed. "I know you, right?"

"Sure, kid." He shoved a thick plastic bag of pills into the boy's chest. "Percs for you and your friends."

"From Zapata?" The kid passed them to a girl in a bikini top and shorts, who poured them into a crystal bowl in the middle of a table and put one in her mouth.

"Yep. A bonus for taking care of the cop."

"Bitchin." The kid went back to the couch and picked up a video game controller as his friends descended on the bowl.

Satisfied that they were occupied, he strode to the closed door down the short hallway.

"What are you doing here?" Ratcliff's eyes popped wide when he walked in.

"Cleaning up my fucking mess," he said. "Didn't I tell you what was expected of you? You ignore the bodies, let him have his fucking fun. Keep the spotlight off this place, and make sure Timmy and his whore are getting back and forth across the border with Zapata's drugs and our guns as often as he wants. In return, we burn your failed piss test and keep your little problem quiet—and supplied."

"I've done all that and then some."

He paced the room, folding his hands in front of his face and trying to breathe.

"Does 'and then some' include calling Faith McClellan to look at remains you know as well as I do are going to turn out to be Freddie?"

"It sure as shit does." Ratcliff grinned. "You're welcome. You don't see it? It's brilliant."

"Have you read one word about this woman? We've kept this quiet for decades and you're gambling it on a very bad hunch? And you thought everyone would be okay with that?"

"If the investigation has her name on it, it's above reproach, man," Ratcliff said. "Think. Freddie had turned. He's been working with the feds. His boss is down here looking for him. Archie Baxter is helping out with that case. So I call Faith, she comes in, she determines it was Timmy or Nava or whoever else we want to point her to, and we're golden. Not only does nobody lose their job, but Zapata has an answer."

"'Zapata has an answer?'" he mocked. "Do you really not even understand what you've done? I have spent half my life working to stay off her radar, and you are not going to fuck it up."

"Simmer down. You know you wouldn't want to be Derek Amin if Zapata found out what really happened to his boy. This way, he never will. Nobody questions McClellan's collars. She's the department darling."

"Not the entire department. I can't fucking stand her. She's headstrong and she breaks rules."

"Pot...kettle." Ratcliff laughed. "You're just afraid she's going to find out what happened to her sister."

He pulled the gun and aimed. "Be very careful what you say there. You don't know what you're talking about."

"I know enough."

He fired two into Ratcliff's head.

"Not anymore."

36

"It's one thing for a group of drug-dealing terrorists to grab Grady's kid," I said, digging through Archie's pantry while Tyler scarfed his dinner. I knew the sitter had likely fed him a few hours ago, but Tyler didn't believe there was such a thing as enough food. "But an actual semi-hostile foreign power taking him is on a whole different planet. I'm not sure anyone would be able to agree on a proportional response."

"I'm sure there are plans for such things in place," Nichelle said. "The president has kids, too."

"Plans are fine, but they go mostly out the window when real people and their emotions get involved." I poured two bowls of Cheerios and grabbed milk from the fridge. "If Miller isn't allowed to go in, we have to call someone else. Clearly, they're out of time for talking. Why doesn't Miller listen?"

"First, I'm sure Kyle is doing everything he can. He jumps through a lot of hoops and his job is half red tape," Nichelle said. "But also"—she frowned, tapping on the edge of the table—"Kyle might be lying."

"Why would he lie?"

"Well...Kyle is a good cop. He hasn't asked me flat out if I was talking to you, but Joey calling him with information about Chen coming to North

America for Grady's son would get him four from two and two really quick. And I did call his dad for help with Gavin, and he knows you were there when Gavin was arrested and that you dislike the border detention center."

"So?"

"So, if he knows I'm talking to you, he might not tell Joey the truth about what he's doing because he doesn't want you running off down there and getting in the middle of it."

"He'd rather let me go alone?" I asked.

"You just said we have to call someone—I'm guessing because you know going alone is suicide. If I can tell you know that, Kyle knows you know it, too."

I sighed and poked my spoon at the cereal. After three bites, I said, "We have to call someone."

"Who are we going to call?" she asked.

"Anyone. The Speaker's office. The CIA."

"Do you remember how politicians work? By the time we convince anyone at either place to take us seriously, Chen will be back in China with Dakota Grady." She poured milk over her cereal.

"I have to get Graham out of there before Chen gets there," I said. "And Grady, too."

"But we don't even know where 'there' is," Nichelle said.

"Trey is a night owl, and he's working on it." I pulled out my phone to text him that it just became more urgent. "You think Miller might go in tomorrow?" I asked her. "Assuming he has intel on where they are?"

"He might."

"So then if I can find the location I'd have a chance," I said.

"But he might not." Nichelle pushed her bowl away, looking alarmed. "You can't go to Mexico alone."

"I'm not sure I have another option," I said.

Nichelle sucked in a deep breath. "Yeah you do," she said, pulling out her phone. "You can go to Mexico with me and Joey."

"I..." I dropped my spoon on the floor. "I cannot take you and Joey to a showdown with Zapata."

"I'm not trying to get us killed before we get to say I do," she said. "Joey and I would stay outside the fence with phones or radios or something, keeping lookout and listening to your end for possible trouble. You would have to go in. Hopefully we beat Chen and his men there and you can slip inside and get Grady's kid and your husband and get out with little fuss."

"You have no idea what you're asking," I said. "Bullet holes or no, you're not a cop. And he works at the trucking company. Thousands of things could go wrong in a situation like the one you're describing. You're not safe just because you're outside."

"We'd be safe enough if they're looking for a big fight from someone and we stay back. You said yourself that Zapata probably wouldn't have anyone with him but his most trusted soldiers and the hostage. And your husband, because he was in the truck Zapata took off in." She fiddled with the spoon and looked up at me. "I know you can tell Joey has experience with this kind of stuff."

"I wasn't going to ask. But it doesn't matter, I can't let a civilian go chasing off after a drug lord if I can stop it."

"Until about a year ago, Joey was the consigliere for the Caccione crime family," Nichelle said quietly. "I'm not saying that I'm sending him with you and waiting for him to get himself killed, but you should know when you're making this decision that he can handle himself in dangerous situations."

I swallowed a half-chewed bite of cereal. "Holy shit...I knew there was something, but that's...you're marrying a mobster?"

"A reformed one. He took down their whole organization from the inside, helping Kyle, and he has an honest job running a trucking company now."

I let my forehead fall to the table. "Jesus."

There hadn't been any kind of update on Graham in days. If Trey could give me a reasonable shot at finding Zapata, I didn't see where I had a choice. Nichelle could pass the location intel to Miller and I would hope he'd bring the cavalry, but I couldn't leave Grady to get dragged off to be the first prisoner of a war that might not start if I could help it, and I couldn't risk never seeing Graham alive again.

It was dangerous. It was incredibly stupid. And I knew every bit of that, but I had to go anyway.

I sighed. "Fine. Call Joey and let him know, and get a text ready to send to Miller when it's too late for him to surround the house and stop us. We need more of a plan than this, but Graham and Grady are out of time. We're going to beat Chen to Mexico. Let's get a little sleep. We'll head out in the morning."

37

I slept fitfully again and was up by four thirty, brewing coffee when Nichelle shuffled into the kitchen just as my phone rang.

I waved at her and took a second cup out of the cabinet. "It's Trey." I held up the phone and touched the talk button.

"Do you sleep at all anymore?" I said by way of hello.

"Look who's talking," he said.

"I've got a few things going on at the moment."

"See, but I never sleep, that's the difference," he said. "Perhaps I can brighten your morning with some news."

"Two seconds, Trey." I poured two cups of coffee and handed one to Nichelle. "It's just regular old Folgers. Tyler's dog sitter picked it up for me yesterday. But it has caffeine."

"That is my only requirement," she said, getting the milk out of the fridge.

"Okay, go." I took a sip of the coffee and focused on Trey's voice.

"So, I spent the last six hours sifting through drone footage. You know there are a lot of damn people who have these things?"

I laughed. "They've gotten far more affordable in the past few years, I think."

"I guess. Anyway, I came up empty. I checked every video from the past three days anywhere near every place you sent me between nine last night and three this morning, and there was nothing. No lights, no people, no nothing."

My shoulders slumped and I sipped my coffee. I couldn't blow up at Trey. He was doing me a favor, and he was trying his best. He stayed up all night looking at amateur video, for God's sake.

"And you checked both companies?"

"I did. But then about 3:45, I went back in to look one more time, thinking I could catch a nap on the couch if I didn't find what you wanted."

"Please tell me you found something."

"Okay, I will. At 3:18 this morning, a user who goes by StarSeeker877 took footage from about five miles outside the country house Governor McClellan told you about—the one outside Carta Rosa? I'm imagining this person was looking for dark-sky star or planet footage out in the desert in the dead middle of the night—I think maybe there's a meteor shower or something, actually."

"There is." I put my coffee mug on the counter. "Graham and I watched it last summer. He said it happens every August."

"Cool," Trey said. "So anyway, I'm thinking this StarSeeker person was pretty pissed because the footage they got was of fireworks. Over Zapata's place."

"Fireworks? At three in the morning?"

"I mean, when I say this joint is in the middle of nowhere...it doesn't do it justice. It's like the back edge of nowhere. And what does a cartel boss care even if there were neighbors?"

"True." I gripped the edge of the counter. "So you think they're there?"

"In the light from the fireworks, even from far away, I made out three laser sights on the ground level with some still-frame enhancement."

"The snipers."

"I'm betting," he said. "Something else—there was a limo there."

"Zapata left the weapons exchange Tuesday in a box truck."

"The kind of limo with flags on the hood. I couldn't zoom in enough to be absolutely sure, but I think they're American flags."

"You think an American official is there at the compound?" I didn't know if that made my situation better or worse.

"I don't think it's, like, the president or anything. I think he's in England, isn't he?"

"I have not watched a minute of the news this week," I said.

"Understandable. No, I think this car came from the US embassy in Mexico City. The Mexican traffic cameras were way easier to hack than the drone company servers."

"You are a goddamn genius, Trey." I blinked hard. "I will never be able to repay you for this."

"No need. Just don't haul off and get yourself killed because I told you this."

"I will do my best." I shot Nichelle a thumbs-up and she smiled. "My father's laptop—were you able to get into the party video, and can you send it to me if you were? Archie's computer—mine was stolen and I didn't think to ask for it back last night."

"Ask for it back? Do you know who stole it?"

"Abbott did. But I can worry about that later."

"You are going to have to tell me that story."

"After I handle this," I said. "The video?"

"I was able to find it and I can send it to you. Rich people do weird shit, you know that?"

"I'm well aware, thanks."

"You good?"

"I'm hoping I will be by this time tomorrow."

"Sur—wait. Are you saying what I think you're saying?"

"I'm saying exactly what I said."

"If you're going down there, I hope you found an arsenal," Trey said. "And you better come back."

"I will."

"Video is on its way. And I'm sending you the coordinates from the drone footage I found, too."

"Thank you."

"Watch your back. Please."

I swore I would and hung up the phone, turning to Nichelle, who was refilling her coffee cup and rubbing one eye. "Did you talk to Joey?"

"He's on his way. He left my mom's about half an hour ago. So he'll be here by the time we're loaded and ready to leave."

I peered out the window at the predawn gloom. "It's about a six-hour drive down if we stick to the speed limit, give or take for the exact location."

"Have you ever in your life stuck to the speed limit?"

"Every once in a while." I winked. "I'd like to make one stop, but I figure if we're on the road by ten or eleven, then we have plenty of time to find a place to stay hidden until it gets dark, even if something unexpected slows us down."

"That sounds reasonable."

"You said you know how to shoot?" I asked.

"When I have to."

"Today you may well have to. Archie has a SIG Sauer pistol that's easy to handle. Will that work?"

"Should be fine." She sipped her coffee, looking a little green.

"You know how to load it?"

"Does it have the clip things?"

I tried not to groan. "Yes."

"Then yes."

I got a banana from the fridge and made some oatmeal. Nichelle tried to refuse food, but I told her she had to eat something because she needed energy for the fight and we had no idea how the day would look.

She got some more Cheerios and downed three cups of coffee.

"You own any normal shoes?" I asked. "You can't chase killers around the Mexican desert in four-inch heels."

"I came here on vacation. I only brought my regular shoes."

"What size do you wear?" I asked.

"Nine."

"My mother has something that will fit you," I said. "I think Archie even bought her some hiking boots, which would be great."

"Whatever makes you happy, Faith." Nichelle finished her cereal and put her bowl in the dishwasher while I went to the study to get Archie's computer.

"Let's see what kind of security we're dealing with," I said, sitting at the table and opening his laptop.

I found the video in Archie's email and opened it, ignoring the guests' shenanigans as well as I could amid Nichelle's observations about naked people and intoxication never mixing well.

Following the lasers on the weapons with my finger and checking the timestamps, I made notes. "Four sentries, making loops of the entire property more than likely, each loop taking thirteen minutes. So there's someone passing every point of possible entry with a gun every three minutes and twenty seconds. I can work with that."

"That's not a lot of time," she said, pointing at an older man wearing nothing but an inflatable pool raft yelling about his penis size as he leapt off a second-floor balcony into the pool. "Wow. I wonder what he was on?"

"Besides Viagra?"

She laughed. "Thanks. I needed that."

"Yeah." I joined her, bending forward in the chair as I closed the computer. "Me too."

"Now what?" she asked when we had quieted.

"We load up the arsenal and find the secret location of Zapata's compound, and save the goddamn day."

"That sounds like a plan."

"Sort of, anyway." I stood and put the computer back in the study before heading to my room. "It's going to be hot as the fifth ring of hell waiting for darkness out there, so I'd advise putting your hair up." I glanced at her outfit: the same pretty white linen pants and green silk top she'd had on yesterday. "Those pants are fine, but let me find you a more muted shirt. I'll bring that and the boots in a few."

"Socks too, if you have any."

"I can do that."

She disappeared into the hall bathroom and I went to the bedroom and ransacked my mother's closet. Wool socks, a linen shirt in eggshell, and a pair of leather hiking boots Nichelle would never appreciate went back to the bathroom door with me. I tapped and set the stuff on the floor, carrying Ruth's navy linen pants to the guest room to get myself ready.

Pinning the tiny camera Skye had handed me a hundred years ago at the coffee shop to my collar, I wasn't sure I was going to give her the video, but I wanted to keep my word—after all, she had promised me she'd get the photos taken down, not that she wouldn't run a bullshit story about my incompetence nearly killing Archie. And she had done what she said she would do. So I probably should, too. Nichelle would get the story first because she was the closest thing there'd be to an eyewitness, but that was Skye's problem, not mine.

I didn't have access to any tactical gear, but Archie had a couple of surplus vests in his guest closet for emergencies, so I rigged one up to fit me, then took the other to the living room. Nichelle shrugged into it and frowned. "This is heavy. And way too big. Why do I need a vest if I'm the lookout?"

"Because the people you're looking out for will be heavily armed and likely have itchy trigger fingers. Come here, I can shrink it." I tightened straps until it fit her about as well as mine fit me. I went to the big gun safe in the corner and pulled out the Ruger Javi had given me, putting it in my holster and passing Nichelle Archie's SIG and all six extra magazines for it. I took the extra ammo for the one I'd chosen, then added a rifle and a shotgun.

I pointed to the two handguns I'd taken from beneath JJ's closet floorboards. "Do either of these look like one you've seen Joey use?"

"I haven't paid super close attention," she said.

I considered that as I loaded my pocket with ammunition for the rifle and the shotgun.

"We'll bring them both," I decided, grabbing a portable case. "He can pick in the car."

Thinking about JJ and that warehouse he had used for storage, I wished I had snagged a grenade or two, but there was nothing to be done for that now.

The doorbell chimed just as I shut the gun case and turned for the door. I picked up the shotgun and walked to the foyer, Nichelle on my heels.

"It's just Joey," she said.

"Last time that bell rang, it did not turn out so well for me," I hissed, moving to the peephole.

It was Joey, who was still good-looking with bedhead and jaw scruff. So was Graham, but in my experience it wasn't common. I pulled the door open and he took in the whole scene, from the gun in his fiancé's hand to my shotgun.

"I hope you have more of those," he said.

"A tactical rifle and three more handguns," I said. "Not what we probably should have, but it's not nothing."

Joey reached for the shotgun. "May I?"

I handed it over.

"Shells?" he asked.

I pulled one from my pocket and he examined it, nodding. "This will work."

"You think we really need all this?" Nichelle asked.

"Absolutely." Joey handed the shotgun back to me and kissed her on the forehead. "I'm afraid it won't be enough."

"Whatever we take, it won't be as much as they have," I said. "That box truck was loaded with some dangerous stuff when they drove away from us on Tuesday."

Nichelle sighed and nodded. "Okay. Let's do this?"

I met her eyes and nodded. Joey asked what he could carry and I pointed to the gun case and our bags in the living room, picking up the rifle and patting Tyler's head.

"Be good, boy. Not too much longer until your people will be back." I hoped.

Nodding for Joey and Nichelle to follow, I led the way to the truck, sliding the large guns into the toolbox that stretched across the bed.

"I'll sit in the back," Joey said, reaching for the shorter door.

"I'm not as tall as you," Nichelle said.

"But you have longer legs than I do." He climbed up and pulled the seat back. "See? I'm set. You ride with Faith."

Her mouth twisted to one side like she wanted to argue, but instead, she just nodded. "Let's go find them."

"Send Miller the text with the coordinates and tell him I'm going in." I started the engine and pointed the car south, praying we weren't walking into a trap—or a slaughter.

The sun was just peeking over the eastern horizon when Ruth called. We were still fifteen minutes outside New Braunfels.

"I have someone here who wants to say hello." Ruth sounded tired. And tearful.

The phone clattered as she passed it over the bed rail. "Hey, new girl," Archie said, his voice thready, but there.

"Thank God." I couldn't stop a couple of tears of my own from falling. "You scared the shit out of me."

"I'm too stubborn to die," he said. "Not right when I'm finally getting everything I've ever wanted."

"That's true." I laughed.

"Your mother said you called last night asking about Abbott."

"I didn't remember him working for Chuck," I said carefully.

"He was there for like ten minutes. There's no reason you would have," Archie said.

"The ledger mother kept of employees said he was there the night Charity went missing."

"He wasn't at the house until after everything went down," Archie said. "I know because he was with me. We were in El Paso with Chuck and didn't get back until late. I remember Abbott being there specifically because he wasn't supposed to go with us, it was a last-minute switch and Chuck thundered at me in his study for ten minutes before we left."

"Do you remember why?"

"You know Chuck. He can't trust himself, so he doesn't trust anyone else either. Abbott was new, we were going to a fundraiser in a blue area of the state, and he didn't want to take the new guy." His voice got weaker as he talked. There was a rattle and Ruth came back on the line.

"He's getting tired," she said. "Is that what you needed to know?"

"Almost. What's in the file box you told me about in the guest room closet?"

"Hold on." She covered the speaker and asked Archie.

"He said that's where he kept the personal file he's kept on Charity's case," she said. "Copies of some of what they have at work but other things he wanted to follow up on, hunches, notes..." She trailed off.

"Of fucking course it is." I shook my head.

"Faith." Ruth's halfhearted objection to my language didn't even sound like her.

"Sorry."

"What do you mean? Archie is asking why you want to know."

"Because Abbott broke into your house yesterday and walked out with the box," I said. "But don't tell him that if you don't think it's wise."

She gasped quietly and said, "I see. You take good care of yourself, honey."

"I will."

I clicked the call off.

"Wow," Nichelle said.

"We can deal with Abbott later," I said. "Like you said last night, he thinks he's already gotten away with this. Well, I accept the challenge. After everyone we care about is out of Zapata's dungeon."

She nodded. "I will help any way I can."

"There's a special place in hell for dirty cops," Joey agreed.

I nodded, trying to focus on the mission at hand, because getting the three of us plus Grady and Graham out of Mexico alive would take every bit of skill and smarts I had ever had.

38

I called Nick Ryan when we were about twenty minutes from his office to ask how he felt about working Saturdays.

"I'm here, so I guess I support it when necessary," he said. "I was going to call you but didn't want to do that too early on a weekend."

"I'm on my way there," I said. "Is that rear door unlocked?"

"It is. And the room I showed you yesterday is exactly how you left it."

The whiteboard wasn't necessary now that I knew all the shooting victims worked in our house the night my sister disappeared—the link was too obvious to question. But I wanted the rest of the files he had printed for me so Nichelle could look over them on the road trip. She had a good eye for detail and an uncanny ability to question things that looked mundane but weren't.

"I have a few interesting things to share when you get here," he said. "I'm in my office. Just come on in."

"See you in a few." I ended the call and put the phone down.

Joey leaned forward over the bench seat. "So who is this guy we're going to see?"

"He works for the state, officially in information intelligence or something. But really the thing is just that he's really good at research—he digs up dirt and makes connections quickly. A damn handy skill, it turns out. Every cop should have a friend like this guy."

"I'm Kyle's friend who does that," Nichelle agreed.

"But this guy is in a little office not getting shot at," Joey said. "Did you know you could use your research skills without getting shot at?"

Nichelle shrugged. "I've never considered it."

"Perhaps it's worth thinking about."

"You want me to go to work for the State of Texas?"

"I'm sure they have something like this in Virginia, too."

I smiled at their pseudo bickering. I missed Graham.

Parking outside the back door at Ryan's office, I turned. "Y'all want to stay here or come in?"

Nichelle's phone buzzed and she wrinkled her nose. "It's Kyle."

"He got your text," I said.

She picked up the phone like she was handling a rattlesnake. "I can already feel that he's pissed. I should stay here and talk to him."

"I'll wait with her," Joey said.

I left the truck and the air conditioning running and stepped into the office building, ducking first into the closet where Ryan had set me up the day before and picking up the other two case files before I erased the whiteboard. Seemed I wasn't going to have time to need it.

Walking back into the hallway, I heard a loud crash, followed by a yelp.

Running, I pulled the Ruger and made sure the safety was off, dropping the files as I went.

Rounding the corner into Ryan's office, I pointed the pistol at the guy who had the older man pinned to the floor. His face obscured by a mask, the intruder wrenched Ryan's arm up behind his back, eliciting a scream.

"There's a nine-millimeter pointed at your head, and I don't miss at this range." I kept my voice calm and clear. "Let him go and get up. Now."

The intruder was clad in black from head to toe, with even his neck and hands covered, not so much as a flash of skin peeking out. He raised both hands and pushed himself slowly to his feet with them still raised.

"Mr. Ryan, you okay?"

Ryan rolled over and sprang to his feet, landing a solid punch to the intruder's jaw before I could blink. His arm seemed okay, then.

"You like sneaking up on people, asshole?" It was hard to take his radio-host voice seriously, but his face...I had rarely seen anyone look so pissed off. I wouldn't want to mess with him.

The mystery guy swung back, almost instinctively it looked like, and with more time to examine him I could see that he was wearing a high-end tactical vest. But I had been aiming at his head at close range, and he wasn't wearing a helmet.

His punch sent Ryan stumbling backward and he landed hard on his desk, his head colliding with a shelf with a nauseating crack.

I lunged toward him, half lowering the gun, and the intruder bolted for the door, his footsteps fading in the direction of the lobby.

Ryan blinked and grimaced as he pulled bloody fingertips away from his temple. "Son of a bitch."

"What on earth was that about?" I asked, putting the gun in the holster and putting a hand out to help him into his chair.

"I have no idea." He settled into the seat and grabbed a tissue to press to his head wound. "I talked to you, put the phone down, and went back to what I was doing. About ten minutes later, I heard a noise. Nothing big, but I'm the only one here and I turned to see if it was you coming in the door. There was nothing there, and then when I turned back to the monitor, this asshole grabbed me from behind. He yanked me out of the chair and put me on the floor before I could even throw a punch."

"Has this ever happened before?"

He laughed, then winced and patted his head gingerly. "I'm a bureaucrat. People don't usually get jumped for being nerds."

"Did the guy say anything?"

"He told me to mind my own business, and before he could say more, you came in," he said. "Thanks, by the way. My hand will hurt tomorrow but it felt good to punch him."

"I can't believe you did that." I laughed. "Most nerds can't swing like that."

"I'll take that as praise from you."

I looked toward the door. "I wish he hadn't gotten out of here," I said. "I'd like you to go home when I leave here, and stay there."

"You think this had something to do with me trying to help you?"

"I think maybe we're poking around in secrets someone thought had been buried long enough to stay that way," I said. "I'm curious about how whoever doesn't want us in them knows that, but I have a theory."

"Care to share?"

"Not just yet." Jim trusted this guy, and he did just get his ass kicked likely because of me, but the fewer people who knew what I was thinking right now, the safer everyone would be. "What did you want to tell me?"

He waved one hand at the monitors and turned his chair around. "The hard drive and the list of weapons you brought me: about two-thirds of the guns on your friend's list were also on the lists in that hard drive. I put all the information I had about them here. I think these people are the people who bought them from the person who owned the drive."

"Probably, but what makes you say that?" I asked.

"Well, because a search of those names in police records shows that all but one of them were arrested or listed as a person of interest in a gun-related homicide," he said.

I leaned forward. "I'll be damned. Are these people affiliated with the Dixie Mafia or the Zapata cartel?"

Ryan's eyes got so big I could see white all around the blue. "Cartel?" He sounded a little faint.

"So no, then?"

He shook his head and then winced. "No. No, mostly domestic cases, a few robberies."

"Was there anyone in Texas JJ wasn't supplying with illegal weapons?" I mused.

"I guess not?" Ryan turned back to the monitor. "The other interesting thing was that several of these guns showed up as being in police evidence in other crimes not connected to the people named as the purchasers. So when I dug a little deeper into that, I found that was because they were evidence in a case before the purchase date shown from this arms dealer guy…JJ you said? They were evidence before he had them."

"Did you by any chance see at which departments?"

He nodded. "All of them at the Travis County Sheriff's Office."

Of course they were. To a deputy assigned to the evidence locker, a

Rangers badge might as well be a Captain America shield—no one would question Abbott coming and going as he pleased.

39

The air cooled appreciably as the sun disappeared behind the roofline of Zapata's massive home. The coordinates Trey had sent from the drone were further away than I would've guessed, more than six miles to the southeast. But we managed to get there, first by following Chuck's instructions, then by asking a woman handing out flyers at a taco stand in the nearest town. I had a flyer in the glove box—her daughter had disappeared five weeks ago, and the local police were so afraid of or infiltrated by the cartel soldiers who roamed the city streets openly with massive automatic rifles that she'd had little help looking. She thought we looked like soldiers and asked if we were there to fight the cartel. I deflected the question, and she passed us a flyer and told us her story: her daughter Pearl was out shopping with friends and caught the eye of a young Zapata soldier with a gun. When she didn't want to join him for dinner, he followed the girls through the shopping center. She stepped away to go to the restroom and never came back.

I asked if the woman knew where to find Zapata's compound and she gave me directions—we left the truck in some brush about a mile away and hiked to a spot a couple hundred yards outside the fence line, directly behind a gap in the wall that allowed us to use binoculars to see part of the yard and the back door. So we waited, crouching behind the low but thick brush ringing and camouflaging the fence line.

Nichelle hid behind a low tree, and Joey had climbed up into the foliage, completely hidden even from a few feet away, but able to see the entire courtyard over the wall.

The stars were just starting to show in the indigo sky when the first sentries passed. I watched for half an hour before I was sure they had changed their routine from Chuck's video. Still four soldiers, still large weapons, but now they walked the property in opposing circles, crossing paths twice every lap. The result was that with the same number of sentries, every section of the property was now watched nearly completely, with less than two minutes passing between soldiers at our obvious entry point. I cataloged other things I would need to know later: a central courtyard stretched maybe 150 yards from the back wall, and several people were moving in and out of the house without tripping motion sensors. The only lasers I saw were on the rifle sights. As long as I was fast and quiet, I could cross the yard, pass the pool, and get inside, especially after the house settled for the night. What might happen once I was inside the house was anyone's guess, though.

I leaned against the trunk and watched the sentries, looking for any change in their pattern. Four hours ticked by and I didn't see one. Night settled over the desert, the temperature dropping to downright chilly, and I stood and looked around, taking a lap around the tree as Joey came down to stretch his legs.

"It's good that there's no moon tonight," he said.

I nodded, wrapping my arms across my chest as the sheer ridiculousness of the situation hit me like a bucket of ice water.

I was a Texas Ranger. A decorated police command officer's wife. A pageant queen. And I was shivering in the Mexican desert discussing the phases of the moon with a reformed mob boss, because I was about to try to break into the well-fortified compound of North America's most notorious drug dealer.

Sure.

"If you go just after the guy in the blue shirt passes, you have three more seconds to get out of sight," Joey said. "The guy in green is slower than the others."

I nodded, my resolve and focus returning as quickly as it had fled. "I noticed that."

"You're sure I can't go in with you?"

"I can't take a civilian into a cartel compound." I shook my head. "Besides, you have some big plans coming up in a few months. It's better if it's just me. There aren't many people here. The ones who are will head to bed soon, hopefully really soon if they were shooting off fireworks at three o'clock this morning. One person can probably slip in and out. As long as I can find what I'm looking for without getting caught."

"You said Grady's kid was in an underground room on the video you saw," Joey said. "So that's something. And I would guess bedrooms for Zapata's guests, which should include your husband, would be on the second floor."

I nodded. I had come to the same conclusions, but it was somehow comforting to know he had, too.

I looked around at the still, peaceful darkness.

"The cavalry isn't coming, is it?"

"Kyle hasn't answered me all day," Nichelle said in a low voice. I flinched. She hadn't spoken in so long I thought she'd fallen asleep. "I'm not sure my messages are sending from here, I guess, but I sent half a dozen before we crossed the border and he didn't answer a single one. I'm sorry. This isn't like him."

Joey's jaw flexed in a way that made me think he disagreed with that, but he stayed quiet.

"I just keep thinking, what if I go in there and Graham and Grady aren't here? Or I can't find them? The place is massive." We had seen a handful of people come and go from the house, but none of them were Zapata, Graham, or Grady.

"I suppose that's a possibility," Joey said. "But you said your old man told you the sharpshooters travel with Zapata. And they're here. So he's here. If he's as paranoid as you said, there's no way Grady is anywhere *but* here. And you said Zapata told Miller's UC that he wanted your husband watched, so again, my bet is that he's here." He kicked at a rock in the sand. "I bet it was hard for you to shoot him."

"It was the hardest thing I've ever done." I didn't hesitate.

He looked at Nichelle. "I bet it was. But so you know—I bet it's the reason he's still alive, too. I've seen some things…"

"She told me," I said.

Joey turned on Nichelle with widened eyes.

"She didn't want to bring us, and she can't go in there without backup waiting out here at the very least," she said.

"Okay. I guess." He shook his head.

"I don't care, Joey," I said. "You've spent the whole week helping a total stranger who happens to be an exiled cop and putting yourself at some degree of risk to do that. That's enough evidence for me that you're a good man."

He flashed a smile. "I appreciate that. Anyway, I was just going to say, don't feel bad about that. If they were watching him with any kind of suspicion, a cop shooting him would kill it. Just so you know."

"Thank you." I didn't have the words to tell him how much that meant to me, so I didn't really try.

He bent forward and touched his toes, then climbed back into the tree, settling into the leaves and taking the binoculars from Nichelle.

"Someone is in the pool," he whispered. "Swimming laps. Short guy, barrel chest, thick gray hair."

"Could be Zapata." I wasn't sure why I was relieved to have possible confirmation of the cartel boss's presence, but it made me feel like we'd accomplished something by finding him.

The three of us had spent hours in the car going over what I'd seen and heard in Ryan's office and all come to the same conclusion: someone inside the TCSO was running a side hustle selling guns out of evidence to JJ, where they were, unsurprisingly, making their way into the hands of criminals. And from the history of the antique pistol used to shoot Adam, it seemed Icepick's story about the housekeeper who stole and fenced weapons to JJ was also true. We knew the gun used on Ratcliff belonged to Abbott's grandfather, and Gavin's description of the person who shot Ratcliff sure could've been Abbott, though we had no way to know that without Gavin giving us a positive ID. If he was still alive.

But all of that was for later. Right now I needed every bit of brainpower

I could muster to get into this house and get everyone I cared about back to American soil still breathing.

"He's out. Drying off." Joey coughed quietly. "Forgot his trunks."

I shook my head, wrinkling my nose. "Thanks for taking that one for the team, Joey."

"He's inside. Lights on in the room behind the pool...something behind that, probably a hallway...upstairs...the room with the biggest balcony and the double doors. Seems like he's gone to bed."

"Any lights on the first floor now?"

"Just a small one in a room to the right of the pool, probably a lamp or night-light. That's all I see."

"It's so peaceful out here," Nichelle whispered. "Hard to believe these people are drug-smuggling murderers."

I nodded, turning to look up the tree at Joey, who was only visible thanks to the faint gleam off the metal binoculars. "What do you think?"

"Give it a little more time. When his light has been off for half an hour."

I settled back against the tree, more afraid than I'd ever been in my life and still somehow about to come out of my skin I wanted to move so badly. Less than a week ago, I had tried and failed to get Graham back from these people. I couldn't fail again tonight.

The light went off, and the longest thirty minutes in the history of the world commenced.

Nichelle dug around in her bag and passed me an earpiece and a microphone. I tucked the battery pack under my shirt and brushed the hair that had escaped my bun in front of the earpiece.

"Can you hear me?" I whispered.

She flashed a thumbs-up.

Zapata was here. But I wasn't here for Zapata, I was here for Graham and Grady.

Joey rustled the leaves over my head as the thirtieth minute passed. I looked up and nodded, not sure he could see me.

The gray-shirt-wearing, east-moving sentry passed the gap. The blue-shirted, west-moving guy would be next, and I needed to go after he passed. I crept to the gap and flattened myself on the right side, so Blue Shirt wouldn't accidentally spot me as he walked. A minute and fifty-six seconds passed, and I could smell Blue Shirt coming. He liked cologne. I held my breath as he passed, then counted ten seconds—long enough for him to get close to the corner of the house, before I picked up the long rifle I'd taken from Archie's gun safe, and turned sideways to slide through the narrow gap in the wall.

I crouched, hurrying silently through the darkness across the tile patio toward the covered porch. Sixty-eight seconds had passed.

Moving carefully at the edge of the porch so I wouldn't trip over a step, I heard the sentry's footsteps approaching from the east.

Shit. I was standing relatively out in the open, the porch supported by wood beams every ten feet or so. The two things I had going for me were the heavy, deep-water country darkness and the shadows under the covered porch.

Scurrying to a solid section of stucco wall outside a door, I leaned against the wall to catch my breath and hoped I was hidden well enough. The sentry passed about ten seconds later but made no noise and didn't deviate from his path.

I pointed to the sky and mouthed a thank-you, looking around what I could see of the courtyard by starlight.

Covered walkways and porches ran the length of every wall, a fountain surrounded by fragrant potted flowers on each end of the pool. The noise from the large, burbling concrete fountains and the height and size of the bigger plants gave me options for cover. On three sides, doors lined the walkways every few feet both upstairs and downstairs, with the corner rooms each sporting a balcony with a table and chairs. Most, but not all, of the doors had some size of glass panes in them. On the first floor, only two rooms had low light spilling through the glass onto the tile of the patio walkway. I looked as carefully as I could but didn't see stairs or anything else indicating there might be an outside entrance to any underground room, which meant I needed to see if there was a way to get down there from inside.

Simple. As long as I didn't get shot. Or caught—and I truly couldn't decide which was worse.

I checked my surroundings, holding the rifle ready, and started moving in a short sidestep. Keeping my back to the wall, I made it to the corner, checking the window into the dim room and finding a large kitchen with a lone night-light plugged into an outlet under the cabinet. A huge island dominated the space, with a butcher-block top and a copper rack full of gleaming pots hanging above it.

Nice digs. I couldn't help wondering both how many bodies were buried around this place and noting how oddly similar Zapata and Chuck were. Probably why they had been what some people might call friends. Except men like Chuck McClellan didn't have friends. He was a demon who drained everyone in his orbit of energy and light and moved on. One needed to look no further than my mother to see how true that was—Ruth was an entirely different person since leaving him than she'd been my entire life. A "blow it up and rebuild" level personality remodel.

I checked my six. All clear.

I kept moving, passing dark rooms that held, in order, a huge grand piano and a harp surrounded by leather couches and chairs; statues and paintings surrounding another fountain; a line of desks that looked like they belonged in a school; and every kind of taxidermied animal I could have imagined plus an entire wall lined with glass-fronted mahogany gun cabinets. Lighted ones. Lifestyles of the rich and violent. I noted a door on the other side of that room that led into an interior hallway and what looked like a dining room across the way.

I contemplated going in, keeping my eyes on the other side of the glass for just a bit too long. By the time I picked a noise out over the fountain's soothing burble and turned to check my six, a broad-chested, muscular Rottweiler barreled across the patio, past the pool and fountain, straight for me.

40

I had about six seconds before the dog would be in range for a tackle, and no idea what to do. I couldn't shoot it—it was only doing what it had been trained to, and I would have nightmares for the rest of my days. People, sure, occasionally deserve to be shot. Never a dog, though.

Of course, my days might end right on this patio as dog chow if I didn't figure something out. I glanced around wildly, looking for something to throw, remembering a park ranger telling me once to make myself as big as possible if I ever ran across a bear in the national park. I stood up as the dog jumped the right side of the fountain and hit the ground still running.

A breeze caught the hem of my pants and blew the leg up, the chilly air making me shiver.

Because I was wearing wide-leg linen pants.

Not my pants.

Ruth's pants.

The dog was ten yards away and closing fast, and I patted the pockets frantically, praying she hadn't washed them the last time she wore them.

Thank you, Jesus and Ruth and Charity. I stuffed my left hand into the pocket and yanked a Milk-Bone free, whistling low and tossing it a few yards to the left of where I was standing. It skittered across the tile and the noise snapped the dog's head to one side. He veered, leaping past me and snatching up the treat. Turning back to me, he barked, the sound so deep and loud the glass in the doors shook.

"*Oso! Silencio!*" a deep voice bellowed from the darkness. "*Perro estúpido. Voy a despertar a toda la maldita casa.*" Stupid dog. Going to wake the whole fucking house.

The dog lay down in the middle of the walkway and whimpered. I pulled another treat out of the right pants pocket, thanking every deity I knew that my mother doted on Tyler to the point of keeping her pockets full of dog treats.

Squatting, I held the treat out to Oso, who stood and trotted over with his stubby tail wagging such that his entire back half moved. Feeding him the treat, I stroked his head. He sat on my foot and leaned back against my leg, closing his eyes and stretching his head back.

"*Buen chico,*" I whispered. Good boy.

One crisis averted. But how was I going to get into the house to find what I came for?

I slid my foot out from under Oso and patted his head, giving him the last bone and whispering for him to lie down. He obliged, and I crept three steps backward, stopping in front of the door to the...rifle parlor. I tried the handle.

It opened.

Sometimes, you just have to try the handle. Zapata was one of the most feared men in North America and he had four armed sentries patrolling the perimeter of his property. I probably wouldn't lock my doors either.

Now if I could just stay out of sight long enough to find Graham and Grady. One room at a time. I stepped through the door, my eyes sweeping the room twice with every step. I needed staircases. Bedrooms were probably upstairs, dungeon down.

I slipped through the gun-and-game room and into the hallway, still pointing the rifle ahead of me. The house was dark and quiet.

I spotted the staircase at the end of the hallway and it was all I could do not to run to it. Running was loud.

I had made it up two steps without a sound when I heard the music.

"*Hola.*" The voice was low and quiet. Familiar.

"*Hola,*" I said, gripping the rifle tighter and stepping back down, rounding the corner into a shorter hallway that led to a dark, cherry-paneled, book-lined study.

"*Este no es muy popular.*" This one isn't very popular.

Beethoven's Fourth poured louder out of the speakers now that I was in the room.

"I told you," Javi said from his seat behind the desk. "I know them all."

"You also told me you were a contract killer who works for Jimbo." I held the rifle steady. He didn't look bothered by it. "But I don't see Jimbo."

"I told you, *bonita*: never trust a criminal."

"Have a seat," Javi said, pointing to a big leather chair on my side of the desk. "Keep your gun, if it makes you feel better."

"Why are you here?" I settled into the seat on the left so I could see him and still see both doors.

"I think you are the one of us who needs to answer that question." Javi watched my face, a small smile playing around the corners of his lips. "Have you come to arrest me, *bonita*?"

He knew who I was.

I shook my head, my brain racing through everything I'd learned in the past nine days. "Abbott sent me," I said. "He wants to make a deal."

"With Zapata?"

"With you."

"I thought you didn't know I was here." Javi looked amused. I was still holding a rifle on him, and he was toying with me. Equal parts annoying and terrifying.

"I'm going to go out on a limb here and say you're not in Zapata's study burning the midnight oil because you're a nobody. Abbott sent me to find Zapata's right hand and cut a deal. So which hand are you?"

"The one you're looking for. What kind of deal?"

"We know Zapata is done. He's grieving Freddie, he wants out of the life he's built here, and that's going to leave a vacuum of power in his wake. Things like this get messy. People die. Zapata is setting up for carnage he can use as cover."

Javi nodded. "So? How can you help me?"

"If everyone thought you had taken Zapata out yourself, and maybe you were to run the Texas Rangers out of Mexico, seizing power would really be no problem."

"So you're offering me the cartel, and Zapata gets what?"

"He gets out."

"And what do you want in return?"

"Well, there's what the Rangers want, and then there's what I want."

"You first." Javi steepled his fingers under his chin, a rapt expression on his face.

"I want to know what happened to my sister." My voice didn't quaver or break.

He nodded and turned his arm, pushing his sleeve up to show off the tattoo. "I saw you flinch when you saw it before. It took me a bit to be sure it was you, you know—you had Jimbo completely fooled. He likes you. But I knew before we got in the Caddy."

"What gave me away?"

"The tattoo. You gave us her name. And your eyes. I watched you for weeks—you were a kid, sure, but the eyes haven't changed."

"You watched me?"

"You were the target." He leaned forward, resting his elbows on the desk. "Faith." Javi shook his head. "Always struck me as ironic, a man like Chuck McClellan naming his kids for virtues he didn't possess for one second of his best day."

"I..." I pressed myself back into the chair, raising the rifle higher. "What do you mean I was the target?" I watched his lips spread into a smile, but my heart pounding in my ears and Chuck twisting his face into a snarl and telling me they took the wrong girl were all I could hear.

I shook my head.

"You were the youngest. So it was assumed you'd be the most valuable. Daddy's little girl and all."

"That was a very carefully crafted image the PR people came up with."

"The photo of you sitting on his shoulders on election night was a nice touch."

"He got pissed that I ruffled his hair." I tightened my grip on the rifle. "This is the strangest conversation I have ever had."

Javi snorted. "Beating out the one where you very convincingly wanted to kill your cheating husband? Are you even married?"

So at least he didn't know about Graham.

If I was going to trust a criminal, anyway.

I shook my head. "I've always considered myself a lousy liar, too."

"I would say you've graduated to decent. Jimbo is a skeptical dude, though a pretty face never hurts with him."

"If you knew who I was, why not tell Jimbo? And why did you take me to get my truck?"

He shook his head. "I don't know, really. I wanted to see what you'd do. McClellan's badass Ranger daughter is the stuff of legend among people I know. I felt like I was in on a secret, knowing who you were when you didn't know I knew."

"You weren't afraid I'd arrest you?"

"Do I look afraid of that now? Jail doesn't scare me, Faith, and neither do you." He shook his head. "I guess I figured our paths crossing again after so many years was fate, somehow. I wanted to see if you remembered."

"I remembered that." I pointed to his arm. "But on someone else's arm. A big man, who had the same thing on his forearm."

"Gang initiation," Javi said. "Before we worked for Zapata. Before anyone worked for Jimbo. There were six of us. I'm the only one left now."

"Were all six of you there the night my sister..."

"Four. They sent a team of four."

"And everyone else is dead now?"

Javi pointed to his chest. "Last man standing." He nodded to the rifle. "Unless you're here to rectify that?"

I held the gun steady, but I could tell he knew I wasn't going to shoot him. Here, three feet away, was the thing I had wished for in Jim's morgue three days ago and a thousand sleepless nights since I was a teenager.

He was right in front of me. Nobody knew we were here. We had time. And he had the answers I had needed for more than half my life.

"Why? Why did you kill her, if they sent you for me?"

"She was coming out of her room as we were walking by. She screamed.

Bruno grabbed her and pushed her back into her room. Told her to shut up." He pinched the bridge of his nose.

I swallowed hard. I remembered. Charity was going to get me a drink because the house was big and I was afraid to go downstairs in the dark. I blinked and refocused. He was still talking.

"She kept screaming 'run.' Jose hit her, but it didn't shut her up. Carlos went looking for you and didn't find you, and the whole fucking thing had already gone sideways—everyone was supposed to be asleep. It was a grab and go, a little girl out of her bed, the door was open, the alarm was off. Easy. We took her because we saw her first, she wouldn't shut up, and we couldn't find you."

"She was telling me to run, but I was hiding in her closet." I sniffled. "That's how I saw the tattoo."

"Bruno was by the closet," Javi confirmed.

"And he was with Zapata in Mexico Tuesday night."

Javi nodded. "He was shot."

"He shot himself in the head," I said, and for the first time since I'd met Javi, a genuine emotion crossed his face.

Shock.

He recovered quickly and merely shook his head.

"I have one more question," I said.

"Shoot," he said, smiling at his own joke.

"Who sent you? I know you guys didn't just up and decide to kidnap the governor's daughter. And I know you had help inside the house. You said there was a door open."

"It was a mercenary job. A guy who had come into the game with McClellan but wanted a bigger cut he wasn't getting, I think. He knew Jimbo, and Jimbo had been selling Zapata Cartel drugs out of his clubs for probably a decade at that point. Jimbo asked Bruno to help persuade McClellan, and Bruno picked the three of us to go along. A hundred grand each to grab you, keep you until your old man caved, and drop you at the lake."

"So why did you kill Charity?"

Javi raised both hands and met my eyes. "Before I answer that, I need you to understand that I have nothing left to lose here, Faith."

"Just tell me why!" I wanted to yell, but I had to keep my voice low and controlled because I had more business to do here tonight.

"We didn't. We kept her for three days, McClellan didn't give in, and we took her to the lake. I didn't know she was dead until I saw it in the paper."

I stared him straight in the eye until mine hurt from not blinking. He didn't twitch, didn't move, didn't breathe harder...

"You're telling the truth," I said.

"I don't know how she ended up dead. She wasn't in great shape when we dropped her off—she fought back and got smacked around for the trouble—but she was alive."

I wanted to sit down on the floor and bawl. A story I had imagined all wrong, wondered about, chased for decades...a murder that had shaped my life more than any other single event...the whole thing was just laid right out in front of me in this utterly bizarre exchange with a career killer in a cartel boss's study. If we'd had beverages, most people would've called this a social occasion. But it still didn't have the ending I needed.

That didn't mean I couldn't find it, though.

I wasn't Charity McClellan's baby sister right then—I was a homicide investigator and I was damn good at my job.

"Who knew you were supposed to leave her there?"

"Jimbo. Probably Zapata. And the guy who arranged the whole thing. He was the one who told us where to take her. Very specific about the location behind the marina."

My brain ran through the scene. There were plenty of places to hide near the water at the marina.

"Abbott, right? Charles Abbott? He was one of my father's bodyguards then."

Javi shook his head. "No, this guy was a cop, but he wasn't a guard. I think he worked at the sheriff's department."

My forehead wrinkled. The sheriff's department. Had Abbott ever worked for TCSO? I didn't know, but I could find out. "Are you sure it wasn't Abbott? He wasn't a bodyguard for The Governor for long."

Javi flashed a sad half smile. "No, this guy had, like, two first names."

My stomach sank. "Nick Ryan?" I had made the same joke to Jim just days ago.

Javi shook his head, snapping his fingers. "Lester? Larry. Larry James?"

My hands went slack on the gun, my voice sounding like it was coming from someone else.

"Larry Jameson?"

"Yeah—that's him. Tall dude. Full of himself. Liked dropping names of important people."

That was him, all right. I couldn't get my head around it. I heard Javi speaking, but my brain flat wouldn't process what he'd said.

Jameson had been my boss. He was still Graham's boss. He was applying to the Rangers to take over my CO's job come December. And Javi was telling me he'd killed my sister.

One of those things didn't fit with the others. Not through a sane and normal lens.

"Jimbo said Larry was the brains behind Chuck's operation," Javi continued. "Amin knew it too. He got rid of Larry when Chuck left office—he didn't trust him. That dude is loco, but he was right about this. I've never had a stronger visceral feeling of dislike toward another human."

I stared, trying to make words come out of my mouth. "It has to be a common name." I waved one hand in front of my face like it could ward off panic—or maybe tears. Or both.

"Probably." He pointed to the doorway. "There's a photo in the trophy room of Larry hunting with Zapata."

I followed him into the room and he picked up a heavy silver frame from a shelf and passed it to me.

I stared until tears blurred the image. I had worked for this man for the better part of a decade. I didn't like him, but I trusted him.

I wasn't sure how Abbott fit into anything, but I could figure that out later. For now, as quiet as it felt, I had an answer, and that was half of what I came here to find.

I tucked the frame in the back of my jeans and whispered, "Thank you," just as the *whuff-whup* flap of helicopter blades split the silence, and the glass in the door that led to the courtyard exploded in a flash of light. A person outfitted head to toe in expensive tactical gear rushed through the opening and shot Javi in the chest with two quick rounds from a military assault rifle.

Having turned when the commando appeared, I was gone before Javi hit the floor.

Diving back into the hallway and scrambling up the stairs, I watched Zapata rush into the hall in his boxers with a gun in each hand. Other men shuffled out of doors, half-awake, until they heard Zapata screech, then they hustled back and returned with weapons.

The commando who killed Javi raced up the staircase, aiming at Zapata, and went down just as fast when Zapata fired one round and the commando's face cascaded down the front of his bulletproof vest, his heavy helmet tipping onto his chest as his skull crumbled beneath it.

Choppers, unidentified soldiers, and exploding bullets flying—the invasion could be the Mexican Army, the Chinese drug lord, or the United States Government, and it wouldn't have changed my mission one bit.

Graham was standing in front of the third door on the right, holding a gun. I didn't think he'd seen me, but I saw him. I needed to grab my husband and locate Dakota Grady and get the hell out of here.

41

"*Muerto, cerdo!*" Die, pig.

Zapata fired four more rounds, running toward me and screeching. He pulled both triggers several more times, but the guns didn't fire. Roaring, he flung them into the air as his closest subordinate shook off whatever combination of sleep and tequila he was fighting and aimed his gun at me.

Zapata's jammed pistol fired when it hit the tile, and a burgundy hole appeared in the left side of said subordinate's head. He crumpled to the floor.

I backed to the edge of the top stair riser and raised the rifle, aiming at the cartel boss's bare chest. "Stop right there," I shouted.

He didn't. I fired. From the tactical rifle at close range, Zapata was dead before he had time to know what hit him.

The echoes of the shot faded, my ears ringing, as four other men in the hallway murmured and pointed, every one of them—including Graham—holding a gun.

I swung the rifle their way and raised it, catching Graham's eye as the briefest flit of surprise crossed his face. His shoulder was bandaged, but the bandage looked clean and he looked otherwise none the worse for wear.

How the hell was I going to get him out of there when everyone was awake and pondering the significance of Zapata's death?

A short guy with a bushy beard turned to me with his pistol raised, and glass imploded all over the house.

Black-armor-clad commandos leapt nimbly through every shattered window and came up firing. The bearded guy tried to swing his weapon around, but it was too late—he hit the floor like a stone when the assault bullets ripped through him.

Graham and the others dove back into their bedrooms.

I heard footsteps double-timing down the tiled downstairs hallway and knew I had about half a second before I was going to be trapped between soldiers. Even though I didn't know whose soldiers they were, I was pretty sure they'd just as soon kill me as look at me, and I'd rather they not.

I dove to the right from the top of the stairs and landed hard on my elbow, watching as a bullet cut through the plaster behind where I'd been standing seconds before. They were shooting at everyone who wasn't them.

I waited to the side, staying on my stomach, for them to decide I was dead.

Five seconds went by. Seven.

Bang bang bang!

Each commando had pounced on a door, beating and kicking it only to pull back bruised fists and broken toes. The walls in Zapata's house were old, thick stucco, and the doors were thick solid wood.

Shouting various swear words, they started firing blindly at the doors. But there were six doors and three of them, and Graham's door was among those they were at least momentarily ignoring.

It was also at the other end of the hallway.

Which meant I had a gauntlet to run.

The good thing about everyone in the hallway filling Zapata's doors full of rounds was that their backs were all turned to the center of said hallway, so Zapata's corpse was the only thing physically standing between my husband and me.

I raised my rifle and stepped over Zapata's body, running full out because nobody in that hallway was escaping with their eardrums intact, so footsteps weren't going to get me noticed. I made it almost halfway to Graham's door before one of the rifles ran out of ammo and its commando saw me when he turned his head to reload. In the half second I had to look up close, I could tell only that the guy had warm brown skin in the dim light of the hallway bulb, but he could've been Mexican or Chinese or any one of a hundred other nationalities.

He clawed at the new magazine attached to his vest and started to open his mouth to alert his partners. I raised my rifle and shot him in the face, not slowing my pace.

Taking a life never gets easy, but it was him or me, and I wasn't ready to die.

When he hit the tile, I was two steps from Graham's door.

The hallway fell silent for three seconds. Shouting started, and it took me a minute to figure out I was hearing Nichelle frantically calling my name through the earpiece and the commandos' muffled shouting at... someone...in Chinese.

"All good," I said, my voice cracking as I whirled with my rifle ready, putting one leg up in a sloppy backspin kick when I felt the floor vibrating from their footfalls.

I hit the closest one dead in the chest with my foot and sent him reeling into the wall. Firing as I turned, I winged the last one across the cheek. Blood bloomed from the cut and ran down his face, but the glancing blow didn't slow him down. His face twisted into a snarl and he grabbed the business end of the rifle, turning and yanking such that I let go to keep it from breaking my wrist.

He threw the gun, a bone-chilling smile replacing the anger on his face as he raised one fist to throw a punch.

I feinted to the left and dodged, and he lost the smile, moving back and throwing a front jump kick into my sternum. Stumbling backward, I barely recovered my balance in time to shoot an arm into the barrel of the other commando's rifle, knocking it just enough astray that the shot he fired went into the wall next to the broken window at the bend in the hallway.

I scurried backward, pulling even with the edge of Graham's door. They advanced, each coming from an angle wide enough that I couldn't keep them both in my full field of vision at the same time. I looked back and forth, trying to anticipate the most urgent threat. The one on my left sprang first, landing a kick to my chin that made my teeth clack together and snapped my head back.

Spinning my arms to keep my balance didn't help. I landed hard on the tile and tried to spider crawl backward to recover my footing, but the commando on my right leapt into the air and landed on my shin. The bone crunched under his combat boots and I screamed, lunging forward to grab my injured leg and pull it away.

He raised his rifle and stepped forward slowly, drawing out his moment of victory as his friend laughed behind him.

I closed my eyes, tears dripping between my lashes. I had made it my life's work to find my sister's killer, and I had done that. So if this was the end, so be it. Nichelle had heard everything Javi told me, and there was a camera on my collar—I had no doubt my new friend would take care of Jameson.

I just barely heard the click from my left before warmth sprayed across my face. It took a few seconds for me to realize the blood wasn't my own—mostly thanks to my leg, which throbbed too insistently for me to be dying or dead.

Opening my eyes, I wiped my face with my sleeve as Graham dropped the last commando standing and crouched next to me. "Can you walk?"

Did he even realize he asked me that in Spanish? There was no time to touch his face, to make sure he was real, to slap the ever-loving shit out of him for scaring me the way he had.

I nodded, because I didn't have a choice.

We were halfway to the staircase when a door opened behind us in the hallway.

Graham turned faster than I could, but it wasn't fast enough to keep me from taking a round in the shoulder. I stumbled forward, hitting my knees as broken ends of bone grated together in my shin.

Vomiting stomach acid onto the tile, I heard Graham swear in English as he fired two shots. The floor trembled when whoever shot me hit it.

"I have to get you out of here." Graham shook his head and caught my eye as he scooped me up into his arms. "I'm so sorry, baby."

"Later," I choked out, kicking my good leg for him to put me down. "You can't shoot if you're carrying me. I can walk."

"You are bleeding and your leg—" He looked down. "Baby, that leg is good and broken."

"Put me down and get me a gun," I said through my teeth. "Any gun that's loaded."

He shook his head but set me on a bench in the alcove at the top of the stairs.

I bit blood out of my lower lip trying not to scream when my left foot touched the floor.

"Okay...bandage. Fabric strips?" I huffed out, looking around. I pointed at the commando I shot. "Take his knife and cut those straps off his vest. I have an idea."

Graham did as I asked and pocketed the knife while I eased the straps over my boot and up my leg to the injury point, pulling the sliding fasteners tight around the break. Splintering pain made me see stars for three beats, but it faded to a throb as I pulled tighter, looping the ends of the straps through both connectors and tucking them into my boot to hold them snug. I put my hand up for Graham to help me to my feet.

He hurried back, carrying weapons and ammo scavenged from the dead commandos, and pulled me up.

I couldn't tell if the stabbing pain in my shin or the warmth of Graham's hand around mine and his breath on my cheek quickened my pulse, but I closed my eyes to center my thoughts and his lips brushed over mine in a kiss so fleeting I might've thought I imagined it if he hadn't whispered, "I missed you," before he stepped back.

I opened my mouth to answer him, my ears ringing less, and heard shouting from downstairs. Chinese and Spanish.

"Fuck. These guys were a distraction," I said, grabbing the railing and hobbling for the stairs.

"That's a hell of a distraction." Graham threw a glance over his shoulder. "Who are they, anyway?"

"Chinese military. They wanted everyone out of the way so they could get to Grady."

"Son of a..."

"Yep. That," I said. "Whoever's guarding him thinks you're cartel. Go. They cannot make it out of this place with him."

42

Gritting my teeth and trying to jog when I got to the bottom of the stairs, I followed the shouting to a door behind the kitchen that concealed a staircase leading down into the bowels of the house.

Dungeon. Check.

"Going after Grady," I said for Nichelle's benefit.

"That guy said your leg is broken. Was that your husband?"

"Yes. And I can't get the leg fixed unless I finish the mission," I said. "I'm fine."

I pulled up the freshly loaded Chinese military rifle Graham had handed me and took the stairs one at a time, finding a standoff at the bottom.

The room was wider than I'd have thought from the video, Grady sitting on the floor chained to the wall as threats and swear words flew in three languages, only two of which I understood.

"Get up!" a commando screamed in English, pointing his rifle at Grady.

They wouldn't kill him. He was no good to them dead.

"You're not going to shoot me. Your orders are to take me with you because of who my mother is," he said dully.

Smart kid.

I backed toward him, finding that walking backward hurt less than walking forward, keeping my rifle on the rest of the room in general.

Four commandos faced off with Graham and two other cartel members. The commandos had assault rifles. Graham had one of their guns from upstairs and so did I, but the other two cartel guys had handguns.

I made it to the wall next to Grady and leaned back, taking some pressure off my injured leg. "You okay, kid?"

He looked up. "Faith?" He blinked. "What are you doing here?"

"Rescue operation?"

"Did my mom...?"

I shook my head. "She wanted to negotiate more. But we got intel that these Chinese guys knew about you and were headed here."

From the Spanish side of the conversation, the commandos were telling the cartel guys to lay down their weapons. Which was about as effective as one would think.

"She doesn't care if I go home. She cares how my death will affect her poll numbers," Grady said. "Voters like seeing her as a mother."

"I...damn." I would've patted his shoulder if I could've let go of my gun. "I understand how that feels, but I'm sorry it's happening to you."

"Why do you think I work at that hellhole?" he asked. "Because if she's going to keep voting to keep it a hellhole, at least I can help people."

I was slightly ashamed of myself for assuming it was nepotism.

"We're going home," I said.

"How do you think we're going to do that?" He nodded a bruised and bloody face at the standoff in front of us as the cartel guy to Graham's left stepped forward. The commando across from him took that as a neutral zone infraction, and fired. From three feet away, the cartel guy's torso exploded.

Six more tac-gear-clad figures clamored down the stairs, guns firing. Their gear was different enough from the Chinese commandos to be noticeable, but I couldn't tell on sight which side they were on.

"Join the party, why don't you?" I muttered, bullets zinging almost every direction as the standoff ended. Stepping away from the wall, I fired two shots at the high end of the chain holding Grady to the stucco.

"Graham!" I screamed. "Out!"

I panicked for half a beat when I turned and didn't see him, then spotted him crouching in the corner, Grady's cot flipped up as a makeshift shield, not that it would do a damn thing to stop a bullet if one went that direction.

Graham popped up and fired twice, hitting one of the commandos in the thigh. Blood spurted and the guy went down. I turned to Grady, shoving a gun into his hand. "Do not move. I will be right back."

I zigzagged through the little outbreak of hell in Zapata's basement, dodging falling bodies and staying as low as I could in the hail of bullets. One grazed my injured shoulder, sending a fresh burst of pain up that arm. I kept moving.

"In the corner!" I heard the voice and placed it just as the shot fired.

Spinning on my good leg, I screamed. "Miller! Hold fire!"

The bullet sailed through the thin metal of the cot with a *ding* that my ears somehow picked out of the deafening racket.

I met Miller's ice-blue eyes over his tactical mask, watching them crinkle with understanding and sorrow.

"Nooooo!" The sound wasn't even human, and my throat ached as it ripped through my vocal cords.

I turned back to the cot as the last commando dropped, a pool of blood spreading way too fast into the sand under Graham's back.

"Hold fire, hold fire!" That was Dean, but he sounded like he was shouting from the other side of a lake.

I hit my knees and tried to crawl, Graham's head turning toward me and his hand coming up. "I'm okay." I think I saw his lips move more than I heard him.

Thick arms wrapped my waist from above and behind, lifting me into the air and turning me away from my husband.

"No!" I kicked and fought, clawing at the hands holding me until they bled. "Fucking put me down and go help him or I swear to God you'll beg me to kill you before I do. Miller!"

"Faith, there's nothing we can do." Dean squeezed my waist so hard he forced the air from my lungs, leaning his forehead against the back of my head. "I'm so sorry."

I remember thinking I didn't want the air back.

And then there was just...nothing.

43

I don't remember the two days after the surgery that put my leg back together with seventeen screws and a metal rod, or the trauma surgeons digging a bullet out of my shoulder blade in a small border town hospital so they could seal up the nicked blood vessels and get me in a helicopter to Austin for the leg surgery.

I'm told I was awake at intervals, that I talked and everything, but nothing about those days stuck with me. Probably for the best.

When I remember waking up, it was Tuesday and I was in a sunny private room at University Medical Center in Austin with a cast on my leg and my arm in a sling. My mother was curled, tired and disheveled, in the small blue vinyl recliner next to the bed. Wires and tubes ran from my hand, arm, and face to machines, and Archie was reading a book in a wooden armchair in the corner.

My mouth felt like I'd eaten four bags of cotton balls.

"Graham?" I felt tears well as I said it, and my mom and Archie sprang from their chairs like someone poked them with a cattle prod.

"Oh thank you, Jesus." Ruth made the sign of the cross and perched on the edge of the bed, taking the hand that didn't have an IV needle in it.

Archie ambled slowly to the other bed rail, his eyes and face the kind of devastated I'd only ever seen on him once before.

"No." I shook my head. "I can't...He's not..." The cotton in my mouth and thickness in my throat strangled everything else I wanted to say.

"Sweetie, he's a fighter, your Graham. They're doing everything they can, but he hasn't woken up," Ruth said, tears spilling down her own cheeks.

I blinked. My head snapped around to Archie. "He's...alive?"

"The doctors say the coma is likely permanent." Archie choked up, holding up one hand and blinking as he cleared his throat. "He lost so much blood it's a miracle his heart is still beating. You have your new friend Nichelle and her fiancé to thank for that, actually. She called for medics when she heard the first shots through the radio you were wearing, so they arrived seconds after Graham went down. They were able to slow his bleeding, and the ATF chopper Miller's team arrived in flew Graham to a hospital in Mexico City. Nichelle and...Joey, is it?"

I nodded, squeezing my mother's hand so tightly her fingers went cold.

"They insisted on going with him, and it's a damn good thing. The blood supply in Mexico City is almost nonexistent because the cartel violence in recent weeks has run them critically low trying to save cops. Nichelle and Joey are both B negative."

"So is Graham," I said, closing my eyes.

"The transfusions saved him. They each gave multiple pints and plasma. Nichelle passed out and had to be admitted for IV fluids and vitamins, but she's okay."

"I want to see him."

"He's still in Mexico, sweetie."

I struggled to sit up. "Then take me to Mexico."

"Faith, you also lost a lot of blood, and you've been out for two days. I don't think the doctors..." Ruth stopped talking when Archie held up a hand and walked to the door.

"I need someone to unhook these machines before she does it herself. She wants to see her husband, and if we don't take her, she'll walk if she has to."

"Damn straight." I used my hands to lift my cast-encased leg over the edge of the bed and hissed a deep breath through my teeth when the blood rushed into it.

"They said keep it elevated," Ruth said.

I glared over my shoulder. "Mother."

"Sorry," she said. "I just don't want you to be in pain."

"If he's still breathing, I have to get to him," I said, nodding to Archie. "You would do the same."

She laid a hand on my good shoulder. "I didn't think about it that way." Squeezing, she stood up straight and started barking orders at medical personnel as she collected my clothes.

"I want enough pain medication to keep her comfortable for the duration of the trip," Ruth said.

"We don't believe in pain medication outside the hospital setting, Mrs. McClellan," the doctor, a small, slight man with a bow tie peeking between the lapels of his lab coat, said without looking up from the tablet he was clicking options on.

"Don't...believe?" Ruth's voice could have refrozen the polar caps. "It's not Santa Claus, young man. It's science. My daughter has been through actual hell, she has metal inside her body and a bullet hole in her shoulder. It is entirely reasonable to think she could use something besides Tylenol for the ride to Mexico City. I suggest you get a prescription pad out. Now."

"Ma'am, these medications can be highly addictive—" the doctor began.

"Doc, I'll take responsibility for it." Archie flashed his badge. "Nothing crazy. Maybe a few Vicodin so she can handle the car?"

The doctor looked back and forth between them for a minute and then touched his tablet screen. "Whatever."

He turned back to me. "Mrs. Hardin, I have to tell you that you're leaving against medical advice."

"I'll sign whatever you want," I said. "I'll even sit in a wheelchair. Just untie me."

"You'll need food half an hour before you take the meds." The doctor waved the nurses lurking in the doorway inside as he left.

The redhead smiled as she leaned over me to unhook the IV port and help me into a clean T-shirt. "What you did for your sister...well. That's really cool."

"Jameson." I looked up at Archie. "Jesus, I almost forgot."

"I made them wait until I was back in Austin, and when I say I have never in my life enjoyed cuffing someone so much, I mean it with every fiber of my being." He winked and nodded. "The only thing that could've made it better is if you could have been there. I was afraid something would spook the bastard and he'd run. We had to move."

"He's in jail?"

"With no bond. Our buddy Jim Prescott really does have friends everywhere."

The nurses finished unhooking everything and an orderly came in with a wheelchair. Archie helped me into it, and I looked up at him as Ruth propped my leg on the rest.

"And Abbott?"

"Left the door unlocked that night. Turns out our assistant chief has a gambling problem."

"Jimbo. Jimbo was running his bets," I said. "Was it him trying to take over the gunrunning from Chuck?"

"No, it was Jameson and Amin, who was only too happy to sacrifice Jameson and Abbott on the altar of avoiding death row."

"What about the other cold cases? The people who worked for us? That was Abbott, right?" I felt sick.

"It was. Remember, I told you he was moved to the trip detail at the last minute the night Charity died? Well, it seems he was supposed to watch the door and make sure it stayed unlocked and the guys knew where to find Charity."

"Me," I said quietly. "Javi said they were looking for me. She went out of her room to get me a drink because I was scared of the goddamn dark, and that's why she's dead." My chin dropped to my chest, my whole body trembling as the orderly unlocked the brake on the chair. "It was supposed to be me."

"Jesus." Ruth sobbed, her hand flying to her lips.

"I'm sorry, Mom," I said.

"Sorry? For what?" She crouched next to the chair. "Faith...you have done so much good in the world. I will never get over losing your sister, but please don't for one second ever think that I would rather their plan had gone as intended. I am so damn proud of the woman you became."

She put her hands on both sides of my face and pulled my forehead to hers, tears falling and mingling on my arm and her pants leg.

“Why those people?” I asked, wiping my nose when I sat up.

We moved as a slow little haggard unit to the elevator.

“Well—Abbott rigged the door with tape to improve his chances no one else would lock it. It was the back door of the garage, and Joe Powers saw him messing with it. Mrs. Ivey, the housekeeper, heard one of the gang members say Abbott’s name and tried to blackmail him years later when she was having money trouble.”

“She was working at a convenience store,” I said as the doors closed.

“Right. And the elderly woman who was killed in the drive-by was a maid, a friend of Mrs. Ivey’s who called the police after her friend was shot. The local officers looked Abbott up, thought the old lady was crazy, and did him the courtesy of a heads-up.”

“And nobody thought it was weird when she was killed?”

“Not weird enough, I guess,” Archie said as the doors opened to the lobby.

Ruth shook her head. “I had no idea.”

“None of us did.” I turned my face up to the sunshine as we stepped out into the heat. “The miracle of ballistics and a good research guy.”

Ruth went to get her car, and Archie took my hand. “I don’t want you to get your hopes up about Graham. We’ve talked to his mother six times a day, and it’s bad. I’m sorry.”

“But you just woke up from a coma.” I waved my other hand in a head-to-foot gesture. “And you’re moving slow, but you seem okay.”

“I was out because of the pressure from the clot, and I am damn lucky your mother managed to marshal good surgeons to clear it before it caused permanent damage,” he said. “Graham’s system started to shut down because of blood loss. It’s not the same thing.”

“I have to go to him, Archie.”

Ruth pulled up and the orderly helped me into the back seat where I could prop up my leg.

“I know,” Archie said. “We’re going.”

44

Nichelle got her story, which was how the nurse in Austin knew what happened.

"Skye was pissed," Archie said as Ruth navigated San Antonio traffic. "She rang my phone at four thirty in the morning when she couldn't get you."

"I wore the camera," I said. "Not my fault I almost died and couldn't give it back to her."

"She said she'll never do another favor for you." Archie laughed.

"I made it almost forty years before I had to ask her for one," I said. "I think I'm set. Besides, I have, God help me, a friend who's a reporter now. Do you have my phone?"

Archie fished it out of his pocket, handing me my badge, too. "If you want to come back, we'd be honored," he said.

"Who replaced...?" I squinted at him. "You? Assistant Chief Baxter?"

"See, it went like this—someone I know wanted me to retire because field work has done a number on me. I was all set to do that, when my daughter figured out the assistant chief was a dirty cop. The governor called me, and...well, you can't say no to the governor."

"No more field work." Ruth grinned triumphantly in the rearview.

"A commanding officer I can trust," I said.

"Which is what everyone in F Company also deserves." Archie turned in the seat. "Boone is still retiring in December."

"I suppose Jameson is out of the running?"

Archie laughed. "He's in a cage where he belongs. So what do you think?"

"More office time." I wrinkled my nose.

"Picking your own cases," Archie corrected.

"Less getting shot," Ruth added.

"For you, Chief?" I laughed when Archie made a face as I tried out the new title. "Sure." Still smiling, I dialed Nichelle.

It rang only once. "My God, I've never been so glad to get a phone call." She sounded like she was going to cry. "You are lucky to be alive."

"Thank you," I said, not bothering to blink away the tears. "Both of you. For what you did for Graham."

"The doctor said he got lucky, some scar tissue from a wound a few months ago helped keep his liver from bleeding as much as it would have if he hadn't been injured before," she said. "But I hear it might not be enough."

"I'm on my way to see him. I just had to thank you and Joey for being heroes."

"You're the hero in this story," she said. "We were the sidekicks."

"You were nothing short of heroic," I said. "Putting yourself at risk to go along, putting your relationship with Miller at risk by telling him you were helping me."

"He risked his career to come in," she said. "Everyone told him no, and he and Dean took a small team and went anyway. Just so you know. He's... distraught isn't a strong enough word."

"I know he didn't know. He's never met Graham. He would've looked like part of the cartel to Miller." My voice thickened. "I've fired shots I wish I could take back. We all have."

Nichelle was quiet for five beats. "I have never seen Kyle like this. He's suspended while they review his conduct, though Joey keeps telling me it'll be okay because y'all got Grady's son back, but he won't leave his apartment. I don't think he's eating. DonnaJo is worried."

I sighed. "I have to see Graham. I'll call him after I see Graham."

“Thank you.”

“Thank *you*,” I said. “I will owe you for the rest of my life.”

“My story got picked up by the international wires and someone called my editor yesterday from Netflix. They want to option the rights.”

“For a movie?” I would’ve been excited by that any other day of my life.

“Or a docuseries. They didn’t say which yet. But if it works out, I’m sending you half the money.”

“You earned it, you keep it,” I said.

“Half is one point three million dollars.”

“Uh.” I pulled the phone away from my head and shook both. “Can I call you about that later?”

“Anytime, friend.”

45

Graham looked small under the blankets, his face an unhealthy ashen shade of gray, stubble turning into a beard along his jawline.

Six different monitors beeped and whirred. From a wheelchair, a kind orderly pushed a few feet into the room before excusing himself, I stifled a sob with one fist.

Graham's mother stood, laying a cross-stitch on the end of his bed. "Baby Jesus in Heaven what did y'all get into?" She crossed the room and hugged me gently.

"What are they saying?" I swallowed tears.

"That if he hasn't woken up yet it's probably because he was down for too long for his brain to recover, but there's still brain activity, so there's a slim chance," she said. "He was dead for five minutes and seventeen seconds before they got enough blood from your friends transfused. The nurse told me at one point they were running a direct line from the young man who came in with Graham to Graham's vein to cut down on the time it took to complete the transfusion."

Jesus. And I had worried about having Joey along to help because of his past.

"So there's a chance?" I asked.

"They don't know how stubborn my boy is." Her eyes shone bright with tears, but she just nodded and pushed me to the edge of the bed. "I need some coffee. The nurse today is Lupe, and she's the sweetest thing. Her baby sister was kidnapped by the cartel a few months ago, so she's been doting on Graham every day."

I nodded and picked up his hand. "Baby, can you hear me?" I asked.

He didn't move.

I clasped his big, baseball-callused hand between my small pale ones and held it under my chin, letting tears fall. "It's okay, love. I'm here. You rest." I sniffled. "Just come back to me when you're ready. Please."

Lupe brought another hospital bed into the room and set it up next to Graham's so that I could hold his hand, even adding a traction getup for my broken leg. I was at least a little more comfortable, though I annoyed Ruth by refusing to take more than one of the Vicodin Dr. We Don't Believe in Pain Meds had sent along with us. "What if he wakes up for ten seconds and I'm out because of these pills?" I asked. "I'm fine."

Graham's mom worked on her cross-stitch, prayed softly over her son, and dozed in the chair. Archie and Ruth went to a Hilton down the block to sleep in a real bed at my insistence.

I figured out international cell service and texted Miller to let him know I was with Graham and there was a chance. He didn't answer for a long time, and then about one a.m., my phone woke me up by buzzing. *Thank you. I will never be able to say how sorry I am. I made you a promise.*

You kept your promise. You came even when they told you not to, I typed.

Nichelle said you were going in. Dean and I couldn't leave you to do that alone. I'm just sorry I didn't see her message earlier, I was in the kind of meetings where they put everyone's phone in a black box all damn day.

Thank you. You probably saved Grady and saved me and maybe stopped an international incident or even a war.

I shot your husband.

It was an accident. He was firing. You didn't know at which side. I blinked hard against tears.

This is more than I deserve.

I have made my share of mistakes. Forgive yourself. It's harder than me forgiving you, but it will help you more.

I put the phone down and turned my face toward Graham's. I could see him breathing, and right then, that was enough.

Eleven days later, I was dozing at two thirty in the afternoon after a heated Spanish argument with a doctor about switching my cast for a walking boot. He said I needed three weeks in the cast before the hardware in my leg would be set well enough to hold up if I wanted to walk on it. I wanted a boot so I could get up without two assistants and a wheelchair, because my shoulder wound was still far too tender for crutches.

I'm not sure how long it took for the pressure on my fingers to wake me, but I opened my eyes to see Graham's mossy-green irises squinting against the sunshine pouring in the windows.

"Am I dreaming again?" I whispered. I didn't think so, because none of the dreams I'd had to that point took place in the hospital.

He moved his jaw and winced, his tongue poking out as he shook his head slightly.

His beard rustling against the pillowcase made me sob, and his mother saw his head move and leapt out of her chair with a yelp. "Graham?"

"I think he's awake," I said.

He nodded. Mom ran from the room screaming for Lupe.

"You came back to me," I said.

"Did you...tell me to rest?" he asked. His words were slightly slurred and came slowly, but he was talking to me. Thanking Jesus and my sister and Granny McClellan, I squeezed his hand back.

"I did say that," I sobbed. "When I first got here."

"We're okay?" He moved his jaw five different directions and shook his head, his eyes going to my leg. "They fixed it. What day is it?" Every sentence sounded a little clearer.

"Saturday. The..." I looked at Lupe's whiteboard. "The third of September."

"September?"

"Two weeks. It took you two weeks, but you're here." I nodded, more tears falling. "You're here."

Lupe and two other nurses came running in with a doctor trailing them, moving the beds apart so they could examine Graham.

The doctor looked up after asking a few questions and checking machines and nodded, a dazed look on his face. "Welcome back, Mr. Hardin."

Lupe turned to me with tears pouring down her cheeks. "It's a miracle," she said, turning her face to the ceiling. "*Gracias, Jesus, muchas gracias.*"

She pushed the beds back together and Graham's hand found mine.

"Would you like anything?" Lupe asked.

"A giant cheeseburger," Graham said. "And a Coke."

"I'll get it. I know what he likes." His mother wiped her face and hurried from the room.

"Anything for you?" Lupe asked me.

"One of those strawberry smoothies you keep bringing me, please," I said. "And a nice, long vacation with my husband. I'm under orders."

The General's Gold
Book 1 in the Turner and Mosley Files

A treasure so priceless, it's worth killing for...

When Mark Hawkins is found dead in a seedy motel, police deem it an accidental overdose. But billionaire computer genius Avery Turner suspects there might be more to the story. Her old friend was on the trail of the legendary General's Gold, and now Avery is determined to pick up where he left off...

Teaming up with Carter Mosley, a deep-sea shipwreck diver and adrenaline junkie turned social media sensation, Avery embarks on a dangerous quest for the treasure—and the truth. From Florida to Maine, and from the mountains of Virginia to the depths of the Atlantic Ocean, they face treacherous gangs, man-eating sharks, and a world of deception and double-crosses.

As they navigate hidden clues and uncertain allies, Avery and Carter must outwit their deadly adversaries and unravel the mystery surrounding the General's Gold. But in this high-stakes game, losing the treasure could cost them their lives.

The Genesis Gold [illegible] 2

Book [illegible] of the Turner and Mosley Files

A [illegible] so priceless [illegible] worth killing for...

When Mark Fitzgerald [illegible] dead in a [illegible], police deem it an [illegible] Investigator [illegible] computer genius Avery Turner suspects [illegible] was on the trail of the [illegible] Genesis Gold, and now Avery is [illegible] to pick up where he left off.

Teaming up with Carter [illegible] wreck diver and [illegible] media sensation, [illegible] truth. From [illegible] the Atlantic [illegible] they face [illegible] and danger.

[illegible] Avery and Carter [illegible] the mystery surrounding the [illegible] cost them their lives.

Get your copy today!

[illegible]

ACKNOWLEDGMENTS

Y'all, this book was a different animal. I have done this 19 times now, and this one was the most difficult for so many reasons. High on that list was that I realized in here somewhere that six books and five years is a long time to have readers wait for the solution to a big mystery that has run through so many books, and so this was more than just an entry in the series I was trying to make better than the one before it: it was *the* entry in the series, and needed to be worthy of all that waiting. There were times when I was writing it that I didn't think I would manage to get it there, days when I told my family I should put it down because I had finally found the one that just wasn't working. And then right at the *very* last minute, with some direction and pointed questions from my editor, it all fell together. Questions I'd been pondering for weeks—months—suddenly conjured up answers out of nowhere. Characters who were unsure what to do next developed clear and logical missions. Characters I thought were going to die didn't. Sue Grafton used to call that part of writing "the magic," and having this book done and in your hands, I wholeheartedly agree.

I know I have said "it takes a village" before, but y'all...this one took half a city. My sincere thanks to everyone who helped, even when you didn't know how much you had: my agent, John Talbot, who is an expert at talking me off ledges after all these years; my editor, Randall Klein, who has superhuman story-whispering skills and has apparently learned over years working together how to keep me sane when a book is testing that boundary; my truly extraordinary team at Severn River Publishing: Amber Hudock, Cate Streissguth, Mo Melten, Andrew Watts, Catherine Farrell, Rohan Hemani, and Julia Hastings, who picked up slack in other areas when I had too much going on with life and writing so I could focus on this story; my partner Bruce Robert Coffin, who is only contractually obligated to work with me on The Turner and Mosley Files, but appointed himself head cheerleader and offered his homicide detective expertise to help me work out chunks of this case anyway; Lisa Gilliam, whose incredibly sharp eyes made this copy sparkle; Cris Dukehart for lending her amazing talents to bringing Faith and her friends to life for so many years now; Kate Schulz for answering all my medical questions (for a book this time!); my friend Maureen Downey who held my hand across miles and encouraged me to keep going when I wasn't sure I wanted to—of all the people the books have brought into my life, Maureen is a favorite; Heather Palmer and Brittany Woods for their super-reader recall of the dog's name when I couldn't find it; and least but never least, Justin and my littles—particularly still-tallest-by-a-hair little, who wouldn't hear any "I can't" or "it's just not working" nonsense because she wanted to read this book. As always, any mistakes you find are mine alone.

ABOUT THE AUTHOR

LynDee Walker is the national bestselling author of two crime fiction series featuring strong heroines and "twisty, absorbing" mysteries. Her first Nichelle Clarke crime thriller, FRONT PAGE FATALITY, was nominated for the Agatha Award for best first novel and is an Amazon Charts Bestseller. In 2018, she introduced readers to Texas Ranger Faith McClellan in FEAR NO TRUTH. Reviews have praised her work as "well-crafted, compelling, and fast-paced," and "an edge-of-your-seat ride" with "a spider web of twists and turns that will keep you reading until the end."

Before she started writing fiction, LynDee was an award-winning journalist who covered everything from ribbon cuttings to high level police corruption, and worked closely with the various law enforcement agencies that she reported on. Her work has appeared in newspapers and magazines across the U.S.

Aside from books, LynDee loves her family, her readers, travel, and coffee. She lives in Richmond, Virginia, where she is working on her next novel when she's not juggling laundry and children's sports schedules.

Sign up for LynDee Walker's reader list at
severnriverbooks.com

lyndee@severnriverbooks.com

Printed in the United States
by Baker & Taylor Publisher Services

Printed in the United States
by Baker & Taylor Publisher Services